IN MILADY'S CHAMBER

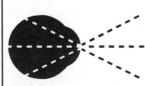

This Large Print Book carries the
Seal of Approval of N.A.V.H.

In Milady's Chamber

Sheri Cobb South

THORNDIKE PRESS

An imprint of Thomson Gale, a part of The Thomson Corporation

THOMSON

™

GALE

Detroit • New York • San Francisco • New Haven, Conn. • Waterville, Maine • London

THOMSON

GALE

LIBRARY OF CONGRESS CATALOGING-IN-PUBLICATION DATA

South, Sheri Cobb.
   In milady's chamber / by Sheri Cobb South.
      p. cm. — (Thorndike Press large print clean reads)
   ISBN-13: 978-0-7862-9877-8 (alk. paper)
   ISBN-10: 0-7862-9877-4 (alk. paper)
      1. Police — England — London — Fiction. 2. Inheritance and succession
   — Fiction. 3. Aristocracy (Social class) — Fiction. 4. London (England)—
   Fiction. 5. Widows — Fiction. 6. Large type books. I. Title.
   PS3569.O755I5 2007
   813'.54—dc22   2007026400

Published in 2007 by arrangement with Tekno Books and Ed Gorman.

Printed in the United States of America on permanent paper
10 9 8 7 6 5 4 3 2 1

20178159

IN MILADY'S CHAMBER

CHAPTER 1
IN WHICH A BODY
IS DISCOVERED IN
THE BOUDOIR

Julia Runyon Bertram, known to the fashionable world as Lady Fieldhurst, sat at her dressing table, resplendent in a high-waisted, low-necked gown of snowy white lace over satin. Diamonds at her ears and bosom winked in the candlelight, trembling slightly as her lady's maid, a handsome Frenchwoman in her early thirties, pinned a jeweled aigrette into her golden curls. Beyond the dressing table, Viscount Fieldhurst stood framed in the doorway that connected his suite to that of his lady. A severe-looking man some fifteen years his wife's senior, he leaned negligently against the doorjamb and studied her with the detached interest of a connoisseur examining the latest oil paintings on exhibit at the Royal Academy. Lady Fieldhurst avoided his gaze, toying with the various articles of toilette littering the dressing table — a silver-backed hairbrush, a pair of nail scissors, a gold-topped bottle of scent.

Abandoning the doorjamb, the viscount advanced into the room. Joining mistress and maid before the mirror, he stroked the side of his wife's slender neck with the back of his index finger. "You shall break hearts tonight, darling. A veritable goddess — Aphrodite, perhaps. Or do I mean Artemis?"

Julia's lip curled. "I am quite certain you meant Aphrodite."

Lord Fieldhurst shrugged. "No doubt you are right. But surely you said something about jonquil crape? Or was the temptation to air the Fieldhurst diamonds too great to resist?" His caressing finger dropped to trace the fall of gems over the bare expanse of flesh.

Striving without success to repress a shudder, Lady Fieldhurst sought to cover her *faux pas* by plunging headlong into conversation. "Indeed, I meant to wear the jonquil, but it is the most tiresome thing! I spilled sherry on the skirt at the Blandford rout, and my good Camille has been unable to eradicate it."

The lady's maid acknowledged this tribute with a tight little smile, but alas, Lord Fieldhurst would not be distracted. "But you shiver, my dear," he said with a piercing look at his wife, sparing not so much as a glance at the discarded gown lying in a heap on the bed. "Shall I ring for the chambermaid to light the fire?"

"That will not be at all necessary," Lady Fieldhurst assured him hastily. "I shall be leaving very soon. Are — are you quite certain you will not accompany me?" The words sounded forced, as if she were hoping for a reply in the negative. If Lord Fieldhurst noticed this, however, he gave no outward sign.

"Would that I might, my dear, but I've an appointment at nine o'clock, after which I shall probably spend the rest of the evening at my club."

"An appointment? Someone from the Foreign Office, I daresay."

The viscount neither confirmed this assumption nor denied it. "You disapprove, my dear? No doubt you would prefer that the Little Emperor be allowed to invade England, so long as he did not interfere with your pleasures. And yet," he tweaked the short, puffed sleeve of her gown, causing it to slip from one white shoulder, "you have no objection to purchasing new frocks with the tribute of a grateful nation."

"Camille, you need not wait up for me. And you may have the jonquil crape as a reward for your efforts, fruitless though they were."

"Merci, madame," murmured the serving woman. She bobbed a curtsy, then bundled up the rejected gown and bore it out of the room, exiting through the small jib door papered to blend into the wall.

"I wish you will not say such things in front of Camille," chided Lady Fieldhurst, tugging her sleeve back over her bare shoulder. "It cannot be comfortable for her, knowing that her wages are paid, at least in part, by our own war efforts against her native country."

One slanting black brow arched toward the viscount's hairline. "Do you truly expect me to consider the sensibilities of a servant?" He chuckled at the very thought. "I have displeased you even more than I knew. I am flattered, my dear. I had no idea my escort was so important to you."

"Much as it pains me to disabuse you of so pleasing a notion, I fear I must inform you that Lord Rupert Latham is to call for me at half-past eight."

"Ah, then you have no need of my escort, after all. I shall trust to Lord Rupert to fill my place admirably."

The smile Lady Fieldhurst bent upon him was somewhat brittle. "Lord Rupert has given every indication that he would be more than pleased to fill your place in whatever capacity I have need of him."

The viscount did not pretend to misunderstand, but took her cold hand and raised it to his lips. "I've no doubt many men would. But I have every confidence in your fidelity, my dear."

And every confidence in my inability to conceive a bastard child with which to embarrass you, Lady Fieldhurst supplied mentally. Aloud, she merely said, "I must not keep Lord Rupert waiting. Goodnight, Frederick."

With head held high, she rose from the dressing table and exited the room in a cloud of white lace.

"Is something troubling you, Julia?" Lord Rupert Latham asked a short time later, as he escorted her from the dance floor.

Lady Fieldhurst unfurled her small ivory fan and plied it vigorously, but the slight breeze it created offered little relief from the heat generated by two hundred wax candles and as many warm bodies. It was ever thus with London society; the mundane reality fell far short of the glittering illusion. Six years of a supposedly brilliant marriage had taught her that.

"Troubling me, Rupert?" she echoed with a trace of defiance, snagging yet another glass of champagne from a tray borne by a passing footman. Was it her third, or her fourth? She decided she did not care. "What could possibly be troubling me?"

"I don't know," said Lord Rupert, frowning as she downed the pale liquid far too quickly. "I only know that you look —"

"Be warned, Rupert, if you intend to make unhandsome remarks about my appearance, I shall be forced to seek more diverting company." She smiled, but her eyes held a reckless gleam.

"I can find no fault with your appearance, Julia. I meant only to say that you look like a woman determined to enjoy herself, even if it kills her."

"I have never heard of anyone being done to death by enjoyment, although if one must go, it sounds as pleasant a way as any other."

Lord Rupert leaned closer and lowered his voice to a husky near-whisper. "Ah, but one may indeed be pleasured to death, Julia, and the best part is that one does not die at all, but lives to, er, die another day."

"Others may do so, perhaps, but not I," said Lady Fieldhurst, not even pretending to mistake his meaning. "My husband assures me that he has every confidence in my fidelity."

"Is that it? Have you quarreled with Field-hurst?"

"My dear Rupert, Fieldhurst never quarrels! He is all that is urbane and charming — provided there are witnesses."

"The bastard! I don't see why you — oh, damn!" muttered Lord Rupert as a portly gentleman emerging from the adjacent card room jostled his elbow, causing him to spill champagne down the front of his form-fitting pantaloons. "If you will excuse me, I shall go home and change."

"Must you, Rupert?" Lady Fieldhurst found herself reluctant to be left alone, even in the middle of a ballroom filled to over-flowing. "It does not look so very bad. I daresay no one will even notice, once it has dried."

"In fact, all I have to fear is being rumored incontinent in the meantime," he observed in accents of profound revulsion. "Never fear, Julia, I shall be back in time to escort you to supper."

The viscountess, painfully aware of having betrayed too much, waved him away with an air of nonchalance. "By all means, go! You need not hurry back on my account."

Lord Rupert regarded her with a sardonic look, then moved away and was soon swallowed up into the crowd milling around the edges of the ballroom. Lady Fieldhurst had not long to mourn his departure, for a dashing Hussar in scarlet and gold lace immediately solicited her hand for the cotillion, and a dandy in high shirt-points and an elaborately tied cravat claimed her for the *contredanse* which followed.

She next took pity on a spotty-faced youth who, stammering, requested her hand for the boulanger, and who repaid her kindness by treading upon her train. Lady Fieldhurst, hearing the delicate lace and satin rip free from the high waist seam, was obliged to finish out the set as well as she might, before seeking refuge in the ladies' withdrawing room set aside for just such emergencies. Holding up her ravaged train to prevent further damage, she pushed open the door to the withdrawing room — and surprised the maid on duty in the lusty embrace of a strapping young footman.

"Oh! Beggin' your pardon, mum," the girl mumbled, red-faced. As her swain beat a hasty retreat, she tugged her starched apron back into place and snatched up the frilled mobcap that had fallen to the floor. "What can I do for you?"

Lady Fieldhurst wondered fleetingly if she had asked the footman the same thing. If so, the girl would be wise to be rather less accommodating. But these were not her servants and therefore not her problem; let the young people take their happiness where they could find it.

"I've a tear in my gown," the viscountess said, turning so that the maid might inspect the damage. "I wonder if you would mend it."

"Aye, mum, I'll have it done in a trice," the maid assured her, all eagerness to please after her earlier *faux pas*.

She helped the viscountess to disrobe behind a large screen, where Lady Fieldhurst was obliged to cool her heels clad in nothing but her shift while the necessary repairs were effected. Whatever her skill with a needle, the girl was not swift. It was fully a quarter-hour later before Lady Fieldhurst returned to the ballroom and noted to her consternation that Lord Rupert had not yet returned.

He did not, in fact, return in time for the supper dance, so she accepted the escort of a noted Corinthian who had recently shocked and delighted Society by shaving a full seven seconds off the London-to-Brighton record held by the Prince of Wales. But though she danced and flirted and laughed at his more outrageous gallantries, she could not quite escape the echo of her husband's voice. Aphrodite or Artemis? Love and beauty, or fertility and childbirth? She had understood his meaning as clearly as if he had spoken the words aloud. In six years of marriage, she had failed to give him an heir, and he silently flung her failure in her teeth every time he took a new mistress.

Her mistake, she knew, was in caring too much. Other ladies, far more well-born than she, were similarly neglected by their husbands and it mattered to them not a whit. But although Lady Fieldhurst might be considered one of Society's most glittering ornaments, in her heart of hearts she sometimes despaired of ever completely throwing off the countrified Miss Julia Runyon, sheltered daughter of a West Country squire.

In retrospect, Somersetshire in 1802 seemed like a different world and in some ways, she supposed, it was. England and France had signed a treaty at Amiens, and the optimism of a world finally at peace had been personified in the young lady who had made her first curtsy at a Bath assembly room. The suave and sophisticated Viscount Fieldhurst, accompanying his mother as she took the waters on her physician's advice, had swept the bedazzled Miss Runyon off her feet and married her in spite of his mother's objections and her own parents' bewilderment. Alas, the Peace of Amiens had proven as short-lived as her own wedded bliss: in less than two years, cannons fired and bullets rained down on far-flung locations from St. Lucia to Copenhagen, and not long after, a colder, quieter war was waged in Berkeley Square — a silent, bloodless battle that left the body unharmed while slowly killing the soul.

She was pulled back to the present by a question from the gentleman seated on her left, a young soldier whose once-handsome countenance was marred by a long scar down his cheek and a black patch over one eye. When he offered to carve for her a slice of the succulent roast beef set before him, she accepted with gratitude and a certain feeling of kinship: they were wounded veterans, the pair of them, albeit of very different wars.

After a supper which seemed interminable despite the pleasures of congenial company (to say nothing of the delights of turbot in lobster sauce, partridge à la Pompadour, and truffles with wine), she returned to the ballroom with the other guests, and was soon rewarded by the sight of Lord Rupert scanning the crowded floor for a glimpse of her. She smiled thoughtfully, tapping her fan against her chin, as he crossed the room in her direction. So Fieldhurst had every confidence in her fidelity, did he? Perhaps it was time his confidence was shaken and the unsophisticated Miss Runyon permanently banished.

It was not as if such things were unheard of in London society, or even particularly frowned upon, provided they were conducted with discretion. Her own dearest friend, the Countess of Dunnington, had been estranged from her husband for years, yet never lacked for intimate male companionship. Indeed, in recent months the countess had urged Julia to follow her own example. Perhaps it was time she did. She snatched yet another glass of champagne off a silver tray, tossed it off in one gulp, and met Lord Rupert halfway across the floor.

"Rupert," she said, gripping the sleeve of his coat, "take me home."

One well-shaped eyebrow arched toward his hairline, but he drew her hand through the crook of his arm without protest. "I am yours to command, my dear."

Together they retraced his steps across the room, heedless of the curious glances and whispered speculations directed their way. They exited the ballroom, descended the staircase, and paused in the foyer only long enough to collect cloaks, hat, and gloves while waiting for the carriage to be brought round. Neither spoke until the elegant equipage drew to a halt before Lord Fieldhurst's town house in Berkeley Square. The windows were dark, Lady Fieldhurst noted; clearly, her husband had chosen not to await her return, but had made good on his expressed intention of spending the night at his club.

Without waiting for the coachman to open the door, Lord Rupert did the honors himself, then lowered the step and turned to offer his arm to Lady Fieldhurst.

"Come inside, Rupert," she said huskily, tugging at his sleeve. "Don't go."

Once again he saw the defiant, almost dangerous glitter in her eyes — although whether the danger was to himself or someone else, he could not begin to guess. Nor, at that moment, did he particularly wish to know. The moment he had long waited for had arrived. Who was he to question it? Nodding in acquiescence, he led her up the stairs to the front door.

"Rogers is not here to open the door," Lady Fieldhurst observed irrelevantly, turning the knob and finding it unlocked. "How very odd."

"I should rather call it fortuitous," Lord Rupert replied.

The viscountess could not but agree. The cool evening air had begun to penetrate the champagne haze that had so emboldened her at the ball — Dutch courage, she supposed — and for the first time since leaving the ballroom, she realized the enormity of what she was about to do. She knew she could rely upon Camille's discretion, but she was less certain where Rogers's loyalty lay. To be sure, Frederick had done little enough to endear himself to his servants, but she was also aware that the servants rigidly adhered to their own code of honor. In the early days of her marriage, Rogers had shown great patience in dealing with a naïve country girl suddenly thrust in command of a large household; he might, however, look less favorably upon a mature woman of six-and-twenty intent upon cuckolding his longtime employer.

A branched candelabrum on a small table beneath the curved staircase provided the only light. Lord Rupert picked this up, and together they mounted the steps to the first floor. Upon reaching the top, Lady Fieldhurst paused before the first door on the left.

"This is it," she said, although she could

not have stated with certainty whether this simple observation referred to the location of her bedchamber, or the finality of the step she was about to take.

She grasped the knob, turned it, and pushed. The door opened some four inches before stopping abruptly with a muted thud. The sudden halt, together with the quantity of champagne she had consumed, caused her to lose her balance, and she stumbled against the door.

"Something is blocking the way," she said, steadying herself in preparation for another attempt.

"Allow me."

Lord Rupert placed the candelabrum on a nearby table, then put his shoulder to the door. It gave only grudgingly, but sufficiently for him to squeeze into the room. A low fire burned in the grate, casting flickering shadows onto a large, dark shape partially concealed behind the half-open door.

"Julia?" said Lord Rupert in a very different voice. "Give me the candelabrum."

She obeyed, asking as she did so, "What is it, Rupert? What is the matter?"

He raised the candelabrum. "Oh, my God," he said, his tone curiously expressionless.

"What is it, Rupert?" she repeated impatiently, standing on tiptoe to peer over his shoulder.

She drew a ragged breath, pressing the back of her gloved hand to her mouth. There on the floor lay her husband in a pool of blood.

"Rupert?" Lady Fieldhurst clutched his sleeve. "Is he — is he — ?"

"Yes," Lord Rupert said curtly. "Undoubtedly."

"Oh. Oh, dear." They were foolish, inadequate words, but then, what in the world was one supposed to say at such a time? Her head suddenly felt stupid and thick — the champagne, she imagined. How much had she drunk, anyway? "We had best send for the watch."

"What, and wake the poor fellow?" replied Lord Rupert in a tone that left no doubt as to his confidence in the night watchman. "No, Julia, I think this is a matter for Bow Street."

"Yes — yes, I daresay you are right."

She tugged the bell pull hanging beside the door. A short time later, a sleepy-eyed footman, breeches pulled hastily on over his nightshirt, appeared. "You rang, my — ? Gorblimey!" he exclaimed at the sight of his recumbent employer.

Lady Fieldhurst, though still alarmingly pale, had by this time regained some modicum of composure. "As you see, Thomas, his lordship has — has met with an accident," she explained, quite as if the viscount had suffered no greater inconvenience than a stubbed toe. "Go as quickly as you can to Bow Street, and summon a Runner."

"Yes, my lady," said Thomas, reluctantly tearing his gaze from the gruesome sight.

Lord Rupert waited until the footman carried out the command, then asked harshly, "Do you really think that is what happened here? That Fieldhurst suffered an accident?"

"He must have!" Lady Fieldhurst cried somewhat wildly. "What else could it be?" She knelt down and reached for her husband's shoulder, but Lord Rupert held her back.

"No, Julia, don't touch him."

"It — it seems barbarous to just leave him here," she protested.

"Believe me, my dear," Lord Rupert drawled, "barbarity is the least of his troubles."

Having received his weekly wages shortly after coming on night patrol duty, John Pickett counted out the coins in the palm of his hand, mentally calculating where they would have to be spent. When he had first been promoted to the Bow Street Runners from the foot patrol, twenty-five shillings a week had seemed like untold riches. It had taken only a few months to discover that this was still barely enough to keep food in his belly and a roof over his head. Furthermore, as his new position occasionally made it necessary for him to testify in court, he was obliged to refurbish his wardrobe by exchanging the distinctive red waistcoats of the foot patrol for clothing more suitable for appearances in the Old Bailey. These did not come cheap, particularly the cutaway coat of black worsted he wore on this particular evening, as the washerwoman was currently striving to remove bloodstains (not his, thankfully) from his workaday brown serge.

To be sure, there was always the opportunity for a Runner to supplement his earnings with lucrative private commissions, but it was unlikely that anyone wishful of hiring private detecting services would seek out a neophyte of four-and-twenty years, with scarcely six months' experience on the Bow Street force. As he looked about the bustling police office, he was forced to acknowledge that he was unlikely to receive any such commissions from his present company. In one corner, a juvenile pick-pocket protested his innocence in a high-pitched whine that turned abruptly to a howl as his victim, impatient with the ponderous workings of the law, boxed the boy's ears. Near the magistrate's desk, a fellow Runner struggled to interpose himself between two inebriates whose quarrel showed every sign of escalating into a bout of fisticuffs. Pickett could sympathize; in just such a way had his brown serge coat become bloodstained, after one of the drunken combatants pulled a knife. By the window, a dark-haired doxy loudly bewailed the trials and tribulations of a woman trying to earn what she very loosely termed an honest living. Pickett, recognizing the voice, pushed his way across the crowded room to tap the woman on the shoulder.

"At it again, are you, Lucy?"

She turned and smiled saucily, giving him ample opportunity to admire the full effect of flashing eyes and low-cut bodice. "Aye, and what if I am, John Pickett? A girl's got to eat, you know. Else what'll happen to my womanly curves?"

She leaned closer, exposing still more of the curves in question. It was, for Lucy, a rare tactical error. Quick as a flash, Pickett thrust his hand down her cleavage. When he withdrew it, the strings of a small coin purse dangled from his fingers.

"Well, Lucy, I'd no idea you counted purse-nabbing among your talents," he remarked. "That's a new lay for you, isn't it?"

"He was going to stiff me, he was!" Lucy protested, snatching ineffectually at the purse. "He promised me five shillings, God's truth, and would have left without paying. So I lifted his purse, I'll not deny it, and all for what? Why, there weren't no more'n a couple o' bob! Now, I ask you, whose crime is worse, mine or his? A fine thing it is, when a woman who's just trying to earn a living the only way she knows how —"

She might have run on indefinitely in this vein, had not a distraction occurred in the form of a new arrival, a rather pale young man clad in the blue and silver livery of a noble house.

"Now, *he'd* be good for more'n a bob, I'll be bound!" pronounced Lucy, the coin purse forgotten as she set off in the young man's direction, hips swaying provocatively.

"Lucy, don't you dare —" began Pickett, hurrying after her.

He caught up to her just as she reached the young man, who was by this time being questioned by William Foote, a fellow Runner some years Pickett's senior who acted as unofficial head of the night patrol.

"Berkeley Square, eh? Very well, I'll be right —" Foote broke off abruptly at the sight of Lucy. "Well, well, what have we here?"

Lucy, never one to miss an opportunity, batted her dark eyes, which now sparkled with tears. "La, sir, I've been cruelly used by a shameful rogue!"

"Have you, now?" inquired Foote, eyeing her heaving bosom with interest. "Well now, we can't let that happen, can we, missy? Here, Pickett, go with this young fellow to Hanover Square —"

"Berkeley Square, sir," put in the footman.

"Yes, yes, wherever. I'll see what I can do to help this poor chick."

"Mr. Foote, sir," said Pickett with some asperity, "this 'poor chick' just nabbed a cove's coin purse —"

"What? Oh yes, I'll take that. Move along now, Pickett, and report back to the magistrate in the morning. Here, now, missy, what's your name?"

Pickett opened his mouth to protest, realized it would be useless, and shut it again. With some resignation, he dropped the pilfered purse into Foote's outstretched hand, reasonably certain that it would be back in Lucy's possession by morning — along with several other shillings, he had no doubt — and set out with the footman for Berkeley Square.

CHAPTER 2
JOHN PICKETT OF
BOW STREET

"Mr. John Pickett, my lady," announced Thomas somewhat breathlessly, "from Bow Street."

Having never had dealings with Bow Street, Lady Fieldhurst was not quite certain what to expect: perhaps a stout fellow past his prime, befuddled with sleep or spirits, with a bulbous red nose — the same sort as might be found in any number of watchmen's boxes across the metropolis. The individual who entered the room in Thomas's wake, however, was very nearly her own age. To be sure, his nose was somewhat crooked, as if it had been broken at some point, but it was far from bulbous, and it was certainly not red. He was quite tall, almost gangly, with curling brown hair tied at the nape of his neck in an outmoded queue. He wore an unfashionably shallow-crowned hat and a black swallow-tailed coat of good cloth but indifferent cut; indeed, his only claim to fashion lay in the quizzing glass which hung round his neck from a black ribbon, and which he now raised, the resulting magnification revealing his eyes to be a warm brown. Julia might have been much reassured as to his competence, had it not been for the fact that his mouth hung open as from a rusty hinge.

As if aware of this unflattering appraisal, the Bow Street Runner abruptly shut the offending orifice and cleared his throat.

"Mrs. Fieldhurst?"

"You will address the viscountess as 'your ladyship,' " interposed the tall, formally attired gentleman at her elbow.

"This is hardly the time to stand upon one's dignity, Rupert," the lady chided him before turning to the Runner. "Thank you for coming so promptly, Mr. Pickett. As you can see, my husband has — has met with an accident. We — we think he must have fallen and struck his head on the corner of the dressing table."

Mr. Pickett found it very difficult to concentrate on anything but the ethereal beauty standing before him, candlelight picking out her features in gold while the dying fire at her back lit her pale hair like a halo. With an effort, Mr. Pickett dragged his gaze away and focused his attention on the dressing table she indicated. He raised his quizzing glass — an affectation, he knew, but one which frequently proved useful in his line of work — and examined the corner of the table. There was no blood, no hair — nothing, in fact, to suggest that anyone had struck his head there, fatally or otherwise. He dismissed the dressing table as irrelevant, then knelt to examine the body. The late Lord Fieldhurst lay facedown in a heap, his form-fitting blue coat pushed off his shoulders, his starched cravat askew. Both, as well as the carpet beneath him, were stained crimson. A lace-trimmed handkerchief bearing an embroidered crest covered the viscount's head, the fine white lawn incongruous against the drying blood.

"The handkerchief is mine," the viscountess explained, as if reading his thoughts. "I thought it best to — it didn't seem right, just leaving him —"

"Quite all right, my lady," Pickett assured her. "Has he been moved at all?"

"No," said the man she had called Rupert.

"Yes," said her ladyship at the same time.

The two exchanged glances, then Lady Fieldhurst plunged into explanation. "The door was blocked, so we — Lord Rupert, that is, since I couldn't get it to budge — had to push it open. We didn't know what

31

— what was on the other side."

Mr. Pickett made no reply, but removed the handkerchief so that he might look for a wound. As the neck had already grown stiff, he could not turn the head, but was obliged to push the shoulders, rolling the corpse onto its back. On the side of the viscount's neck, bright red blood congealed along a short but ugly gash. Where the body had lain, a small metallic object gleamed. Pickett picked it up, and Lady Fieldhurst gasped as he held it up to the light.

"You recognize it?" he asked, watching the candlelight play along the short blades of a pair of silver nail scissors.

"Yes," she said. "They're mine."

Lord Rupert stepped forward, as if to shield her. "That doesn't prove anything!"

"I'm not accusing her ladyship of anything," Mr. Pickett replied blandly.

"Really, Rupert, there is no need for this posturing," protested Lady Fieldhurst. "Mr. Pickett is merely performing his duty. Of course he must know whose scissors they are, and how they came to be —"

She shuddered, running a hand across her eyes as if to eradicate the sight of her dead husband on the floor at her feet. She looked unutterably weary, and Pickett, though "merely performing his duty," felt like a cad for doing so.

"I don't have to know it all tonight," he found himself saying. "You've had a nasty shock. I'll need to ask you some questions, but I can do it tomorrow, after you've got some rest."

Her smile, though feeble, made him tingle all the way down to his toes.

"You are most kind, Mr. Pickett," she said, her voice warm with relief and gratitude.

"Kind," he muttered to himself a short time later, as he plodded eastward. He could think of more fitting words: *gullible*, for one, or just plain *stupid*. What had possessed him to give the pair of them all night to concoct a pretty story? Hard on the heels of this damning question came another: how was he to explain this fit of gallantry to the magistrate?

The sky was beginning to lighten by the time Pickett reached his hired rooms off Drury Lane, allowing him only a few hours of rest before presenting himself in Bow Street. Alas, he was to be denied even this brief respite. Mrs. Catchpole, the woman who was both his landlady and (for a modest sum in addition to his monthly rent) his charwoman, was already up and bustling about the shop. Upon hearing her boarder's tread on the stairs, she fell into her habitual harangue.

"Is that you just getting in at this hour, Johnny?" she called, her tone slightly accusing.

"It is, Mrs. Catchpole. I'm sorry if I disturbed you."

She waddled over to the staircase, a large rosy-cheeked woman whose starched mob-cap covered once-beautiful tresses now more silver than gold. "Lord love you, you're not disturbing me! I've been up this half-hour and more. But what's kept you out and about all night?"

"Bit of a dust-up in the West End," Pickett explained wearily, pausing halfway up the stairs with one hand resting on the banister. "I'll tell you about it later, but now I'm for bed."

"Aye, I don't doubt it! What you need, Johnny, is a wife. Give you a woman waiting at home, and you'd be eager enough to seek your bed before sun-up, I'll be bound!" She chuckled richly at the prospect, then returned to her scold. "Trouble is, the only females you meet in your line of work ain't the right sort for marrying. Dolly-mops, most of 'em, or pickpockets, or both."

Pickett could not dispute this home truth.

He knew almost every prostitute from Long Acre to the Strand by name, yet he'd never "known" a woman in the biblical sense. He'd seen too many men wracked by disease, too many women selling their bodies to feed their bastard children, to avail himself of those all-too-fleeting pleasures. But he was not about to make a present of this information to Mrs. Catchpole; if she ever got wind of it, she wouldn't rest until she saw him wed.

"You'll be happy to know, then, that tonight I met a woman who is none of those things."

Mrs. Catchpole saw the little half-smile playing about his mouth, and hope flared within her ample bosom. "You don't say! Is she married?"

"Widowed."

"Recently?"

He nodded. "Quite — quite recently."

"Hmmm." She frowned, pondering the difficulties inherent in courting a newly bereaved woman. "She'll need plenty of time to mourn her husband, you know. Best not press her for a hasty marriage."

"I won't be pressing her for a marriage at all — at least, not marriage to me. She's a viscountess."

If Pickett had hoped for assurances as to

love's ability to conquer all, he was much mistaken in his confidante. Mrs. Catchpole collapsed into cackling laughter that set her numerous chins quivering. "A viscountess? Lord love you, Johnny, how you had me going! Here I was, thinking you was ready to post the banns!"

Pickett hastily demurred, professing himself to be quite satisfied with his bachelor state.

"Aye, that's what you young fellows always say," said Mrs. Catchpole, still chuckling. "You'll change your mind when you meet the right girl, mark my words! Would you care for a spot of tea, or a bit of bread and butter? You'll sleep all the better for a full belly."

Pickett wanted nothing more than to escape a conversation which he found uncomfortably personal, but at Mrs. Catchpole's mention of breakfast, his stomach reminded him urgently just how long it had been since he had last eaten. He accepted, although he had no illusions that this indulgence would somehow come without a price.

Nor did it. "You should meet my niece, Alice," Mrs. Catchpole said, as she dispensed steaming tea into two mismatched cups. "As pretty as a morning in May, she is, *and* she knows how to hold household, which I'll wager is more than anyone can say of this viscountess of yours!"

By the time she had plied him with food and drink, and bethought herself of no less than three promising local girls, any one of whom would have been a more fitting object for his affections than any viscountess, it was time for him to report to his magistrate in Bow Street, and he had not yet shut his eyes.

He was not surprised to find Mr. Colquhoun there ahead of him, and scarcely had time to wonder if the energetic Scotsman had already heard the news from Berkeley Square when the question was answered for him.

"Hear you'd some nasty business in Mayfair last night," observed the magistrate, regarding his most junior Runner from beneath bushy white brows.

"Yes, sir," agreed Pickett. "Viscount Fieldhurst, stabbed in the neck in his wife's bedchamber. Found some time later by her ladyship and —" He paused for a moment to consult the small notebook in the breast pocket of his coat. "— Lord Rupert Latham."

Mr. Colquhoun's forehead creased, and his eyebrows wriggled together like twin caterpillars. "And why didn't Foote investigate?"

Pickett recalled the senior Runner's avid interest in Lucy's exploits. "He was, er, otherwise occupied."

Upon reflection, the magistrate conceded that Pickett's handling of the case might be a good thing, on the whole. Aside from an unexpectedly keen intelligence, the young man possessed a gift for mimicry, picking up and echoing back the speech patterns of the people around him, apparently without conscious effort. In fact, there were times Mr. Colquhoun could detect traces of his own Scots brogue in his protégé's conversation. Perhaps the Fieldhurst clan might find Pickett's reasonably genteel accents less objectionable than William Foote's cruder tones. Not being given to lavish praise, however, he merely grunted. "Hmph! Well, I suppose you'll have to do, but I don't mind telling you I would have preferred a more experienced man on the job. No offense, mind you, but the upper classes don't like to have their dirty laundry aired in public, and what they don't like, they can make downright unpleasant. Still, I suppose it can't be helped. Any sign of the murder weapon?"

Pickett nodded. "A pair of nail scissors

belonging to her ladyship."

"Any signs of a struggle?"

"None, sir. Although his lordship's coat was pushed down off his shoulders."

Colquhoun gave a grunt of satisfaction. "Taking it off preparatory to giving the little lady a tumble, no doubt. But she's got this Lord Robert on her mind —"

"Lord Rupert, sir."

"Yes, yes. So she sees her opportunity and, while his lordship's arms are effectively pinned behind his back, she stabs him with the scissors. Classic love triangle, crime of passion — should be simple enough."

"Perhaps," Pickett said doubtfully, "but I don't think so."

"Come now, Pickett, don't be naïve! What else would this Lord Rupert have been doing in Lady Fieldhurst's bedchamber at such an hour?"

"Yes, sir, but among other things, the timing isn't right. The blood was already beginning to congeal by the time I arrived. My guess is that he'd already been dead for an hour, perhaps two."

"What makes you so certain you were summoned at once? The pair of them may well have plotted to kill Fieldhurst, then 'discovered' the body some time later to avert suspicion."

"Maybe," Pickett said grudgingly, considering this possibility with some reluctance. "I don't mind telling you that Lord Rupert strikes me as the sort who wouldn't stick at much. But her ladyship — well, sir, you should've seen her. All white and scared, she was, and trying hard to convince me — and herself too, I'll be bound! — that his lordship's death was an accident."

"A clever pretense by a guilty woman."

"But she was so pale and — and sort of dazed, as if she couldn't believe what was happening. She wasn't pretending, sir. I'm sure of it."

"You have lodgings in Drury Lane, do you not?"

Pickett was somewhat taken aback by the sudden change of subject, but he nodded. "I've a couple of rooms above a chandler's shop."

"Then I daresay you've been to the theatre there?"

Pickett recalled many enjoyable evenings spent in the pit at Drury Lane and wondered if Lady Fieldhurst might have been in one of the boxes above. It was strange to think that he had been unaware of her existence a scant six hours ago.

The magistrate took his silence for agreement. "Then you know that there are

40

women — yes, and men too, we won't forget them — who make their living 'pretending,' as you say, emotions they don't feel. Some of them do it very convincingly."

"Yes, sir, but —"

"Tell me," interrupted Mr. Colquhoun, his eyes narrowing in suspicion, "would you say Lady Fieldhurst is an attractive woman?"

Pickett did not hesitate. "I'd say she was the most beautiful woman I've ever seen."

The magistrate heaved a sigh at this unforeseen complication. "John, your instincts are among the best I've ever come across — God knows you wouldn't be here if they weren't — but you still have a lot to learn. You must never, *ever,* allow yourself to become personally involved in a case. Always maintain a professional distance."

Pickett regarded him with limpid brown eyes. "Like *you* did, sir?"

Although his tone was innocent enough, Mr. Colquhoun was not deceived. He remembered all too well a lanky youth, already an accomplished pickpocket at age fourteen, whose parents he had just sentenced to transportation to Botany Bay. A circuitous route had brought that same youth back to Bow Street ten years later, this time on the other side of the law.

"Harrumph! One moment of weakness, and you see what it's got me: an impertinent young cub who had one lucky guess, and now thinks he knows everything there is to know about police work! Well, you don't, my lad, not by a long chalk, but you've got too much sense to let your head be turned by beauty in distress. Besides," he added, lowering his voice as he leaned forward to prop his elbow on his desk, "Fieldhurst was highly placed in the Foreign Office, and what with the war on, it's a bad time for them to lose an important man. There might be a lucrative reward for the man who brings his killer to justice."

"I have every intention of doing so, sir. But it won't be Lady Fieldhurst. I'd stake my reputation on it."

"You have, Mr. Pickett." Mr. Colquhoun leaned back in his chair and folded his arms across his chest. "You have."

With this dire warning ringing in his ears, Pickett left Bow Street and set out for Lord Rupert Latham's rooms in the Albany. The door was opened to him by Lord Rupert's man, who looked down his nose and stated that his master was breakfasting while managing to convey his unspoken opinion that anyone worthy of being admitted to the lordly presence would have known better than to call at the uncivilized hour of ten o'clock. Pickett held his ground, however, and in the end the manservant was forced to content himself with a disdainful sniff before going in search of his master. He returned a short time later and grudgingly requested that Mr. Pickett be so good as to follow him to the breakfast room.

Pickett obliged and was soon treated to the sight of Lord Rupert Latham, gorgeously arrayed in a dressing gown of Oriental design, addressing a plate of eggs, ham, cold chicken, and toast; all of which were washed down with coffee. Clearly, the events of the previous evening had no effect on his appetite.

"So, Mr. Pickett, we meet again," said Lord Rupert. "I trust you've no objection to seeing me *en déshabillé.* Do sit down!"

He waved his fork in the general direction of the chair opposite. Pickett sat.

"I'll not trouble you long, your lordship. I only need to ask you a few —"

"Yes, yes, of course you do. But first, do tell me: whom do you intend to hang for the murder — the fair Lady Fieldhurst, or my humble self?"

"I don't intend to hang anyone — at least not right away. I'm only trying to fix the time of death."

"You relieve my mind."

"Then perhaps you won't mind describing your movements last night." Pickett withdrew his occurrence book from the breast pocket of his coat.

"Not at all." Lord Rupert fortified himself with a long pull from his coffee cup. "I called for Lady Fieldhurst at half-past eight. We drove straight to Lord Herrington's residence in Portman Square. We returned to Berkeley Square at promptly two o'clock, as evidenced by the tolling of bells from a distant church; I regret that I cannot say with certainty which one. I escorted Lady Fieldhurst upstairs to her bedchamber and, finding the door partially blocked, shouldered it open to discover her husband dead upon the floor. The rest you know."

"Tell me, your lordship, what is the nature of your acquaintance with Lady Fieldhurst?"

Lord Rupert's cup froze halfway to his mouth, and his eyebrows arched. "My good fellow, I should think it was obvious."

"Humor me," suggested Pickett, tight-lipped.

"Very well," Lord Rupert said with a shrug. "I first met Lady Fieldhurst — Miss Runyon, as she was then — in oh-two, when she came out."

"Came out where?"

Lord Rupert looked pained. "Came out in Society! Bath, to be precise, where I was obliged to economize, following a particularly unhappy night at the tables."

"The tables?" echoed Pickett, uncertain as to whether Lord Rupert had been driven to the medicinal spa by indigestion or some more serious complaint.

"Gaming, my good man, gaming!" explained Lord Rupert, beholding his audience all at sea. "Pray, Mr. Pickett, are you by any chance acquainted with an establishment in Jermyn Street by the name of the Monastery?"

"No, I can't say that I am."

"Accept my felicitations! As they say, ignorance is bliss. Would that I might have remained equally, er, blissful."

Pickett, uncomfortably aware of an insult so ambiguous in nature that he could not be certain whether it was intentional or not, forced himself to swallow his spleen and steer the conversation back to the matter at hand.

"About Lady Fieldhurst — you were saying?"

"Ah, yes. She was the belle of the Season that year. I proposed marriage to her —

45

several times, in fact — but it soon became evident that Miss Runyon had ambitions. Alas, the mere third son of a marquess cannot hope to compete with a viscount. She married Fieldhurst, and I —" He paused to drain the last of his coffee from the cup.

"And you — ?" prompted Pickett, when Lord Rupert seemed disinclined to continue.

"I waited for the bloom to fade, then renewed my attentions to the viscountess."

"With the intention of becoming her lover," concluded Pickett.

Lord Rupert inclined his head. "As you say. Unfortunately, she seemed unmoved by my, er, manly charms — until last night; upon which momentous occasion we arrived at the rendezvous only to discover Fieldhurst's dead body waiting to greet us. Ironic, is it not? Even in death, he cuts me out."

"I should think you'd be pleased. After all, with Lord Fieldhurst safely underground, you're free to wed his widow."

"Lest you seek to credit me with a motive for murder, Mr. Pickett, I must point out that, if I had murdered Fieldhurst with marriage in mind, I could not have served myself a worse turn. Lady Fieldhurst will now be obliged to spend the next twelvemonth mourning her husband — in letter, if not in spirit — and I will be obliged to hold my ardor in check for the duration. Why, I ask you, should I take such risks only to obtain, after a year's delay, what the lady was already prepared to give without, as they say, benefit of clergy?"

Pickett, finding himself possessed of a sudden urge to plant Lord Rupert Latham a facer, judged it high time to take his leave. After cautioning his lordship that he might well call again, should other questions arise over the course of his investigation, he collected his hat from the dour-faced manservant and stumbled out into the street. His pride was rather stung; he could not shake the nagging conviction that he had not emerged victorious from the encounter. Still, he knew Mr. Colquhoun well enough to know that the magistrate would not have been pleased to learn he had come to blows over a suspect (least of all that particular suspect), so he was left with no choice but to depart, and that right speedily. It was none of his affair, he reminded himself sternly. Adulteress or no, murderess or no, Lady Fieldhurst was not for the likes of John Pickett.

CHAPTER 3
BEAUTY IN DISTRESS

Lady Fieldhurst awoke the next morning with a throbbing head and a vague sense of lingering nightmare. When at last she summoned sufficient resolve to open her eyes and found herself not in her own suite, but in the best guest room, she knew that the disturbing images that had so troubled her sleep had been no nightmare. Her husband was dead, stabbed in the neck with her own nail scissors. He had been lying on the floor when she returned from the Herrington ball. Lord Rupert Latham had been there, too — in her bedchamber, no less. Good heavens! Just how many glasses of champagne had she drunk? And there had been a Bow Street Runner as well — not a highly intelligent man, by the looks of him, but he'd had such nice eyes . . .

And he would no doubt be calling soon to question her. Bracing herself against the pain she knew would follow, she sat upright and swung her legs out of bed. Delaying the unpleasant tasks which lay ahead would not make them go away: arrangements must be made for transporting Frederick's body to the family crypt at Fieldhurst Hall; mourning clothes must be obtained, and some of her old gowns dyed black to carry her through until new ones could be made up; her family must be notified, as well as that of her husband. The prospect of facing the dowager Lady Fieldhurst brought a queasy feeling to her already unsettled stomach.

She tugged on the bell pull, and a moment later Camille entered the room, a black gown draped over her arm.

"Bon jour, madame," she said with a solemnity suited to the occasion. "I have taken the liberty of brushing *madame*'s black bombazine, if it would please *madame* to put it on."

Lady Fieldhurst recognized the gown as one of several she'd had made during the year following the death of some distant Fieldhurst relative. "Then you have heard?"

"The news, she travels *rapidement* in the servants' hall, *madame*."

Lady Fieldhurst could not dispute it; nor could she deny the speed with which gossip spread from one house to another, due in large part to friendships and family connections between servants. She must send word to her husband's cousin at once; it would never do for the heir to learn of his inheritance from his valet.

"Thomas must deliver a message to Mr. George Bertram," she told Camille. "Pray fetch me paper and pen, and I shall write it at once."

"*Un mille pardons, madame,* but the pot boy has already gone to inform Monsieur Bertram, as Thomas cannot be spared."

The viscountess merely nodded, too overwhelmed to wonder why the kitchen boy should have been dispatched on an errand more suited to the footman, or, for that matter, why Thomas's presence had suddenly become indispensable.

"I shall require a great deal of you today, Camille. Some of my dresses will have to be dyed — the figured muslin, I think, and the blue crape should suffice, so long as the ribbons are removed."

"*Oui, madame.* It seems a pity, though. Such lovely gowns —"

"Nevertheless, it must be done," said Lady Fieldhurst in a voice that brooked no argument.

"*Oui, madame,*" Camille said again, then left the room.

She returned a short time later with a

steaming kettle, which she emptied into the large porcelain bowl on the wash stand. Lady Fieldhurst washed her face and hands, then put on the black bombazine and allowed the maid to dress her hair before dismissing the woman. She then went down to breakfast, averting her eyes as she passed the closed door of her bedchamber on her way to the stairs. She was no more than halfway to the ground floor when Thomas the footman hurried forward to meet her.

"Beg pardon, my lady," he said, "but Rogers has done a bunk. He's not been seen since last night, and his bed hasn't been slept in."

Lady Fieldhurst dashed a hand over her eyes. Would she never awaken from this nightmare? "Thank you, Thomas, I shall look into it. In the meantime, you must take Rogers's place."

"Yes, my lady." Thomas bowed, then left her to seek her morning meal in peace.

The breakfast room, which faced east to catch the morning sun, was almost obscenely bright. Squinting against the light, Lady Fieldhurst drew the curtains, then fortified herself with strong coffee. Although the smell of buttered eggs and bacon made her feel ill, she somehow managed to choke down a single slice of dry toast. Scarcely had she risen from this Spartan meal, when Thomas came forward once more.

"The dowager Lady Fieldhurst, my lady, and Mr. and Mrs. George Bertram."

"Oh, dear!" said Lady Fieldhurst, glancing about the breakfast room as if seeking an escape route. "Put them in the —"

"Julia! My poor child!" Thomas was pushed aside by a stout woman swathed in black, who advanced upon Lady Fieldhurst with every apparent intention of clasping her in a fond embrace.

"M-Mother Fieldhurst," stammered her daughter-in-law, submitting to her fate. "Cousin George, Cousin Caroline. How good of you to call."

She gave Mr. Bertram her hand, and he bowed over it, clicking his heels together sharply in a gesture that, along with his drooping mustache, was one of the last vestiges of an undistinguished military career. It seemed ludicrous to think of poor, ineffectual Cousin George (who had once obeyed his commanding officer without question, and now performed that office for his wife) as the new viscount. Whatever his shortcomings as a husband, the late Lord Fieldhurst had been a political force to be reckoned with, both in Parliament and in the Foreign Office. How he had hated the idea of his cousin stepping into his shoes! Never had Julia regretted her barrenness more.

"We came as soon as we heard the news," said the younger of the two females, a sharp-faced woman of forty whose filmy black draperies gave her the appearance of a large crow. "I was never more shocked! But we cannot talk here. We shall be much more comfortable in the drawing room."

Exactly as though she has already taken possession of the house, thought Lady Fieldhurst resentfully, as Mrs. Bertram herded the party into the drawing room.

"I felt I must come at once to offer you a place in my home," the dowager said, settling herself upon a sofa covered in bronze-green satin. "So distressing for you, staying here. Why, who knows but what next time a housebreaker might murder you in your bed!"

"A — a housebreaker, ma'am?" echoed Lady Fieldhurst, still somewhat dazed by the suddenness of the invasion.

"Of course it must have been a housebreaker! Who else would have reason to do such a thing to my poor son? Really, one wonders what the watchmen are being paid to do!"

"And this house contains so many valuable things," put in Mrs. Bertram, examining the furnishings as if calculating their worth. "There is certainly more than enough to tempt any thief."

"We have talked it over, and it is all settled," announced the dowager. "Caroline says that you are more than welcome to remain in this house after she and George move in —" Here Mrs. Bertram nodded her agreement in a flutter of black draperies. "— But she is convinced you would be most uncomfortable, sleeping in the very room where it took place —"

"Not the *very* room, Aunt Lavinia," tittered Mrs. Bertram. "I shall have that one, of course, as it adjoins the master suite. Although, Julia, you will be pleased to hear that I plan to redecorate the whole house so you would never know it for the same place. Lady Blandford has had the most cunning Egyptian furnishings from Mr. Hope, with the sofas and chairs supported by gilt sphinxes —"

"For now, my dear Julia, you may accompany us to Fieldhurst Hall for the funeral," said Cousin George, with the air of one bestowing an unexpected favor. "Not that you ladies will be expected to attend the service, of course, although I will naturally do so. But you may watch the procession from the window, if you wish."

"And afterwards we shall remove to the Dower House," put in the dowager. "You will want to live very quietly during your period of mourning, of course, and I am sure I will be very glad of your company. You may take my dear little pug for long walks about the countryside, and you may read to me in the evenings. Alas, my eyesight is not what it once was —"

"And, of course, when George and I are in residence at the Hall, you must dine with us for a special treat. I confess I look forward to seeing the Hall again. I told George just this morning that I think the rose garden should be dug up and a folly situated in its place, but I cannot decide between a Grecian temple and a Gothic ruin! I should value your opinion, Julia, if you will favor me with it."

Lady Fieldhurst, who had designed the rose garden and planted some of its more exotic species with her own hands, thought it wisest not to express her opinion on this particular subject; but she need not have worried, as she was given no opportunity to voice it in any case.

"So," declared the dowager, "all that remains is for you to have your woman pack your bags, and we may set out early tomorrow morning."

"Begging your pardon, ma'am, but I'm afraid that won't be possible."

At the sound of an unfamiliar voice, the entire company turned toward the open door. The dowager and Mrs. Bertram scowled at the somewhat shabbily-dressed man framed therein, but Lady Fieldhurst welcomed the interruption much as a drowning swimmer might a rope thrown from a passing ship.

Pickett, finding himself the recipient of a smile that rivaled the sun in its brilliance, was emboldened to continue. "I'm sorry to interfere with your plans, ladies, but I must insist that Lady Fieldhurst remain here until the investigation is complete."

Julia, recovering her composure, hastened to explain, "This is Mr. Pickett, the Bow Street Runner who will see that Frederick's killer is brought to justice. I'm sure he has many questions to ask me, so if you will excuse us —"

The visitors needed no further urging. With renewed outpourings of sympathy and promises to call again upon their return to Town, they took their leave. As they passed Pickett, the ladies carefully held their black skirts aside, so as not to contaminate them through contact with so humble a personage. Once they were gone, Lady Fieldhurst turned to regard her rescuer with a rueful smile.

"Well, Mr. Pickett, I hope you are pleased with yourself. You have put me in the intolerable position of having to thank you for making me your chief suspect."

"Not at all, your ladyship, but — if you don't mind my asking, who *were* those people?"

"The dowager Lady Fieldhurst — my mother-in-law — and Mr. and Mrs. George Bertram. Mr. Bertram is my husband's cousin and heir presumptive to his title."

"Oh." The thought that these dreadful creatures might be her nearest and dearest had not occurred to him. "Did you *want* to go with them?"

"I should rather go to Newgate!" As the unfortunate implications of this speech became clear to her, she stammered, "That is, I — I did not mean —"

"I know," he said simply, and had the felicity of seeing her wary expression yield to a cautious smile.

"So long as you understand that I am not making a confession, Mr. Pickett, is there anything you desire I should do for you?"

The possibilities raised by this simple query were so outrageous as to make him blush. He was both relieved and disappointed to see that she was not similarly affected, but he was not surprised; it was highly unlikely that such a lady would entertain the sort of thoughts about him that he'd had of her from the moment he'd first laid eyes on her.

"If I may, I'd like to have another look at your — at the scene of the crime." Seeing her smile fade, he added quickly, "You need not come with me, if it upsets you."

She squared her shoulders and took a steadying breath. "No, I shall come with you," she said resolutely. "You may have questions that I can answer."

"We don't have to go right away," he assured her. "First, I'd like you to tell me about last night."

"Very well," said Lady Fieldhurst, more than willing to postpone the unpleasant task. "What do you wish to know?"

"Everything — and nothing in particular. Just sit down and tell me about it, like you were telling a friend."

Her black skirts rustled as she settled herself on the bronze-green sofa so recently vacated by the dowager. "Where do I begin? I was promised to attend a ball given by Lord and Lady Herrington. Rupert — Lord Rupert Latham, that is — called for me at half-past eight, just as we had agreed."

"Did you often attend such things without your husband?"

"I don't know what you would call 'often,' but it was not unusual. As with most Society marriages, he had his interests, I had mine, and we rarely interfered with one another. On this occasion, he could not have escorted me in any case, for he had an appointment at nine o'clock."

"Did he, now? With whom?"

"He didn't say." She watched with mingled exasperation and amusement as he withdrew a small notebook from his coat pocket and began to write. "If you truly wish for me to speak to you as a friend, Mr. Pickett, I must point out that my friends rarely take down my words."

He gave her a rueful smile, but kept writing. "A necessary evil, I'm afraid."

"In that case, I suppose I must resign myself." In spite of these brave words, she turned slightly away from him, sparing herself the reminder of Pickett's official capacity while at the same time unwittingly presenting him with a view of her elegant profile. "As I said, Lord Rupert called for me at half-past eight, and we were driven to the Herrington house in Grosvenor Square. We returned several hours later. I did not note the exact time."

Pickett flipped back a page or two in his notebook and scanned the notes he had taken earlier that morning. Lord Rupert Latham had said quite decisively that they had returned at two o'clock. If they had concocted a story together, they had made a very poor job of it.

"And while you were at the ball? Were you together the entire time?"

She turned to regard him with an indulgent smile. "You do not understand how these things work, Mr. Pickett. Just because a lady accepts a gentleman's escort to a ball does not mean she must sit in his pocket the entire evening. Indeed, it would be very bad *ton* to do so."

"Even if the gentleman were her lover?"

"*Especially* if the gentleman were her lover." The implication of her words wiped the smile from her face. "Mr. Pickett, I realize that it must look very bad for me, but I must tell you that Lord Rupert is not my lover."

"I'm no guardian of the public morals, my lady," protested Pickett, blushing like a schoolgirl. "You've no obligation to explain to me —"

"Nevertheless, I wish to do so. Whatever else my failures as a wife, I have always been faithful to my husband. But I'd had too much champagne, and Rupert was — indeed, I don't know what I was thinking! I have asked myself a hundred times if I would have actually gone through with it. I still don't know the answer."

"You'd quarreled with Lord Fieldhurst, perhaps?"

"Quarrel is too strong a word for it. Certainly we were not in perfect charity with one another, but I believe such a state is not uncommon among married couples." She glanced at the notebook on his knee, his hasty scrawl now filling its pages — with her own incriminating remarks, no doubt. "Goodness, how I have prattled on! You have a talent for making people say more than they ever intended to."

"It comes in handy in my line of work," he said with a smile.

"And it has no doubt sent more than one person to the gallows."

"And saved more than a few others. Come, your ladyship, you've nothing to fear from me. I want only to find someone who can prove that you'd no opportunity to kill your husband."

"But this is absurd!" protested her ladyship. "How could I have done so, when I was in plain view of almost three hundred people the entire —"

She faltered, and Pickett, seeing consternation writ large upon her face, prompted, "You've thought of something?"

"I — It seems I would not have been in plain sight the *entire* time, after all," she said slowly. "During one of the sets, my gown was torn, and I was obliged to withdraw from the ballroom long enough to see to its repair."

"How long would you say you were gone?"

"Fifteen minutes, perhaps, no more than twenty."

Pickett, making a note of this in his occurrence book, looked up. "Does it really take that long to shove a couple of pins in?"

Her ladyship colored slightly. "Your knowledge of ladies' clothing is obviously not extensive."

"No, I can't say that it is," confessed Pickett with a rueful smile.

Her color deepened. "Suffice it to say that I was obliged to remove the gown entirely."

"Did anyone see you?" asked Pickett, firmly banishing the mental image this confession inspired. "I mean — that is, did any other lady enter the room during this time, anyone who might vouch for your presence there?"

"No, no one but the maid on duty. I do

not know the girl's name, but I daresay Lady Herrington could furnish it — unless, of course, she was hired as extra staff for the occasion. If that is the case, the employment agency that placed her would be the most reliable source of information."

Pickett wrote down this suggestion, but privately hoped for a less circuitous line of investigation. "What about Lord Rupert?" he suggested. "Was he perhaps awaiting you in the corridor? If he could swear that you were at that ball from eight-thirty to two —"

"Oh, but he couldn't. He was gone for part of the evening himself."

Pickett's pencil fell to the floor with a clatter. "He *what?*"

"He spilled champagne on himself — or rather, someone jostled him and caused him to spill it — and so was obliged to return to his rooms in the Albany for a change of clothes. He did not return until after supper."

As Lady Fieldhurst recounted the incident, Pickett once again sought confirmation from his notes. As he'd thought, there was no mention of Lord Rupert's having left the premises. An innocent oversight on that gentleman's part, he wondered, or a deliberate attempt to deceive? It might well be the former, but he would not put the latter past his lordship.

"At what time was supper served, my lady?"

"Midnight."

At first glance, it would appear that Lord Rupert had just been promoted to chief suspect. Unfortunately, the timing of Lord Rupert's movements did not square with those of the murder quite as well as Pickett could wish. Nor could it have been Lord Rupert whom the viscount had arranged to meet at nine o'clock; surely Lady Fieldhurst must have remarked upon it if Lord Rupert had called for her at half-past eight, only to abandon her early enough to visit her husband a scant half-hour later. That mystery, at least, should be cleared up easily.

"Lady Fieldhurst, I should like to have a word with the butler who admitted your husband's visitor last night."

Her lips twisted in a humorless smile. "So should I, Mr. Pickett, but it appears that Rogers has disappeared."

Mr. Pickett's eyebrows rose. "Done a bunk, has he?"

"You sound just like Thomas."

"Thomas?"

"The footman who met you at the door," she explained. "He was the one who informed me of Rogers's disappearance. He will be acting as butler until Rogers returns, or until another butler can be engaged."

"I'll want a word with him before I go."

"Of course. But surely you don't think Rogers —"

"I think," said Pickett with great deliberation, "that whoever Rogers showed in at nine o'clock last night was very likely the last person to see Lord Fieldhurst alive."

CHAPTER 4
IN WHICH
A CLUE DISAPPEARS

"And you think the visitor — and therefore the murderer — was Rupert."

Lady Fieldhurst's tone was slightly accusing, and Pickett realized that the cautious camaraderie of a moment earlier had been no more than a brief illusion. However welcoming her smile, however amiable her manner, she was still a viscountess, and he was still a thief-taker.

"I don't know what to think, at least not yet," he said. "Might I have a look at the room where your husband received his guests? Perhaps he left some clue to his visitor's identity."

She nodded in understanding. "You mean a calling card, or some such thing. Yes, certainly you must see Fieldhurst's study."

She led the way across the tiled entrance hall and opened the door to the room directly opposite. The curtains were tightly drawn and no candles burned, but the room gave off a masculine aura discernable even through the gloom. Pickett rather thought it lay in the smells that hung in the air: old leather, fine liqueur, and snuff. Then Lady Fieldhurst drew back the heavy curtains, and the pale March sunshine flooded through the tall windows, illuminating the sources of the various scents. Bookcases lined two walls from floor to ceiling, their shelves groaning under the weight of calf-bound volumes, all neatly arranged alphabetically. Canisters of snuff marched with military precision along the mantle, each one labeled and dated. The late viscount, it seemed, was an organized man — far too organized, unfortunately, to Pickett's mind. There was no sign of the brandy he'd undoubtedly offered his visitor, nor was there any calling card left lying about which might serve to identify the mystery guest. Even the gleaming mahogany desk had been swept clean of all but a quill pen, an ink stand, and a stack of franked letters awaiting the post. Pickett thumbed idly through these and then paused. He could neither read nor speak French, but he recognized the language when he saw it, and the letter beneath his hand was unmistakably directed to a Paris address.

Without looking up, he asked, "Did your

husband have correspondents in France, my lady?"

"He may well have done," she said, crossing the room to join him at the desk. "We are at war, Mr. Pickett, and my husband was highly placed in the Foreign Office. Under the circumstances, I always felt it best not to inquire too closely into his correspondence."

He tucked the letter back into the middle of the stack and restored it to the desk. "No doubt you're right. Now, if I might have another look upstairs?"

"Of course."

Together they left the viscount's study. Pickett followed Lady Fieldhurst up the gracefully curving staircase to the closed door at the top of the landing. She paused for a moment and took a deep breath, then turned the knob and opened the door.

The last time he had been in this room it had been in darkness, illuminated by nothing more than a single branch of candles and a dying fire. In sunlight it was a thing of beauty, all blue and pink and delicate rosewood furnishings. Only a large, brown stain on the carpet gave silent testimony to the violence perpetrated here a scant twelve hours earlier. Except for the removal of Lord Fieldhurst's body, the room appeared untouched; not even the cold ashes had been swept from the grate. If he were a gambling man, Pickett thought, he would bet a week's wages that the servants were afraid to set foot in here.

"You will find the room essentially unchanged," Lady Fieldhurst told him, as if reading his thoughts. "I gave orders to the maids that it was not to be cleaned — not that they needed a great deal of persuading."

He nodded but offered no reply, his attention being at present occupied with a survey of the room. In addition to the door they had just entered, the only other entrance to the room appeared to be a door set in the adjacent wall. He tried the knob. It turned in his hand, and the door swung open to reveal a second bedchamber, this one somewhat larger and furnished in royal blue and berry red.

"My husband's bedchamber," said Lady Fieldhurst by way of explanation.

"Was this door usually left unlocked?"

Color flooded her cheeks, but the glitter in her eyes gave him to understand that her uppermost emotion was not embarrassment, but affront. "I realize, Mr. Pickett, that you think me immoral and possibly murderous, but I was never so derelict in my duty to my husband that I should lock my door against him!"

Pickett opened his mouth to protest, then decided against it. If that was what she imagined he thought of her, it was perhaps better that she remain unenlightened. He shut the door connecting the two bedchambers, then turned his attention to the window, which, if his sense of direction could be relied upon, should look out the front of the house onto the street. He crossed the room and drew back the filmy curtains. As he had expected, the view was of the square below. The hedge-lined walking paths of the common area bisected the square into geometric patterns, while the wrought-iron railings about its perimeter protected the pleasant island of greenery from trespass by undesirables. Beyond it, a row of almost identical edifices faced the Fieldhurst abode and its neighbors, like duelists confronting one another on the field of honor.

Finding the window unlocked, he pushed the casement open and leaned his head out to inspect the pavement two stories below. A nimble man might manage to scramble down without serious injury, but he would be forced to do so in full view of his neighbors, any one of whom might glance out the window at any time. That fact alone would appear to put paid to the house-breaker theory. No, it was far more likely that the viscount's killer was someone who had the run of the house, someone who could do the deed and then stroll down the stairs without arousing suspicion.

Almost as if she had read his thoughts, Lady Fieldhurst raised another possibility. "If you are considering how my husband's killer might have made his escape, you should be aware of the servants' entrance to your left."

Pickett turned to the adjacent wall, but saw only a wainscoted surface picked out in cream and rose. Lady Fieldhurst stepped forward and pushed against the panel. It yielded under her hand, revealing a narrow, uncarpeted staircase descending into the shadows.

"It leads to the kitchen," she explained. "Camille, my abigail, uses these stairs when she brings my morning chocolate, or hot water for bathing. There is a similar entrance in my husband's room, employed by his valet."

"Forgive me, my lady," interrupted a voice from the corridor. Thomas the footman hovered in the doorway, warily eyeing the bloodstain on the carpet. "Sir Archibald Stanton is below, asking for his lordship.

What should I tell him?"

"Tell him — no, I had best see him myself. If you will excuse me, Mr. Pickett?"

She closed the concealed door and joined Thomas in the corridor, raising her skirt slightly as she stepped past the grisly stain, and thus unwittingly affording Pickett a glimpse of shapely ankle. With an effort, he tore his gaze from this intriguing sight and forced his mind back to the matter at hand.

He crossed the room to stand before the fireplace, from which vantage point he could see all three entrances to the room. The position of the bloodstain on the carpet, along with the combined testimony of both Lady Fieldhurst and Lord Rupert Latham that the viscount's body had blocked the entrance, meant that the door to Lady Fieldhurst's bedchamber must have been closed at the time of the murder; thus, the murderer must have made his escape another way. Lord Fieldhurst's bedchamber was the obvious alternative but, as the service staircase proved, by no means the only one. Any household servant with a grudge against his master might have crept up the concealed stairs, seized her ladyship's scissors, buried them in his lordship's neck, and returned to the kitchen without provoking comment. Even the housebreaker theory was not beyond the realm of possibility, though he could not but think it unlikely: when closed, the concealed door was rendered so nearly invisible that no one without certain knowledge of the house would be likely to know of its existence.

As he drummed his fingers on the mantelpiece, he gradually became aware of the sound of voices from below.

"My dear Lady Fieldhurst, may I say how very sorry I am for your loss," said a masculine voice, undoubtedly that of Sir Archibald Stanton. "I came to see your husband on a matter of business. I never dreamed that he — shocking business, absolutely shocking!"

"Thank you, Sir Archibald," responded Lady Fieldhurst. "The manner of Frederick's death must be a dreadful shock to all who knew him."

"All but one, anyway," Pickett muttered under his breath to no one in particular.

Though not loud, the viscountess's words were surprisingly clear. Pickett realized that the study was situated directly below, and that the two rooms shared the same chimney. Sounds from below were carried up the flue to the room above. He glanced at the plastered ceiling overhead, and wondered if anyone had been in the room above this one — anyone who might have heard a murder being committed. Upon closer inspection of the fireplace, however, he was forced to abandon this promising line of investigation. The remains of a fire had been smoldering in the grate when he arrived on the scene, the ashes of which were even now cold on the hearth, thanks to the chambermaid's unwillingness to enter the room. Surely the crackling of the fire would have prevented the passage of any sound up the flue.

"I would not wish to impose upon you at such a trying time," Sir Archibald was saying in the study below, "so I shall take my leave without further ado. I wonder, however, if there is any small service I might render. I see, for instance, that your husband had written letters. I should be happy to post them for you on my way to the Foreign Office, if you wish."

Pickett, listening, could find nothing improper in Sir Archibald's offer, but the memory of one letter bearing a French direction made his hackles rise all the same. He bolted out of the room and clattered down the stairs, reaching the study just in time to hear Lady Fieldhurst's reply.

"— several letters of my own to write, in fact — relations who must be notified, instructions for the staff at Fieldhurst Hall.

When I am finished, I shall have Thomas post them all at once."

Any relief Pickett might have felt upon hearing these words was tempered by the sight of Sir Archibald Stanton turning away from Lord Fieldhurst's desk, withdrawing his hand from the inside pocket of his coat.

"Mr. Pickett?" Lady Fieldhurst blinked as he burst into the room, but quickly recovered her poise. "I trust you were able to find everything you needed? Sir Archibald, Mr. Pickett is the Bow Street Runner who is investigating Frederick's death."

Sir Archibald nodded in Pickett's direction, but made no attempt to offer his hand. Pickett, however, was less disturbed by the social slight than by the growing conviction that the late Lord Fieldhurst's French correspondence now reposed within the bosom of Sir Archibald's coat. For one brief moment, he thought of challenging the other man to turn out his pockets. A moment's reflection, however, forced him to abandon this idea. Such a demand would very likely meet with a crushing rebuff. At this point, he could not afford to antagonize suspects — particularly important and highly influential suspects. For now, at least, he must maintain the respectful attitude toward his betters of one who knew the lowliness of his own place in the world.

"You were a friend of his lordship?" Pickett asked, returning Sir Archibald's nod.

"Our acquaintance was primarily a political one — Lord Fieldhurst was attached to the Foreign Office, as am I — but yes, I believe I can claim friendship with him. Certainly, I mourn his loss personally as well as professionally."

"I may have a few questions to ask you in the future."

"Of course, of course. I shall be glad to help Bow Street any way I can. Lady Fieldhurst, I am, as always, your very obedient servant."

"You are too kind, Sir Archibald," she said, following him to the door. "I shall show you to the door myself, as Thomas is busy polishing the silver. Did I tell you our Rogers has disappeared? It is most peculiar . . ."

Their voices grew fainter as they moved across the hall, their progress marked by the clicking of Sir Archibald's boot heels against the marble tiles. As soon as he was assured of their continued absence, Pickett seized the stack of correspondence from the viscount's desk and quickly ruffled through the letters.

Just as he had feared, they were all written

in English. The one addressed in French was gone.

CHAPTER 5
INTERROGATIONS
BELOW STAIRS

Staring at the stack of letters in his hand as if he might make one reappear through sheer force of will, Pickett castigated himself for a fool. He'd been so thoroughly rattled at the prospect of being alone with the beautiful Lady Fieldhurst — and in her bedchamber, no less — that he'd allowed a valuable clue to go astray. Not, to be sure, that he had any proof that the letter was connected with Lord Fieldhurst's murder, but its sudden disappearance told its own tale. Sir Archibald Stanton obviously had something to hide, and he, John Pickett, had very obligingly given him the opportunity. He did not look forward to the prospect of explaining his lapse to the magistrate.

"I apologize for the interruption," said Lady Fieldhurst, returning to the room with a gentle smile curving her lips. "Was there anything else you needed?"

It struck Pickett that she did not appear to be heartbroken by her husband's demise. Last night she had certainly been distraught, but today, in spite of her somber attire, she had the appearance of a prisoner who has just been granted an unhoped-for pardon. He wished for some sign of grief on her part. Or did he flatter himself that, were she to cry, he would somehow be the one to dry her tears? Clearly, it behooved him to solve this case and get away from this woman before he lost all pretense of objectivity.

"I'd like to have a word with the servants, if I may," he said quickly. Perhaps some time spent below stairs amongst the household staff would serve to remind him of his proper sphere.

She reached for the bell pull and gave it a tug. "It appears poor Thomas's silver polishing is doomed to be interrupted, in any case," she said with a mischievous smile, as if the tormenting of Thomas were a private joke between the two of them.

Thomas answered the summons a moment later, the smudged apron covering the front of his livery bearing silent witness to his aborted occupation.

"Mr. Pickett has some questions to ask the staff," Lady Fieldhurst told him. "You are all to render him any assistance he may require."

"Yes, my lady," said Thomas, acknowledging this command with a bow.

He led Pickett through the green baize door at the back of the hall and down the narrow stairs leading to the kitchen. Thomas had taken temporary possession of the butler's pantry, where a stout table bore an assortment of gleaming candlesticks, an ornate tea service, and a miscellaneous collection of plate.

"You'll have a bit more privacy in here, sir, as some of the maids do like to talk. If you'll give me half a minute to put away the silver — Mr. Rogers not being here to take care of it himself —"

"There's no hurry," Pickett assured him. "Perhaps while you finish, you can tell me what happened last night."

"Well, now, that's more than I can say," declared Thomas, picking up a silver candlestick and wiping it vigorously with a cloth. "It started out just like any other night. Her ladyship had gone out for the evening, and his lordship was in the study with a visitor —"

"Who was this visitor? Did you let him in?"

"No, sir. Mr. Rogers did that, and brought them refreshment, too." Thomas's polishing slowed, and his expression grew pensive. "I never saw neither one of them again. Leastways, not alive."

"You've reason to believe the butler is dead?"

"No, sir!" Thomas amended hastily. "That is, I don't know what's happened to Mr. Rogers, but when I next saw his lordship, he was dead as a doornail."

"When was that?"

"After her ladyship returned. Well after midnight I'd say, though I didn't think to look at the clock — the sight of his lordship drove everything else from my mind."

"Understandable enough, under the circumstances. I expect you were sleepy too, having been awakened in such a manner."

"Aye, that I was, but I woke up quick enough when I saw his lordship," said Thomas, shuddering at the recollection.

"And the rest of the household? Was anyone else awake?"

"Only her ladyship and that Lord Rupert what brought her home. And I reckon Mam'zelle de la Rochefort, her ladyship's maid, might have been waiting up to undress her ladyship."

The thought of Lady Fieldhurst undressing, with or without assistance, was one Pickett judged it best not to dwell on.

"What of Lord Fieldhurst's man?"

"His valet? Gilmore was given time off to visit his sister in Knightsbridge, she being taken ill. His lordship had been mostly doing for himself, though I'd been polishing his boots and such-like."

Pickett made a note of the valet's name and direction. If his investigation warranted, he would go to Knightsbridge himself to confirm the valet's presence there. For the nonce, however, he had more than enough in London to keep him occupied.

"Were you still awake when Lord Fieldhurst's visitor left?"

"Aye, waiting to take his lordship's boots downstairs for cleaning. After the gentleman had left —"

"You are certain the caller was a gentleman?"

Thomas frowned thoughtfully. "Not for certain, but — hold on! This morning when I laid the fire in the study, I noticed a tray on the desk with a brandy decanter and two glasses. That would be a strange beverage for a female to be drinking, wouldn't it?"

"Unusual, perhaps, but not unheard of," agreed Pickett. "But I was in the study earlier and saw no such tray."

"No, for I brought it down to the kitchen — as Mr. Rogers would have done, if he'd still been here."

Pickett experienced a sinking feeling in the pit of his stomach. Potential clues seemed to be disappearing at an alarming rate. "Perhaps it would have been better if you'd left the tray where you found it," he pointed out gently.

"Aye, sir, and I'm sorry if I've done anything I shouldn't. But I don't mind telling you, I've never been a party to no murder before, and don't care to again!"

"Yes, well, never mind. What did you do after this guest had gone?"

"I allowed time for his lordship to prepare for bed, then I went up to fetch his boots. But his lordship wasn't in his room, and I heard —"

Here the footman broke off his narrative, and Pickett was obliged to prompt him. "You heard what?"

Thomas continued reluctantly, as if the words were being wrung from his unwilling throat. "I heard a woman's voice coming from her ladyship's room."

"Had her ladyship returned early?" Pickett asked, dreading the answer.

"No, sir. Leastways, I don't think so. It didn't sound like her. But then, folks do sometimes sound different when they're angry, don't they?"

"And the voice you heard, did it sound angry?"

"Aye, that it did."

"Could you understand the words?" Sensing the footman's reluctance, Pickett assured him, "You don't have to be eavesdropping to overhear a conversation, especially when the speaker is making no attempt to prevent being heard."

"That's true enough," conceded Thomas. "But the words — they don't make no sense."

Pickett smiled. "Perhaps you'd best let me be the judge of that."

"Very well." Thomas took a deep breath. "They said, 'The tomb of Deacon Toomer may shut the door on the poor sod.' "

And that, reflected Pickett, his smile fading, *will be a lesson to me to be less smug in the future.* "You're right. They don't seem to make any sense. Do you have any idea who this Deacon Toomer might be?"

Thomas shook his head. "None at all."

"What time would you say this was?"

Thomas's brow puckered in concentration. "I know it was after midnight, for I remember hearing the clock chime. Closer than that, I couldn't say."

"You recall hearing the clock strike twelve, but you didn't hear it strike one?"

"Aye, I did, but that's the problem. The long-case clock in the hall marks the hour and half-hour. So, after the twelve strokes at midnight, it would strike once for half-past twelve, once for one o'clock, and once for half-past one. So, even if I'd heard the clock strike one — which I can't say for certain, as I hear that single stroke so often during the day that I take no special notice of it — I couldn't say for sure what time it was marking."

"I understand, Thomas. Thank you for being so frank. Now, if I may borrow your pantry a bit longer, I'd like to have a word with the housekeeper."

"Yes, sir. I'll fetch Mrs. Applegate."

Thomas set off at once on this errand, leaving Pickett to ponder the footman's cryptic testimony. *The tomb of Deacon Toomer may shut the door on the poor sod . . .* The "poor sod" in question would appear at first glance to be his late lordship; the time — if Thomas's estimation was anywhere near accurate — would seem to bear this theory out. Was it possible that Thomas had unwittingly overheard a murder being planned? Or was Lord Fieldhurst not the one spoken *of,* but the one spoken *to?* Had the viscount been in the room at the time, and had his connection with the unknown

Deacon Toomer — whatever it might be — somehow led to his death? Pickett sighed. How was he to solve this case when every new development raised more questions than it answered?

"Excuse me, sir. Thomas said you was wanting me?"

The pantry door had opened to frame a middle-aged woman as plump and round-cheeked as her name implied. Pickett found himself liking her on sight. Her high-necked black dress was covered by a voluminous white apron, and a black-hemmed cap adorned her graying locks — tokens of mourning for her late employer that somehow sat oddly against a naturally cheerful countenance. In her hands she cradled a steaming cup, which she presented to him with a maternal air. "I thought you might be ready for a spot of tea. Milk and sugar?"

"Thank you, Mrs. Applegate. Sugar please, no milk."

As he watched her make the necessary improvements to his tea, Pickett remarked, "I appreciate your kindness, Mrs. Applegate. This must be hard on all of you. I daresay the household is at sixes and sevens."

"Lawks, yes! Here I've been in service since I was a girl of fourteen and thinking I'd seen it all! Well, I don't mind telling you

I've never seen nothing like this, not by a long chalk! And now there's Mr. Rogers gone, and Sukey swearing she'll not set foot in my lady's bedchamber again for love nor money —"

"Yes, a curious thing about the butler," observed Pickett, seizing his opening. "Have you any idea where he might have gone?"

"No, for he had no family, apart from a son who enlisted in the army. Young Billy Rogers might have had a good position as a footman — might have stepped into his father's shoes someday, come to that, for the Rogerses have served the Fieldhursts for generations. But he was mad to see the world, so he up and took the king's shilling, nigh breaking his father's heart in the process. Last I heard, the lad was somewhere in the Mediterranean."

"And Mrs. Rogers?"

"Dead these ten years and more, God rest her soul. She was housekeeper here before me."

"So you've known the butler quite some time."

"Lawks, yes! Never knowed him to behave so oddly, though. Wouldn't have thought him capable of it, neither, for he was always that particular about his work."

"What about earlier during the day? Did

he seem upset, or act in any way unusual?"

"Truth to tell, I can't rightly say," admitted Mrs. Applegate. "He spent most of the day in the wine cellar, having just received a new shipment from Berry Brothers. I do remember him fetching up a fresh bottle of brandy for his lordship at about ten o'clock, but I didn't see him again, as he didn't come down to dinner. Nor," added the housekeeper, her jolly air quite vanished, "did that French creature, neither, until the meal was half over."

"French creature?"

"Her ladyship's maid. Calls herself Camille, she does, although *I* could call her a thing or two! Gives herself airs, speaking that foreign gibberish and strolling into the servants' hall in one of her ladyship's gowns, like she was the Queen herself!"

Pickett, who dealt every day with the most sordid of crimes, found himself slightly shocked by this comparatively minor infraction. "The maid wears Lady Fieldhurst's gowns?"

"Her lady's maid," reiterated Mrs. Applegate. "A lady's maid is often given her mistress's cast-offs," she added somewhat regretfully, as if reluctant to admit that, in this case at least, the despised Camille was within her rights.

"And what time did the staff eat dinner?"

"At about twelve-thirty."

Pickett's eyebrows rose. "Isn't that rather late?"

"Not for the Season, for we don't eat until after the family has gone out for the evening — or, like last night, until the guests have gone home. In the winter, of course, or at Fieldhurst Hall, it's different, for there we keep country hours."

Pickett scarcely heard the last part of this speech, for a thought had struck him. If Rogers had chosen to make his escape while the rest of the staff was at dinner, was it possible that Camille, arriving late, might have surprised him at some point along the way? At any rate, her position would give her ready access to Lady Fieldhurst's bed-chamber without attracting undue attention. He would do well to have a few words with the lady's maid — provided, of course, that he could make heads or tails of her "foreign gibberish." He thanked Mrs. Applegate again for the tea and dismissed her, with a request that she send Camille to him. A twist of the housekeeper's lips gave him to understand that she had no liking for this errand, but she apparently performed it nevertheless, for a scant ten minutes later, the door to the pantry burst open and a woman entered the small room.

Anyone less like the matronly Mrs. Applegate — or, for that matter, the ethereal Lady Fieldhurst — would have been hard to find. She wore the prim black dress of a serving woman, its only ornamentation the round, black buttons which fastened the bodice tightly from waistline to throat, but the oppressive modesty of this garment somehow only served to emphasize the lushness of the figure beneath. The tightly-bound locks of hair visible from underneath her mobcap were jet black, and the expression in her dark eyes was haughty. Her nose was straight, as was her backbone; her posture would not have shamed a duchess. Pickett had never seen anyone look less servile.

"Camille de la Roquefort?"

"Oui," she said, with a toss of her head which Pickett, who knew no French, took for agreement.

"You are Lady Fieldhurst's personal maid?"

"Oui."

"How long have you held that position?"

"Since her marriage to *le vicomte.* Six years."

"And before that?"

Her expression could have frozen water. "Before that, I had maids of my own."

Pickett had been scrawling notes in his occurrence book, but this assertion was so unexpected that his pencil paused in mid-sentence. "I take it this was in France?"

Again that inclination of the head: half agreement, half defiance. He understood it a little better now; she had come down in the world indeed, one of the *emigrées* who had fled the Terror of the previous decade. He felt a momentary pang of sympathy but resisted the urge to express it. This proud creature, he suspected, would scorn pity, particularly from the likes of him.

"What of your family?" he asked instead. "Are they still in France?"

She shrugged. "*Oui,* those who survived the Terror."

"Do you write to them?"

"Our countries are at war," she reminded him. "Communication, she is *très difficile,* but *le vicomte* has always been most help-ful."

Pickett nodded. That might well explain the letter on Fieldhurst's desk, although Sir Archibald Stanton's interest in it still mysti-fied him. Was there more to the letter than simple family correspondence, or was Sir Archibald, that bastion of the Foreign Of-fice, in the habit of seeing spies behind every bush? Once again Pickett wished he'd possessed the foresight to pocket the letter himself. Although he could not have read the French words, he had no doubt Mr. Colquhoun could have.

"When was the last time you wrote such a letter?"

"Yesterday, or perhaps the day before." She passed a shapely but slightly chapped hand over her eyes. "Forgive me, *monsieur,* but time, he has stood still. It is all too terrible!"

Were her tears genuine, Pickett wondered, or had hers been the angry voice Thomas had heard shouting about Deacon Toomer? He allowed her a moment to compose herself before continuing.

"Did you wait up to undr — er, did you wait up for her ladyship to return last night?" The idea of the viscountess in a state of undress was far too distracting to think about, much less put into words.

"*Non, monsieur. Madame* told me I need not so do."

"So what did you do after she left for the ball?"

The Frenchwoman gave a Gallic shrug. "I put her ladyship's room in order; then I went down to supper."

Pickett consulted his notes. "Lady Fieldhurst left the house at half-past eight, and supper in the servants' hall was not served until after midnight. Did it really take four hours to clean her ladyship's room?"

The look she gave him was one of pure scorn. "I do not 'clean her ladyship's room,' *monsieur.* I am not a chambermaid! When I say I put her ladyship's room in order, I mean I put away her jewels, launder her linen, repair her torn lace, and iron her gowns."

"I beg your pardon," said Mr. Pickett, with deceptive meekness.

"*Pas de tout,*" Camille conceded with a wave of her hand. "*Madame* had also given me a gown of yellow crape. This I put on and wore to dinner."

Since this admission coincided with Mrs. Applegate's account, Pickett changed tactics. "Did you see the butler, Mr. Rogers, anywhere along the way? On the stairs, perhaps?"

"*Mais non.* No one was on the stairs, and the butler was not at dinner last night. *Moi,* I believe he was already gone."

"And after dinner? Did you, at any time during the evening, hear voices coming from her ladyship's room?"

"Milord and milady conversed as I dressed milady's hair, but after that — *non.*"

"Were Lord and Lady Fieldhurst angry

with one another? Did they quarrel?"

"Milord had long been unhappy over *madame*'s failure to conceive a child, but they did not quarrel over this last night, at least not to my knowledge."

"Do you know, or have you heard of, anyone called Deacon Toomer?"

Again she bent on him that look of disdain. "I am of the one true faith, *monsieur*. I know nothing of these English deacons."

Pickett made a last notation in his book, then dismissed the lady's maid. Alone in the butler's pantry, he dug his fingers into his hair as he scanned the scrawled pages of notes. His outlook was not optimistic. Now, in addition to finding a killer, he had to locate a missing butler, identify a deceased churchman, and unearth a pair of wine-stained breeches. And while he was about it, he might as well toss the falsely accused viscountess across his saddle-bow and rescue her single-handedly from the gallows. At this point, one seemed no more impossible to achieve than the next.

CHAPTER 6
VISITORS, BOTH
WELCOME AND
OTHERWISE

While Pickett interrogated her household staff, Lady Fieldhurst received yet another caller; this one far more welcome than her husband's family had been. Lady Dunnington was almost ten years the viscountess's senior; nevertheless, a firm if unlikely friendship had blossomed between the two very different women. And if the countess was said by some to be a trifle "fast," certainly no one could find fault with the appearance of the lady who now swept into the room with the air of one accustomed to command. Her lilac muslin walking dress and gold-braided, purple pelisse were in the first stare of fashion, as was the matching bonnet that covered her dark tresses. The dyed ostrich plumes adorning this confection fluttered as she sailed across the room to seize her hostess's hands.

"My dear Julia, I was never so shocked!" she declared, kissing the air on either side of Lady Fieldhurst's face. "How very obliging of Frederick, to be sure! Who would have thought it of him?"

The viscountess acknowledged this sally with a weak smile. "Trust you to say something outrageous! But you cannot have heard the whole, Emily. Frederick's death was no accident. He was murdered."

Lady Dunnington's face paled at this pronouncement, and she sank onto the nearest chair, but she was a resilient creature, and quickly recovered her composure. "Is it as bad as that, then? Truth to tell, I scarcely believed it when I heard he was dead."

"Oh yes, it is quite true! There is a Bow Street Runner below stairs even as we speak, questioning the servants."

"My poor Julia, how dreadful for you! You must tell me about it at once!"

Lady Fieldhurst was more than willing to unburden herself to a disinterested party, and one, moreover, who possessed neither the authority nor the inclination to clap her in irons and haul her off to Newgate. In one particular, at least, she could not have had a more sympathetic audience. Since Lady Dunnington's estrangement from her husband and subsequent string of lovers were common knowledge among the *beau monde,* she expressed no shock, much less disapproval, at Lord Rupert Latham's presence in her ladyship's bedchamber.

"And about time, too!" she declared roundly. "But how dreadful that it should end this way, before it even began! What will you do now?"

"I daresay I shall do as you have been urging me, and set up my own establishment, for live in the Dower House with Mother Fieldhurst I will *not!* Nor do I have any particular desire to return to my father's house. I do not know how it is, but I can never remain beneath Papa's roof for five minutes without feeling as if I were still eight years old."

"You could always come stay with me in Audley Street," suggested Lady Dunnington. "Heaven knows I have plenty of room."

The viscountess arched a skeptical eyebrow. "Wouldn't Mr. Blakeney-Hughes find my presence a bit *de trop?*"

Lady Dunnington dismissed her latest lover with a wave of her hand. "Mr. Blakeney-Hughes and I are quite exploded. I gave him his *congé* these three days past."

"Indeed?" asked Lady Fieldhurst, her mind distracted, at least for a time, from her present difficulties. "But you seemed so taken with him!"

"Indeed, I was — taken with him, and taken in *by* him! His wife was brought to bed of a son a fortnight ago, and the wretched infant looks just like him! If I am going to cuckold Dunnington for his sake, the least he can do is be faithful to me. And so I told him," she added with a self-righteous sniff.

"Really, Emily!" scolded Lady Fieldhurst, choking back a wholly inappropriate urge to giggle. "The things you say! I think you delight in shocking people."

"You are quite mistaken, my dear; I only delight in shocking *you.* In some ways, you are just as green as you were when you first came to London."

"And in some ways, I only wish I were," said the viscountess with a sigh of unexpected longing for her childhood home in the West Country. "You realize, do you not, that I am the most likely suspect? It is no secret that Frederick and I were not upon the best of terms."

"Nonsense! If that in itself were a motive for murder, half the *ton* would be gallows-bait, and the other half would be dead."

"I daresay you are right, and Bow Street Runners interrupt me at breakfast merely for the pleasure of my company," suggested Lady Fieldhurst with gentle irony.

"No, but they would, if they knew how fetching you looked in black — rather fragile and innocent. If you must stand trial, my dear, take care to wear black. No jury in the land would convict you."

The soft sound of the door opening on well-oiled hinges made Lady Fieldhurst look around. Thomas, his expression one of well-trained impassivity, stood with one hand on the doorknob. Pickett, apparently finished with his interrogations below stairs, stood framed in the doorway, twisting the brim of his shallow-crowned hat in his hands.

"I — I beg your pardon, your ladyship," he stammered, glancing at the footman for assistance, but finding none. "I was just coming to take leave of you. I didn't realize you had guests."

"Think nothing of it, Mr. Pickett. Lady Dunnington is quite like one of the family."

"When one considers her nearest and dearest, one can hardly be flattered by the comparison," put in Lady Dunnington. "Still, I shall strive to accept the encomium in the spirit in which it was no doubt intended."

"Pray hush, Emily! You will give Mr. Pickett the oddest notion of the company I keep!"

Pickett hastily denied having any such thoughts in his head and imparted the additional information that, should her ladyship have further need of him, she had only to send to Bow Street for him. Having delivered himself of this communication, he made his bow and betook himself from the room.

The door had scarcely closed behind him when Lady Dunnington gave vent to the peal of laughter held in check since Pickett first appeared in the doorway. "*That* is your Runner? I was not aware that Bow Street was in the habit of employing babes in arms! Still, I daresay he will do you no harm — although I question his ability to do you much good, either."

Thomas, being thrust all unprepared into the role of butler, had yet to acquire several of those sterling qualities which had made the absent Rogers so indispensable to the Fieldhursts' comfort; chief among these being an exquisite sense of timing. As a result of this lack, he was both a bit early in opening the drawing room door and a bit late in closing it.

Pickett, therefore, both entered and exited the room to the accompaniment of Lady Dunnington's candid impressions of him, both personally and professionally; neither of which was flattering, and both of which cut a bit too close to the bone. He was forced to concede the lady's point where the former was concerned, as he could do nothing about his years or lack thereof; however, he took umbrage with the latter. Not only was he persuaded of his ability to do the viscountess a great deal of good, but that morning's interview with the magistrate had left him convinced that he was the *only* one who might do so.

Granted, things looked awkward for her ladyship, but she was not the only one who might stand to profit from the viscount's death. Nor, for that matter, was her would-be lover, Lord Rupert Latham, although Pickett felt no such chivalric tendencies where his lordship was concerned. There was, for example, Mr. George Bertram, heir presumptive to the title, whose wife appeared eager to assume her new status. Mr. Bertram himself had been more restrained, but the fact that he did not flaunt his ambitions did not necessarily mean they did not exist. Or had he perhaps murdered his cousin in order to please his wife? Mrs. Bertram hardly struck Pickett as the sort who might drive a man to murder for love of her, but human nature being what it was, one never knew.

Then there was the matter of the disappearing letter. Had Sir Archibald Stanton killed Fieldhurst in order to gain possession of it, after trying without success earlier in the evening to procure it by less drastic means? The disarrangement of the viscount's coat could have been due not to any amorous intentions on Fieldhurst's part, as Mr. Colquhoun had suggested, but to a frantic (and apparently unsuccessful) search on the part of Sir Archibald after the viscount was already dead. Every instinct urged him to demand an answer of Stanton at once, before the letter found its way into the post or onto the fire.

As luck would have it, a crisp, white rectangle of paper lay on a small side table near the front door. Pickett had the impression that Lady Fieldhurst's friendship with her present guest had long since moved beyond such formalities as calling cards, and dared to hope that the card might have been left earlier that morning by Sir Archibald Stanton. He bethought himself of a clever bit of sleight of hand learned in his misspent youth, and paused beside the table as Thomas opened the door for his departure.

"By the bye," he asked, "how long have

you been in the viscount's employ?"

"Ten years," the footman said with a hint of pride.

"You must have been just a lad, then."

"Aye, that I was. Worked my way up from kitchen boy, I did."

Pickett encouraged these reminiscences, and when he left the house a short time later, he was on excellent terms with the footman and the card was secreted up his sleeve.

He progressed up Charles Street, well past Berkeley Square, before examining his ill-gotten gain. As he had hoped, it was engraved not only with Sir Archibald Stanton's name but also with his direction, which proved to be a very short distance away in Curzon Street. He turned his steps southward and was soon knocking upon the door of Sir Archibald's domicile. It was opened by a dour-faced butler who looked at him as if he were a particularly repugnant species of insect.

"John Pickett, Bow Street," said the Runner, handing the butler his unfashionably low-crowned hat, "here to see Sir Archibald Stanton."

The butler took the hat by its brim, holding it gingerly between thumb and forefinger as if fearing contamination, and placed it on an elaborately carved and gilded console table, where it looked ridiculously out of place even to its owner's untrained eye. The butler then flung open the door to a small sitting room. "If you will wait here, sir, I will inform Sir Archibald of your arrival."

As the sound of the butler's measured tread faded away, Pickett took stock of his surroundings. Besides being cramped, the little room was cold and dark. No fire burned in the grate and, although one wall contained no fewer than three tall, narrow windows, any warming sunlight was blocked out by heavy, brown velvet curtains. As for the furniture, the straight chairs along the walls looked decidedly uncomfortable — an impression which was confirmed the moment Pickett sat down on one of them. He suspected unwelcome guests were left in this room for extended periods of time in the hope that they would give up and go away. He was not surprised, therefore, when fully half an hour passed before his host put in an appearance.

"Good afternoon, Mr. — Plunkett, is it?"

"Pickett."

"Yes, yes. So sorry to have kept you waiting. Now, what may I do for you?"

"I've just come from Lord Fieldhurst's house, where I managed to — misplace — a potentially valuable bit of evidence. Since you were there at the same time, I wonder if you might have walked off with it — purely by accident, of course."

"Misplacing valuable evidence? Tut-tut, Mr. Pickett, how very careless of you. I regret that I am unable to assist you."

Pickett rose from the uncomfortable chair and regarded Sir Archibald from his superior height. "Then you have no knowledge of the letter that disappeared from Lord Fieldhurst's desk at the same time you left the viscount's house?"

Alas, Sir Archibald was not so easily intimidated. "Did I say that? I am quite certain I did not. In fact, I am fully aware of the letter and its contents. I said merely that I am unable to assist you. You may console yourself with the knowledge that it was valueless as a clue, in any case."

"I think I would be the best judge of that."

"Perhaps, but as the letter has been disposed of, we shall never know, shall we?"

"Disposed of?" Pickett seized upon the telling phrase. "How? In the post, or on the fire?"

"Does it matter? It is lost to you either way. Suffice it to say that it has been dealt with in such a way that it need cause a lady no distress."

"Lady Fieldhurst?" demanded Pickett, rapidly losing his composure. "What has she to do with it? Just what was in that letter?"

"Come, Mr. Pickett, we are both men here, well versed in the ways of the world. Surely Lady Fieldhurst has suffered enough already, without discovering amorous correspondence among her husband's papers."

"You would have me believe that the letter was a communication between Fieldhurst and his mistress? But it was written in French and directed to a French address. That's a long way to go for a tumble."

"Perhaps it was written in that language to confound prying eyes," Sir Archibald said pointedly.

"If the Fieldhursts' marriage was as troubled as everyone seems to believe, it's unlikely her ladyship would be shocked to discover that her husband had a mistress in his keeping."

"Perhaps not, but why take the chance? Sometimes, Mr. Pickett, it is best to err on the side of caution."

"It would seem you think so, at all events. Sir Archibald, where were you last night between the hours of midnight and one o'clock?"

Sir Archibald bristled, and Pickett was more than ever convinced that his motives in taking the letter went beyond mere gallantry. "I was here, reading in my library."

Pickett hoped for his sake that the library was furnished with more comfortable chairs than the sitting room they now occupied. "Would anyone else in your household be prepared to swear to that?"

"Why the devil should they? A fine thing it is, when a man can't enjoy the comforts of his own fireside without a damned Nosey Parker from Bow Street treating him like a common criminal!"

Pickett, realizing no more information was to be had from his belligerent host, quitted the cheerless little room and picked up his hat from the console table near the door. As the butler opened the door to speed his departure, Pickett turned back for one parting word of advice. "Sir Archibald, a man has been murdered and you, by your own admission, removed something from his house the next morning without his widow's knowledge or permission. If I were you, I would make it my business to find someone who could testify to my whereabouts at the time of Lord Fieldhurst's death. Good day, sir."

CHAPTER 7
THE HEIR
PRESUMPTIVE AND
HIS MATE

The Bertram domicile in Half Moon Street was not nearly so imposing as the viscount's Berkeley Square residence but, as if in compensation for this deficiency, it was far more ornately decorated, with much gilding and numerous pieces of frankly fake Grecian statuary. Upon stating his business with the master of the house, Pickett followed the butler to a small, cluttered study, where George Bertram sat behind a desk whose top was scarcely visible for the piles of papers littering its surface.

"So it's you, is it?" Mr. Bertram complained in a tone which, in a less reedy voice, would have been a growl.

"I told you I would come," Pickett reminded him.

"You certainly didn't let any grass grow beneath your feet."

As Pickett approached the desk, Mr. Bertram swept a number of papers into the long, shallow drawer in the center, but not before Pickett (who in his short time on the Bow Street force had developed the useful talent of reading upside down) had recognized the names of a number of fashionable shops in Bond Street. They were, in fact, tradesman's bills; most containing numbers with double or triple digits, and several of which had "past due" scrawled boldly across the top. Here, it seemed, was motive enough, even for Mr. Colquhoun.

"But so long as you're here," continued Mr. Bertram, "you might as well make yourself useful. My strongbox was broken into last night — there, what do you make of that?"

He lifted the small metal box from the desk and turned it around so that Pickett might inspect the damage. The lock itself was intact, but long scratches on the face of the box surrounding the lock bore mute witness to the fact that it had been breached with a sharp object.

"Interesting," remarked Pickett, although he could not see precisely how this relatively minor crime might fit in with the viscount's murder, if in fact the two were related at all. Still, robbery and murder within the same family, all in a space of less than twenty-four hours, were rather too coincidental for his liking. "When did you discover the burglary?"

"This morning, shortly after I returned from my late cousin's house in Berkeley Square. I entered my study, and discovered — that." A sweep of his hand indicated the ravaged strongbox.

"Was anything taken?"

"Sixty-five pounds in five- and ten-pound notes."

Pickett crossed the crowded room, carefully skirting several occasional tables and a large bust of an obscure Greek philosopher, and examined the windows for any sign of forced entry. He found none.

"Don't you think," complained Mr. Bertram, "that the public would be better served if you fellows did more to prevent this sort of thing?"

As he offered no suggestions as to precisely what might have been done to prevent such an occurrence, Pickett wisely ignored this question and instead put forth one of his own.

"I will look into your burglary later, but for now, Mr. Bertram, I must ask you where you were last night between the hours of midnight and one o'clock."

George Bertram scowled. He was obviously attempting an air of belligerence, but succeeded only in sounding peevish. "So it has come to that, has it? Very well, Mr. Pickett, I will answer your question momentarily, but first you can answer mine. If I intended to kill my cousin, why should I have waited until now? Surely the time for murder would have been six years ago, after his betrothal was announced and it seemed likely that he would soon beget a son to supplant me in the succession. Why take such a risk once my position was assured?"

It appeared Mr. Bertram was well aware of the chief argument against him and had prepared a counterattack. Indeed, he had made such a good job of it that Pickett wondered if a written draft of his defense might be found among the papers covering his desk.

"Was your position so assured?" he asked. "You seem very confident."

"My good fellow, I have every reason for confidence! It is common knowledge that all was not well between my cousin and the lovely Lady Fieldhurst. Not to be indelicate, but he had formed the habit of taking his pleasure elsewhere, so, even if she had not been barren, there was also the matter of opportunity, if you take my meaning."

Pickett took his meaning very well, and wished he did not. He hated hearing Lady

Fieldhurst discussed in such a way, as if she were a brood mare. More specifically, he hated the thought of Lady Fieldhurst participating in the activities necessary for giving her husband an heir. But it had, he reminded himself, nothing to do with him, and he was determined not to be drawn into reacting emotionally. He had made that mistake once already with Lord Rupert Latham, to the detriment of his investigation.

"Husbands and wives can always reconcile," Pickett pointed out. "But even if they did not, it could not be pleasant for you, having to wait for a man still in his prime to die before you could collect your inheritance. I daresay this house must cost a pretty penny to maintain — more than I'll ever see in my lifetime, I'll wager."

Whether subconsciously or by design, a wistful note crept into Pickett's voice as he glanced around the cluttered but expensively furnished room.

"It's not cheap, I'll grant you that," Mr. Bertram admitted grudgingly. "Add to that my wife's determination to be a leader of fashion amongst a set of women whose husbands have twice my income at their disposal, and — well, much as I regret the manner of Fieldhurst's death, I'll not deny the timing was providential."

"Providential," echoed Pickett thoughtfully. "An interesting word for murder. Somehow I'd never pictured a Divine Providence going about sticking scissors into the necks of mortal men."

Mr. Bertram flushed an angry scarlet. "You are impertinent, sirrah! You ask where I was last night between midnight and one; very well, I shall tell you. I was at my club. I only returned this morning, just in time to be informed of my cousin's death."

"Which club was this?"

"White's. The Bertrams have been members there for generations."

Pickett jotted down this information in his notebook. "Were you often in the habit of spending the night there?"

"Not often, no," Mr. Bertram conceded. "But I'd had, er, unpleasant words with Mrs. Bertram earlier in the evening, which left me disinclined to endure more of her company."

"You quarreled over her spending habits?"

A stiff inclination of the head was the only reply, but it told Pickett far more than any number of words. Had the quarrel left Mr. Bertram so desperate for funds that he had stormed out of the house, not to spend the night at his club, but to remove the only impediment standing between himself and a fortune? A word with the porter at White's should supply the answer to that question, but another emerged. Had Mrs. Bertram, desperate for a style of living just beyond her reach, taken advantage of her husband's absence to secure the fortune for herself? There was still the puzzle of how she came to be in the viscountess's bedchamber, but here, too, a possibility arose. She had no doubt heard from her husband of the estrangement between the Fieldhursts; had she then, in an attempt to catch the viscount off his guard, offered him those favors he no longer obtained from his wife? Ludicrous, of course, to think that any man married to the beautiful Lady Fieldhurst could be tempted by the likes of Mrs. George Bertram, but there was no accounting for tastes.

He thanked Mr. Bertram for his time, feeling well pleased with this interview. He thought he had acquitted himself rather well against the new viscount; it was only with her ladyship — and, it must be confessed, Lord Rupert Latham, her lover — that he tended to make a fool of himself. He thought again of her insistence that nothing had happened between herself and Lord Rupert. Had she been telling the truth, or did he believe her because he wanted so desperately for it to be so?

"Mr. Pickett?" George Bertram's voice penetrated Pickett's reverie. "Have you anything else to say?"

With an effort, Pickett forced his attention back to the matter at hand. "I should like a word with Mrs. Bertram, if you please."

"Very well."

Mr. Bertram tugged the bell pull, and a moment later a footman came to show him to the drawing room where he might await Mrs. Bertram's pleasure. Pickett followed him as far as the door, then paused and turned back.

"By the bye," he addressed Mr. Bertram, "are you acquainted with a deacon named Toomer?"

"Never heard of him," Bertram stated decisively. "Why do you ask?"

Pickett shook his head. "No special reason."

The drawing room was as expensively and tastelessly furnished as the rest of the house. Mrs. Bertram entered the room in such a flutter of black crape that one might have supposed it was her husband, rather than his cousin, who had died.

"I can only spare you a moment," she informed him without preamble. "I have an appointment with my dressmaker. I must have new blacks made, you know, for square necklines are quite out of fashion this year, while as for trains, why, one might as well wear homespun! Still, at least it is only for a few weeks — not like my dear cousin, who must spend the next twelvemonth in a color so very unbecoming to her! Really, I thought the poor thing looked quite haggish. But so it always is with ladies who possess that pale sort of beauty: dark hues steal what little color they have."

Jealous old bat, thought Pickett. Aloud, he said, "I'll not take much of your time, your ladyship —"

"Oh, you must not call me that!" simpered Mrs. Bertram, in a voice which clearly communicated her pleasure in hearing herself thus addressed. "At least, not until after the funeral. It wouldn't be proper."

"As you wish, Mrs. Bertram. Can you tell me where you were last night between the hours of midnight and one o'clock?"

Her brow furrowed in concentration as she considered the question — trying, no doubt, to decide how best to answer without dredging up her quarrel with Bertram, Pickett thought.

"George and I — Mr. Bertram, you know, at least until after the funeral — attended the opera last night. It finished at about eleven — interminable, all that caterwauling, but simply everyone attends! — and we returned home."

"Where you both remained for the rest of the night?"

Mrs. Bertram nodded. "As you say."

Pickett made a great show of flipping through the pages of his notebook. "Then I must have been mistaken. I understood your husband to say that he had spent the night at his club."

Mrs. Bertram's face grew pale beneath her black-bordered lace cap as she rushed into speech. "Did he say so? And so he may have done. I daresay he left for White's after I had retired for the evening." She gave a brittle laugh. "Between you and me and the lamppost, Mr. Pickett, my husband and I were quite put out with one another. I fear he has little understanding of what it costs for a woman in my position to dress appropriately. But I am sure that is all settled now, for I know he will not wish to be behindhand in any courtesy due Fieldhurst or his widow."

"His widow?"

"Why, yes, for it is not her fault that she failed to give Fieldhurst a son. I believe such is often the case with these frail beauties.

But since George and I have three sons — one at Oxford, one at Eton, and one still in the nursery — it is not as if the line will die out due to her negligence. Indeed, if she does not wish to live with the dowager, I think we must consider letting little Edward's nanny go, and giving him over to his dear auntie's care. I daresay the boy will eventually become like the son she never had, and she may be assured that she is still one of the family."

The prospect of Lady Fieldhurst spending the rest of her life as unpaid drudge to her successor momentarily deprived Pickett of speech. "You seem to have matters well in hand," he said, when he could talk at all. "I only hope her ladyship will give your offer the consideration it deserves."

Mrs. Bertram, oblivious to irony, preened. "Yes, well, as Shakespeare said, blood is thicker than water."

Pickett, living only a stone's throw from Drury Lane Theatre and frequently to be found occupying its pit, was fairly certain that Shakespeare had never said any such thing, but declined to argue the point. He only wished Mr. Colquhoun had been present to witness this interrogation. Here was evidence aplenty of Lady Fieldhurst's innocence, for what woman of beauty, wealth, and position would willingly cast herself upon the charity of the new viscount and his wife?

"And so," continued Pickett, returning to the subject at hand, "you returned from the opera shortly after eleven, quarreled with Mr. Bertram, and then retired to your room. What time would you say this was?"

Mrs. Bertram shrugged her shoulders, setting her black draperies aflutter. "Goodness, I don't know! Midnight, perhaps, or a little after? I fell asleep so quickly, I never even heard the clock chime."

Pickett could not have said why he was so certain she was lying. Perhaps it was the way her gaze slid away from his, or the manner in which her unquiet hands twisted her black-bordered handkerchief. He made a note in his occurrence book, watching her all the while out of the corner of his eye.

"You are a very fortunate lady, Mrs. Bertram. I understand you might have been murdered in your bed."

Her agitated hands grew still, and her handkerchief floated to the floor unnoticed. "I beg your pardon?"

"Your husband tells me you suffered a burglary last night. His strong-box, to be exact."

"Oh, that!" Finding her hands unexpectedly empty, she spied her handkerchief on the floor and stooped to pick it up. "Yes, shocking, is it not? Really, one wonders how much a single family must be called upon to endure!"

Pickett regarded her with a puzzled frown. "Unwelcome though it is, surely the theft of sixty-five pounds hardly compares with the murder of a man in cold blood."

"Of course not," agreed Mrs. Bertram, flushing an unbecoming red. "But surely anyone capable of cold-blooded murder would not balk at petty thievery."

"You believe, then, that the murderer and the thief are the same?"

"Surely they must be!"

"I wonder," said Pickett thoughtfully.

"Some low person with a grudge against the family," suggested Mrs. Bertram, warming to this theme, "or riff-raff hoping to initiate a revolution in the French tradition. Most uncomfortable for us all, if that should prove to be the case."

Pickett agreed rather mechanically and took his leave. Once on the street, however, he paused to look back at the house. Something about the Bertram burglary did not ring true, in spite of the incriminating marks defacing the front of the strong-box.

Obeying a sudden impulse, Pickett vaulted

the low wrought-iron railing and hurried down the narrow staircase leading to the service entrance below ground level. He knocked on the door and was soon admitted to the kitchen, which was already bustling with preparations for an elaborate evening meal.

" 'The funeral baked meats did coldly furnish forth the marriage tables,' " quoted Pickett, before recalling that Shakespeare's lines dealt with a new widow's too-hasty second marriage. He wondered if Lord Rupert Latham's courtship would prove more successful this time, then pushed away a thought too repugnant to contemplate. He reminded himself sternly that any union between Lady Fieldhurst and Lord Rupert was none of his affair; he had all he could do merely seeing that she escaped execution.

Still, it was a rather deflated young man who requested of the housekeeper a private word with Mrs. Bertram's abigail. He was shown into the housekeeper's own parlor, where a frightened, somewhat mousy young woman soon joined him.

"Yes, sir? You wanted to see me?"

Pickett gave her a reassuring smile. "Only to ask you a few questions."

She slid into a chair and sat ramrod-straight, hands clasped tightly in her lap. "I don't know if I can answer them, but I'll do my best."

"That's all I ask. Tell me, what is your name?"

"Nancy, sir."

"Well, Nancy, what time did your mistress retire last night?"

The nervous Nancy hesitated for a moment before replying. "She came home from the opera at almost half-past eleven."

"Yes, but what time did she go to bed? Surely you must have helped her undress, put away her clothes. What time was that?"

"I can't rightly say what time she came upstairs. The master wanted a word with her first, and — well —"

"Yes, I know all about that." Pickett grinned. "I'll wager you got a rare earful afterwards."

The allure of a sympathetic ear, particularly one attached to the head of a handsome young man, proved too powerful to resist. The last vestiges of Nancy's fear vanished. "Aye, that I did! All told, it was going on for two o'clock by the time I put my mistress's pelisse away and sought my own bed."

"Her pelisse?" echoed Pickett, thinking of the well-dressed ladies occupying the boxes of Drury Lane Theatre, as glimpsed occasionally from his place in the pit. "Her opera cloak, surely?"

"No, for I'd put it up right after she came in. But soon after her confab with the master, she changed into a walking dress, put on her pelisse, and went out again. The master had already gone out by then, too. I heard — that is, I understand he was going to his club."

Pickett cocked a knowing eyebrow. "Descended to a shouting match by that time, had it? But surely it was a bit late for Mrs. Bertram to be going out alone. Is your mistress always so capricious?"

"Oh, no — leastways, she'd never done anything like that before, but mayhap she'd never had reason to. I shouldn't like to say anything against her, for she's always been good to me, giving me her castoff ribbons and such. Although," she added, "what she thinks I can do with a couple of bent and broken hair pins, I'm sure I don't know!"

"Bent and broken hair pins? Did she truly give you such things?"

"Oh, yes! Just last night, after I'd put up her coat. I didn't like to seem ungrateful, so I just thanked her kindly and put them in my pocket."

"Do you still have them?"

Nancy plunged a hand into her capacious pocket and withdrew two hair pins. The end was broken off one, while the other was bent at so sharp an angle as to render it useless.

"May I?" Pickett took the bent one and examined it through his quizzing-glass, thinking again of the scratch marks on the face of the strong-box. "Will you show me upstairs, Nancy? I think I need to have another word with your mistress."

Caroline Bertram, silently congratulating herself on a narrow escape, was not at all pleased to discover Pickett still on the premises.

"Yes, what is it now? I thought you had gone."

"I beg your pardon, Mrs. Bertram. I have one more request to make, if I may. I should like to have another look at your husband's strong-box."

"Oh, if that is all — ! Mr. Bertram is still in his study, if you would care to knock."

"I'm afraid you misunderstand. I should like you to show me the box, if you would be so kind."

Mrs. Bertram opened her mouth as if to protest; then, thinking better of it, turned and, with one last, furtive look in Pickett's direction, disappeared down the corridor in the direction of George Bertram's study.

She returned a few moments later, bearing the small metal box in both hands.

"Thank you." Without waiting for an invitation, Pickett sat down on a nearby chair and set the box on his knee. As he produced the bent hair pin, he heard Mrs. Bertram's gasp, quickly suppressed. He inserted the pin in the lock and, with one flick of the wrist, the lock sprang open.

"But — but — oh, that wicked Nancy!" exclaimed Mrs. Bertram, clearly grasping at straws. "Who would have thought it of her?"

"Come now, Mrs. Bertram, Nancy never opened that box," Pickett chided. "The pins were already in that condition when you gave them to her."

"What — what are you saying?"

"I am saying," replied Pickett, "that you broke into your husband's strong-box yourself, after he had departed for his club, and that you removed from it notes in the amount of sixty-five pounds."

"Nonsense! Even if I wished to do such a thing, I should not know how to go about it."

Pickett traced the longest scratch with one finger. "No, not at first. But never fear," some demon of mischief prompted him to add, "it grows easier with practice."

A dull red suffused her cheeks. "Insolent

man! I daresay you will expound this absurd theory to George!"

"No, for I expect he has already guessed. Besides, I am more interested in your movements afterwards. What did you do with the money?"

"You may search the house, if you wish," declared Mrs. Bertram, gesturing expansively. "You will not find the missing notes anywhere on the premises."

"No, for you went out again, did you not? And what, pray, was your errand? Did you call in Berkeley Square, by any chance?"

"No!"

"Or perhaps you hired a henchman to speed your husband to the succession by killing his cousin? Sixty-five pounds seems a rather low price for a viscountcy, but perhaps your cohort was as much a newcomer to murder as you were to burglary."

"I tell you, no! I confess, it was I who broke into George's strong-box, but not for any nefarious purpose. In fact, I did it for poor Harold!"

"Harold?" echoed Pickett, all at sea.

"My eldest son. He is presently at Oxford, and — well, you should know what young men are, Mr. Pickett, being so young yourself. They need the wherewithal to amuse themselves without being beholden to their parents for every last farthing."

Privately, Pickett felt that sixty-five pounds might amuse any number of young men for a year or more. Aloud, however, he merely said, "Surely you cannot expect me to believe that you traveled to Oxford and back in the space of less than two hours!"

"No, no, of course not! But I had to get the money out of the house before George returned, and it was far too late to catch the Mail. So I took it to my dear friend Clara Beauvoir, whose husband is just as clutchfisted as George, and who would naturally sympathize with a mother's need to provide for her child, no matter how great the risk to herself."

"And where does Mrs. Beauvoir live?"

"Why, here on Half Moon Street, only two doors down."

Alas, when, immediately upon leaving the Bertram domicile, Pickett attempted to confirm Mrs. Bertram's extraordinary tale, he met with a blank wall: Mrs. Beauvoir, as her butler informed him in no uncertain terms, was Not Receiving. This constituted no small setback, as Pickett's efforts on Lady Fieldhurst's behalf would have been aided considerably by Mrs. Beauvoir's vehement denial of a story which, it must be said, seemed too far-fetched to be believed.

Unfortunately, Pickett could not shake the lowering conviction that it was probably true.

CHAPTER 8
JOHN PICKETT
PAYS A CALL

"It won't do, John," the magistrate said some time later, when Pickett's findings were presented to him. "You know it won't. Good, solid evidence is what you need, and you haven't a shred of it."

Pickett leaned against the railing that separated the magistrate's bench from the rest of the room. "Not yet," he confessed reluctantly. "But the porter at White's can't recall seeing Mr. Bertram leave the premises, and Mrs. Bertram turns out to possess a ruthless streak that wouldn't stick at much. And both of them had sufficient reason to want Fieldhurst dead. As for Sir Archibald Stanton, I don't know yet what his motive might be, but I'll be bound he never stole that letter out of pure gallantry. Her ladyship is not the only possible suspect."

"But it was she who discovered the body."

"Exactly!" Pickett came up off the railing

like a rifle shot. "Why should she bring a lover to the very bedchamber where she knew her husband was lying dead?"

"I should rather ask, why should she succumb to Lord Rupert's advances on this particular night, when she had steadfastly resisted up to this point? Perhaps because she knew she would not be obliged to go through with an illicit union? Perhaps because she wanted a witness present to attest to her shock and horror upon discovery of her husband's dead body?"

Seeing that his most junior Runner had lapsed into silence, the magistrate pressed his advantage. "It was still she who had easiest access to the bedchamber, and it was she who knew the nail scissors were readily to hand. She wanted only the opportunity. If you truly want to establish her innocence, you must first eliminate that."

"And so I will, sir, as soon as I —"

Here he caused no small damage to his argument by yawning hugely. Mr. Colquhoun waited patiently until his Runner's mouth was closed, then asked, "How long since you've slept, John?"

Pickett glanced at the clock on the mantel. "Just over twenty-four hours, sir."

The magistrate nodded. "I thought as much. Go home and go to bed. I promise you, no one will arrest the viscountess while you sleep."

She wanted only the opportunity . . . To establish her innocence, you must first eliminate that. The magistrate's words accompanied him all the way to Drury Lane, where he discovered to his relief that Mrs. Catchpole was occupied in the rear of the store. Feeling incapable of facing another inquisition — for Mrs. Catchpole's questioning could be twice as ruthless as Mr. Colquhoun's, once that redoubtable female had got the bit between her teeth — he tiptoed up the stairs so as not to attract her attention. Once upstairs, he paused only long enough to remove his coat and boots before collapsing onto the narrow iron-framed bed.

Alas, his slumber was not the peaceful oblivion he had hoped for. He was troubled — if that was the word for it — by vaguely erotic dreams in which Lady Fieldhurst, clad in the white ball gown in which he had first seen her, twined her slender arms about the neck of a man who was somehow both himself and the viscount. As he lowered his head to kiss her, firelight flashed off the silver blades of a pair of nail scissors concealed in her hand, and he awoke shaken and damp with perspiration. When he slept again, the setting had changed to the gallows, where a hooded executioner approached Lady Fieldhurst with a length of rope stretched taut between his hands. But even as he reached to lower the noose over her head, Pickett seized the lady, tossed her across his saddle-bow, and carried her in safety to his rooms above the chandler's shop, where she rewarded his heroism in a manner which, when examined in the harsh light of wakefulness, was as embarrassing as it was improbable.

But whatever else they may have done, these dreams served to strengthen Pickett's belief in Lady Fieldhurst's innocence. A moment's reflection was sufficient to inform Pickett that, if he truly wished to rescue Lady Fieldhurst from the gallows, his best course of action lay not in tossing the lady across his saddle-bow (an awkward proposition in any case, as he possessed neither saddle nor horse), but in eliminating any possibility that she might have had either the inclination or the opportunity to do the deed. Unfortunately, there was little he could do about inclination. He had already heard from the lady's own lips that all had not been well between herself and her husband, and this unhappy state of affairs had been confirmed by Camille de la

Rochefort as well as Mr. and Mrs. Bertram.

His efforts, then, must focus on opportunity. Pickett's experience of balls was slight to the point of nonexistence, but common sense informed him that, if Lady Fieldhurst had indeed spent the evening thus engaged, her presence must surely have been noted. There must be gentlemen somewhere in London who would remember dancing with her, ladies who would recall admiring her gown. It remained only for him to locate these anonymous beings and piece together a complete accounting of the viscountess's movements on the night of her husband's murder. With this end in view, he rose, washed, and dressed, then set out for Lady Herrington's house in Portman Square.

Herein he made a tactical error, for it was by now almost half-past three — that time of day at which the *ton* made what it erroneously referred to as morning calls. Lady Herrington, when interrupted by her butler, was in the act of dispensing tea to a roomful of these callers. She took no particular pleasure in this act of hospitality, as her guests had been quick to inform her that her recent entertainment, which she had believed to be quite the *succès fou,* had been eclipsed in the public eye by the violent death of Viscount Fieldhurst.

"Beg pardon, my lady," murmured her ladyship's butler, "but there is a man from Bow Street below, requesting a word with your ladyship."

"Dear me!" she exclaimed, setting her teacup down with a clatter. "And he wants to see me? Show him into the small saloon, and tell him I shall be with him directly. I wonder, does one offer tea to such a person? Best not, I suppose."

Lady Herrington rose with a rustle of silk skirts and excused herself to her guests. A moment later she entered the small saloon at the back of the house, her expression carefully, if imperfectly, schooled into an expression devoid of curiosity.

"John Pickett of Bow Street, my lady," intoned the butler, then withdrew, leaving her ladyship alone with a young man whose slightly shabby dress and outmoded queue appeared glaringly out of place, even in this least formal of receiving rooms.

"Your ladyship," said this worthy, rising awkwardly from his rigid perch on the edge of a straight chair covered in cherry-striped satin. "I hate to take you away from your guests, but I understand you held a ball here last night."

The lady inclined her head, somewhat mollified by the information that word of her humble amusement (only four hundred invitations sent, and, by some quirk of scheduling, in direct conflict with a rout given by a rival hostess) had spread so far eastward.

"And you numbered among your guests the viscountess Lady Fieldhurst?"

Again that inclination of the head.

"I should be grateful if you could give me, as well as you are able, an accounting of her ladyship's movements last night."

At this simple request, Lady Herrington abandoned all pretense of indifference. "Good heavens! Never tell me you believe *Julia — !*"

Mr. Pickett had no intention of telling her any such thing, even had he been able to find his tongue after being unexpectedly presented with the gift of Lady Fieldhurst's Christian name. *Julia.* It suited her, somehow. But this fact, though undoubtedly interesting, was a matter of irrelevance where her ladyship's guilt or innocence was concerned, so he mentally filed it away for future study, and returned his attention to the matter at hand.

"Merely a routine interrogation, my lady," he assured Lady Herrington hastily. "I believe Lord Rupert Latham was also present?"

"Yes, for he escorted Lady Fieldhurst," concurred her ladyship, recovering her composure.

"You were not surprised to see them together?"

"Lud, no! Sir Rupert was mad for her before her marriage — Miss Runyon she was then, of course. I wonder if she will marry him, now that Fieldhurst is dead? She is far too young and beautiful to wear black for the rest of her life."

Pickett found himself in complete agreement with this assessment, although he was less than enthusiastic at the prospect of her marriage to Lord Rupert Latham.

"So she arrived with Lord Rupert. What next?"

"I believe they had the first dance together, although I could not swear to it, for I was still greeting guests at the door. My husband partnered her for the second, as she was the next-highest ranking lady present, after the countess of Farnsworth."

"Did she dance a great deal?" Pickett asked, duly taking notes as Lady Herrington prattled on.

"Oh, Lud, yes! I daresay she reserved the supper dance for Lord Rupert — no, that cannot be right, for I saw her at the table with Mr. Fretwell —'tis a wonder he didn't break his neck, dashing off to Brighton in that rackety way! And before that, Captain Sir Charles Ormond had partnered her in the cotillion — now *that* I do remember, for I noticed particularly what a handsome pair they made, he in his scarlet regimentals and she all in white."

Pickett, deciphering this speech with some difficulty, came to the conclusion that Lady Herrington might well prove to be a veritable font of information, provided he was able to curtail the occasional rabbit-chase (precisely when, and for what purpose, Mr. Fretwell had made his perilous trip to Brighton, for instance, he knew not and cared less) and steer her ladyship gently back to the subject at hand. In this manner, he was able to piece together a fair accounting of Lady Fieldhurst's movements, particularly after Lady Herrington conceived the happy notion of retrieving the invitation list from her escritoire. Armed with this voluminous document (which, Mr. Pickett was rather surprised to observe, ran to more than a dozen pages), she was able to provide him with a roll-call of gentlemen with whom she had seen the viscountess paired, in an approximation of the order in which these dances had occurred.

Alas, her recollections were incomplete, as

she had frequently been distracted by her duties as hostess. Pickett foresaw that he would be obliged to spend several hours in questioning a number of unknown gentlemen for whom he had unaccountably conceived a violent dislike. But even if every one of these gentlemen recalled dancing with the viscountess in vivid detail, there still remained a period of a quarter-hour in which Lady Herrington could not recall having seen the viscountess at all.

"Perhaps," suggested Pickett blandly, "her ladyship was obliged to withdraw from the ballroom in order to check her hair, or her gown."

"Indeed, yes! I can see you are well acquainted with the idiosyncrasies of my sex, Mr. Pickett. If Lady Fieldhurst withdrew for such a reason, my Jane should have known of it, for I instructed her to remain at my guests' disposal all evening."

"Would you send for her, if you please?"

"Would that I might, Mr. Pickett, but I was obliged to let the girl go." Leaning forward in her chair, she lowered her voice to a scandalized whisper. "One of the guests discovered her in *flagrante delicto* with the second footman. I was obliged to dismiss the pair of them. One simply can't tolerate that sort of thing, you know."

"Do you know where I might find this — Jane, was it?"

"Jane Mudge. As for where she might be found, I have no idea. To be quite frank, Mr. Pickett, I hope I may never set eyes on the wretched girl again!"

Having pursued this line of investigation to a most unsatisfactory conclusion, he thanked Lady Herrington for her trouble and assured her that she had been most helpful. He asked if he might borrow her invitation list and, permission being granted, thanked her again, bade her good day, and took his leave. It was perhaps as well for his peace of mind that he was out of earshot by the time the lady returned to her guests, and so could not hear her breathlessly exclaim, "My dears, you will never credit it! I have just had the most *extraordinary* interview!"

CHAPTER 9
IN WHICH JOHN PICKETT CONDUCTS AN EXPERIMENT

Methodically working his way down Lady Herrington's guest list, John Pickett was somewhat daunted by the scope and variety of Lady Fieldhurst's male acquaintance. There were Lords and Sirs and Honourables, to say nothing of the plain Misters who compensated for their lack of more exalted titles with an assortment of hyphenated surnames. There were military men and fops, dissipated rakes, and one besotted youth who grew quite truculent when he realized the direction of Pickett's questioning. While some of these gentlemen had more relevant information to offer than others, one constant remained: there was a fifteen- to twenty-minute period of time in which no one could recall having seen the viscountess.

Worse, without the maid to corroborate her statement, he had only Lady Fieldhurst's word that she had torn her gown at all. While that might be good enough for him, he had no illusions as to how far it would get her in a court of law.

His steps slowed as he neared Bow Street. It appeared he might have spoken too soon when he had assured the magistrate of her innocence. For beyond the damning circumstances of her bedchamber and her nail scissors, it now appeared that she had both motive and opportunity to rid herself of a husband she no longer loved. And yet, try as he might, he could not reconcile the memory of the newly-widowed viscountess, dressed in unrelieved black and beset by her husband's domineering relations, with the image of her ladyship's white-clad figure fleeing down the gas-lit streets of Mayfair with malice aforethought.

The picture that formed in his mind caused him to stop in mid-stride halfway across Long Acre, inspiring the driver of a passing hackney to shake his fist as he struggled to regain control of his startled horses. But Mr. Pickett had no thought to spare for such mundane matters, nor did he hear the verbal tirade directed against loitering pedestrians who considered their own leisure to be more important than the business of honest tradesmen. For he had suddenly recollected in vivid detail Lady Fieldhurst's appearance on the night of her husband's murder. He had been kneeling over the viscount's body, and she standing nearby, the dying firelight flickering over the hem of her gown and the toes of her soft kid slippers.

Was it possible for any woman, dressed as she had been, to travel on foot from Portman to Berkeley Square and back again within, at most, twenty minutes? Of his own ability to do so, he had no doubt; not for nothing were the members of the Bow Street force called "Runners." But a lady in evening dress, to say nothing of those shoes —

He was abruptly startled from his reverie as a plump arm looped through his. Pickett looked down to see a pert young female in a faded bonnet falling into step beside him.

"Bone chewer," she caroled in cheerful, if unrefined, accents.

"Lucy! You startled me. But — what did you call me?"

"It's French," Lucy explained, preening herself on this new, if dubious, accomplishment. "It means 'good day.' I've a young gentleman who's teaching me."

Pickett had little doubt as to what this obliging "gentleman" — Lucy's concept of class structure was surprisingly fluid — was receiving in return for his expertise. But her assistance as an informer had been invaluable on more than one occasion, so he continued to supplement her income, while turning a blind eye to her less reputable activities.

"He says French girls can find work as lady's maids. So I figures I'll learn to speak French, then go to work for a fine lady in a big house."

Pickett thought of Lady Fieldhurst's French maid and wondered whether the haughty Camille de la Rochefort would recognize her native tongue on Lucy's lips.

"Lucy!" he exclaimed as an idea took form. "You're just the person I want!"

"And about time, too, John Pickett," she retorted with a saucy sway of her hips.

"Can you meet me tonight, very late? Two o'clock, say? You'll be well compensated for the inconvenience, I promise you."

"I don't doubt it," Lucy purred, looking him up and down in a manner which, had he been less caught up in his own plans, would have made him extremely uncomfortable.

He arrived by hackney carriage at the designated hour, and disembarked before the ramshackle dwelling where Lucy shared a room with two other young women of the same profession. He climbed the narrow, uncarpeted staircase up three flights, and rapped with his baton on a wooden door from which the paint had long since peeled. Lucy flung it open, wearing a frilly but threadbare dressing gown and an expression of high dudgeon.

"We've got to go someplace else," she informed him without preamble. "Moll thinks her new cully is too fine to share a roof with the likes of us!" This last was delivered in ringing tones, and directed somewhere over Lucy's shoulder. Suddenly Pickett realized that Lucy had definite, and quite erroneous, ideas about the evening's entertainment.

"That's not what I meant," he protested feebly. "Lucy, you know that's not what I meant!"

"Well, I thought it would be a new lay for you, who've never once tried to take advantage of a poor working girl, more's the pity. And as for what Moll will say, when she hears I wasted the whole night jawing with a prig-napper —"

"You can tell Moll that I called to take you for a carriage drive, just as if you were a fine lady."

This interruption, couched in soothing

144

tones, had the desired effect. Lucy forgot her grievances with a readiness which, while hardly flattering to Pickett's manhood, boded well for the success of his mission.

"Go on with you!" Lucy exclaimed, torn between hope and doubt. "You don't really mean it!"

"Yes, I really mean it."

As Lucy's world was largely confined to the streets where she plied her trade, a ride in a hired hackney constituted untold luxury. As Pickett flagged down a vehicle and settled himself and his fair passenger on its worn and poorly sprung seats, she entertained herself hugely with predictions of Moll's envy and wrath upon learning of Lucy's adventures. It was not until the dark and narrow streets of Covent Garden gave way to the broader thoroughfares of the West End that she thought to inquire as to their destination.

"We're going to Mayfair," Pickett informed her. "Portman Square, to be exact."

"Not amongst all the nobs!" exclaimed Lucy, her cup by now running over. "But why?"

"I need a favor from you, Lucy. I need to know how long it takes a lady to travel on foot from Portman to Berkeley Square."

The hackney had by this time rolled to a

stop, and Lucy, without waiting for Pickett to assist her, flung open the door and leaped to the pavement. She stood at one end of an elegant square lined with tall, narrow dwellings whose pilastered façades and long, arched windows gave the impression of aristocratic faces gazing haughtily down patrician noses at a trespasser. Halfway down the square, one building blazed with light in spite of the lateness of the hour, and lilting violin music drifted on the night breeze.

"Gor!" Lucy breathed, awe-struck. "You *are* flying high these days, aren't you?"

Pickett merely shrugged and consulted his watch. "Murder looks much the same in Mayfair as it does in Seven Dials. Now, if you're ready, let's go."

"Murder?" echoed Lucy in thrilling tones, falling into step beside him as they set out on foot across the square. "Who's got hisself rubbed out?"

"A viscount by the name of Fieldhurst."

"And this lady you want me to pretend to be?"

"His wife — widow, I should say. Lady Fieldhurst."

"Lud, it's better nor a play!" Lucy exclaimed with ghoulish zeal. "Did she snuff him?"

"No!"

This denial was uttered with such vehemence that Lucy stopped in her tracks. She resumed her steps at Pickett's urging, but cast a coy sidelong glance in his direction. "Is she pretty?"

"Yes."

Lucy waited for him to elaborate on this rather curt reply and, when he did not, drew her own conclusions. "You'd better watch yourself, John Pickett, before you get in over your head."

He offered no response to this cryptic warning, and the remainder of the trek passed in silence, punctuated only by Lucy's labored breathing as she struggled to maintain the pace set by the determined Runner. At last he took her elbow as they drew abreast of an elegant residence whose door knocker was tied up with black crape.

"We can stop now." As Lucy gawked at the splendors of Berkeley Square, Pickett consulted his pocket watch, and was pleased with what he found there. "Lucy, you're an angel! Eight minutes, forty-three seconds. Allowing her ladyship, say, five minutes to reach her room, quarrel with his lordship and stab him with the scissors, then the return trip to Portman Square — no. Impossible for her to do it in less than twenty minutes."

"Unless she took a coach," suggested Lucy eagerly, apparently not nearly as angelic as Pickett had supposed.

"There is that," acknowledged Pickett, somewhat deflated. "I'll have a word with Lord Rupert's coachman."

"Or," persisted Lucy, "she could've hired a hackney."

"Faugh!" snorted Pickett, dismissing this suggestion out of hand. "Did you ever know a hackney to turn up just when it was wanted? And well off the main roads, too!"

As if determined to prove him a liar, a hackney carriage chose that moment to lurch round the corner into Berkeley Square, stopping before an imposing edifice and disgorging a rather unsteady gentleman in rumpled evening dress who whistled tunelessly as he staggered up the front steps. Lucy, arching a knowing eyebrow at Pickett, merely grinned.

Mr. Colquhoun, the magistrate, was not grinning several hours later, when apprised of his youngest Runner's nocturnal activities. Indeed, the revelation of Lady Fieldhurst's apparent innocence garnered no response from him save the lowering of bushy white brows over his hawk-like nose.

"Tell me, Mr. Pickett," he intoned, scowling over the wire rims of his spectacles, "why are you so determined to believe this woman innocent?"

Pickett, unintimidated, answered the question with one of his own. "Meaning no disrespect, sir, but why are you so determined to believe her guilty?"

"You cannot deny that all the evidence thus far appears to point in her direction: *her* bedchamber, *her* nail scissors, *her* discovery of the body, conveniently accompanied by a witness — *her* lover. To say nothing of her relationship to the victim. If she was indeed unhappy in her marriage, there was little else she could have done to emancipate herself. Even had she prevailed upon her husband to apply to the House of Lords for a divorce, you may be certain that august body would not have dealt kindly with her."

"I'll grant you she was at odds with his lordship, sir, but there's quite a difference between divorce and murder. Lady Fieldhurst is innocent, and I intend to prove it."

Mr. Colquhoun heaved the weary sigh of one who has echoed the same argument too many times. "I would suggest, Mr. Pickett, that you concentrate less on proving who did *not* murder the viscount and focus your attentions on proving who did. Or have you given any thought to that matter at all?"

If Pickett noticed the magistrate's sarcasm, he chose not to acknowledge it. "Yes, sir, I have. I can't rule out the heir, George Bertram, but to my mind, Lord Rupert Latham is the likeliest suspect."

Mr. Colquhoun unbent sufficiently to cock one eyebrow. "Lord Rupert Latham? Lady Fieldhurst's lover?"

"Only in his dreams, sir," said Pickett, not without satisfaction.

"I see," observed the magistrate, who apparently saw a great deal more than Mr. Pickett intended. "And is your case against Lord Rupert built upon evidence or — dare I say it? — envy?"

Pickett flushed scarlet, but replied woodenly, "I hope I know my place, sir."

"Good. See that you don't forget it."

Pickett, his pride stung by his magistrate's parting shot, deemed it high time to pay another call on Lord Rupert Latham. He had not looked forward to this undertaking, being uncomfortably aware that he had not come off well in his initial interview with Lady Fieldhurst's would-be lover. Not that Pickett doubted his abilities at detection; indeed, it was a source of some pride to him that he had been promoted from the Foot Patrol at the tender age of four-and-twenty. But although he had told Lucy that murder was the same, no matter one's part of Town, he was not entirely convinced of the truth of his own words. Something about Lord Rupert Latham made him feel not only his shortage of years but, worse, his lack of sophistication. Even more galling was the suspicion that his lordship was fully conscious of his advantage, and used it to full effect. Was it, as Mr. Colquhoun suggested, the bitter knowledge that it was Lord Rupert, and not John Pickett, who was Lady Fieldhurst's choice? If that were so, he would do well to find the killer quickly and have done with her ladyship at once, before he made an utter fool of himself.

With these melancholy thoughts for companionship, he arrived at Lord Rupert's rooms in the Albany, and requested the indulgence of a word with his lordship. Lord Rupert's man opened his mouth — to say something crushing, Pickett had no doubt — but was forestalled by the appearance of Lord Rupert himself. On this occasion, his lordship was not seated at the breakfast table *en déshabillé,* but was dressed for the day in a long-tailed morning coat of dark blue cloth and skin-tight pantaloons unmarred by creases. Dual rows of brass buttons gleamed on his chest and, as for his glossy black boots, Lord Rupert might have seen his reflection in them had his starched cravat not prevented him from lowering his chin. Pickett, painfully aware of his serviceable but outmoded brown serge coat, felt not only unsophisticated, but shabby as well.

"Ah, Mr. Pickett, my friend from Bow Street," drawled his lordship. "To what, pray, do I owe this honor?"

"It's come to my attention, my lord, that you left Lady Herrington's ball at some point during the evening, and did not return to Portman Square until some time after midnight," Pickett replied without preamble.

"Who says so?" demanded Lord Rupert.

"Lady Fieldhurst."

Lord Rupert, engaged in extracting a pinch of snuff from an elegantly enameled box, froze with one slender white hand suspended scant inches from his aquiline nose. "Interesting. I wonder what other disclosures you had from the artless Julia's lips."

"And *I* wonder, my lord, why you saw fit to withhold the information."

"Perhaps," suggested his lordship, after a pause during which he raised the pinch of snuff to one nostril and inhaled sharply, "I withheld it because it was none of your business."

Made bold by righteous indignation, Pickett held his ground. "Murder is everyone's business."

"There, sir, you have me," acknowledged Lord Rupert, bowing with exaggerated civility. "Should I ever commit murder, you will be the first to know. Alas, I did nothing more remarkable than douse my person with champagne — unworthy of me, I confess, but hardly illegal."

"I'd like to see those breeches, if I may."

Lord Rupert arched an eyebrow. "My dear Mr. Pickett, surely you do not suppose I would wear stained breeches! I gave them to my man, Farley. Farley, be a good fellow and fetch my damaged breeches for Mr. Pickett."

"Not to be disobliging, my lord, but I regret that I cannot," said the servant, breaking the disapproving silence he had maintained since first opening the door. "I sold them yesterday morning to the rag-and-bone man for two shillings tuppence."

"Two shillings tuppence!" echoed Lord Rupert in mournful tones. "And when one considers what one's tailor charged for them! Ah, well, I daresay it can't be helped.

As you see, Mr. Pickett, I can be of no further assistance to you."

"One moment," Pickett said, addressing himself to Farley. "What of this rag-and-bone man? Do you know his name or direction?"

"I am hardly upon intimate terms with such a person, sir," intoned Farley in haughty accents that equaled anything his master might have employed, "but I believe, by certain things the man let fall, that he had formed the intention of selling the article to a second-hand clothing store."

"Any idea as to which one?" Pickett asked, making a notation in his notebook.

"As I am not in the habit of frequenting such establishments, sir, I am sure I could not say."

The disappearance of the stained breeches was a bit too facile for Pickett's liking, but the recollection that Lady Fieldhurst frequently disposed of her own cast-offs in a similar manner served to lend credence to the tale. Still, it was a lead, and in a case with so little hard evidence, any lead was worth pursuing. Searching the numerous second-hand shops in London's seedier districts was, he decided, a task that would suit Lucy down to the ground.

CHAPTER 10
SIR THADDEUS
RUNYON, SQUIRE OF
SOMERSETSHIRE

Over the next forty-eight hours, Lady Fieldhurst was overwhelmed with visitors paying
condolence calls. Lady Dunnington, with
her usual candor, characterized them as a
flock of vultures come to pick over the dead
man's bones, but the viscountess could not
but be grateful for their concern. She attributed the unusual number of visitors to
her late husband's influence in government
circles, and so dispensed tea and cakes with
all the graciousness of a seasoned political
hostess performing the office for perhaps
the last time. However else she must have
disappointed her husband, she felt she had
not shamed him in that role. She accepted
condolences on the viscount's death, gently
but firmly discouraging any speculation as
to how it came about, and steered the
conversation to less personal subjects. The
Herrington ball of two days ago was one of
the more convenient topics to hand since,

now that she thought of it, most of her current guests had been present on that occasion, also.

Alas, she was in for a rude awakening. During a brief lull in the conversation, young Mr. Ned Gibson, the same stammering youth who had stepped on her ladyship's hem during the night's festivities, declared in a fervent voice, "I don't care what anyone says! I *know* you didn't kill him!"

A shocked silence greeted this pronouncement; whereupon Mr. Gibson, seeing the reproachful looks cast in his direction and feeling the evil eye of his mother upon him, felt it incumbent upon him to make matters worse by adding, with undiminished fervor, "And so I told that fellow from Bow Street, you may be sure —"

"Dear me, look at the time!" interrupted Mrs. Gibson, seizing her hapless son by the ear and hauling him to his feet as if he were still in the nursery. "I shall be late for an appointment with my dressmaker. Good day, Lady Fieldhurst — tragic loss — so sorry —"

With this disjointed farewell, she all but dragged her disgraced offspring from the room in her wake. An awkward silence reigned for only a moment, before the entire company burst into loud and cheerful conversation. This unnatural jollity lasted perhaps five minutes, until Lady Fieldhurst demanded of the lady seated on her left, "What of you, Martha? Has Mr. Pickett questioned you, as well?"

"N-no, my dear," stammered the lady, "he merely called to make a few inquiries of my husband. Robert did dance with you, you know, and that Bow Street fellow wanted to know if he could recall what time —"

"And you, Lydia?" challenged the viscountess, turning to a trembling woman on her right.

"No, but I was at Lady Herrington's on the morning after her ball, when the Bow Street officer came to question her. They were gone for quite a long time."

And so it went. One by one, each caller admitted that, yes, they had heard of Lady Fieldhurst's implication in the crime, if not from "that Bow Street fellow" himself, then from Lady Herrington or one of her guests. The viscountess's head was buzzing by the time the bravest of her callers deemed it safe to take her leave and crept sheepishly from the room. The others quickly followed and, within ten minutes, the viscountess was alone with Lady Dunnington.

"What did I tell you?" sniffed the countess. "Vultures, every one of them, come to sniff out what gossip they can."

"And who can blame them?" asked Lady Fieldhurst, slumping in her chair. "I thought he believed me. I suppose I was naïve."

"No more so than I," said Lady Dunnington, sipping her now tepid tea. "I said the man-child from Bow Street could do you no harm. It appears I was wrong."

Lady Fieldhurst was not finished entertaining for the day, for shortly after tea, Thomas ushered Lord Rupert Latham into the room.

"Rupert!" cried her ladyship, pressing a hand to her blackclad bosom. "Thank heaven it is only you!"

"My dear Lady Fieldhurst," Lord Rupert said with excruciating correctness, bowing over her hand. "I trust I have not come at an inconvenient time, but I had to see for myself how you are bearing up."

"As well as may be expected, considering that I have spent the better part of the day pouring tea for the most voracious set of busybodies in London," she replied, gently withdrawing her hand from his, when he might have retained it a bit longer than propriety decreed.

Thomas, still acting in the capacity of butler, took himself from the room and closed the door behind him. Lord Rupert, hearing the click of the latch, abandoned his pursuit of Lady Fieldhurst's hand, only to pull her into his arms.

"Rupert!" protested her ladyship, struggling to hold him at arm's length. "We must not!"

"I can think of a time when you were not so unwilling," he reminded her.

"Under the circumstances, this is hardly —"

Lord Rupert released her, nevertheless objecting, "Come now, Julia, this is doing it much too brown! Surely you don't think to enact the role of the grieving widow?" He broke off and raised his quizzing glass, the better to admire the effect of sunlight spilling through the long window, turning her fair hair to gold and giving her an angelic appearance which contrasted sharply with the unrelieved black of her gown. "Although I must confess that you are one of the few women to whom mourning is becoming. Accept my compliments."

"Oh, *bother* your compliments! Rupert, when you left Lady Herrington's ball, where did you go?"

"Why, here, my sweet. Surely you must remember?"

"Not then — earlier, after you spilled your champagne."

"I returned to my rooms to change my raiment, just as I told you at the time. Why do you ask?"

Too late, it occurred to the viscountess that it might be wisest to keep her doubts to herself. She knew from experience that Lord Rupert could be unscrupulous where his own interests were at stake; indeed, the *frisson* of danger which surrounded him had always been a great part of his appeal. But, while a ruthless admirer might be all very well for provoking the ire of a jealous husband (not that Frederick had ever shown any signs of jealousy), he might not be the safest confidante for a woman in her present circumstances. If Lord Rupert had indeed committed one murder, he might not scruple to commit another in order to conceal the first. Suddenly his air of tightly controlled passions seemed much less appealing, and far more menacing. Although she would have scoffed at the idea only moments before, she was now uncomfortably aware of the fact that she was very much alone with him, and that Thomas — and indeed all the rest of the staff — seemed very far away.

She shrugged, making a valiant attempt at nonchalance. "No particular reason. It merely seemed to me that you were gone a very long time. You did promise to return before supper, and when you did not, I began to wonder —"

"The devil you did! Has that damned thief-taker been here? What has he been telling you?"

"He has been here, yes — it appears he has been all over Mayfair! — but he didn't say anything about you. In fact, he didn't know anything about your absence from the ball until he suggested you might vouch for my presence there from half-past eight to almost two. Honesty compelled me to say that you could not do so, as you had been absent for a brief time yourself."

"Destroying not only your own alibi, but mine in the process," Lord Rupert pointed out. "I see now why I was forced to endure another visit from Bow Street. At least this time the diligent Mr. Pickett had the courtesy to wait until I had finished my breakfast before descending upon me."

She regarded him warily, her blue gaze narrowed. "If I placed you in an awkward situation, Rupert, I'm sorry. I didn't realize you were in such dire need of an alibi."

"Nor did I, until I had the honor of breakfasting with our friend from Bow Street. I had the distinct impression that he would cheerfully send me to the gallows in order to save your pretty neck. You appear to have made a conquest, my dear, and a very useful one at that. I congratulate you."

"I wish you will not talk nonsense! You didn't kill him — did you?"

"Our friend from Bow Street? Oh, you mean your husband! How very gauche of me, to be sure. It is truly amazing what one learns about oneself in a time of crisis," Lord Rupert marveled. "Before yesterday, I had no idea so many people considered me capable of such bloodthirstiness. My dear Julia, no one needed your husband to remain among the living more than I. Should you doubt it, you have only to consider the coolness with which you greeted me only moments ago."

"But," said the viscountess, wisely ignoring this rider, "if *you* didn't do it, and *I* didn't do it — and I assure you I did not, no matter what the gossips may say! — Rupert, is it possible that Frederick killed himself?"

"By stabbing himself in the neck with a pair of nail scissors?" scoffed Lord Rupert. "Highly unlikely, my dear. I daresay most gentlemen so inclined would prefer to use a pistol. Messy, to be sure, but, if done properly, infinitely less painful."

Lady Fieldhurst made a moue of distaste,

but whatever she might have said to this rather graphic analysis was interrupted by a tentative knock on the door.

"Yes, who is it?"

The door opened a crack, and Thomas's head appeared in the opening. "Begging your pardon, my lady, but Mr. Crumpton is here."

Lady Fieldhurst, recognizing the name of her late husband's solicitor, recalled that her husband's will was to be read that day, and resigned herself to an afternoon of dealing with the more mundane aspects of her husband's demise. "Very well, Thomas, show him into the — no, bring him here. Lord Rupert was just taking his leave."

Lord Rupert raised an eyebrow, as if ready to contradict this statement, but remained silent.

Thomas, blushing furiously, bowed himself from the room, shutting the door behind him.

"Now, what do you suppose is wrong with him?" Lady Fieldhurst wondered aloud.

"Er, I fancy young Thomas supposed himself to be interrupting a romantic tryst," offered Lord Rupert.

"Good heavens! Did he think to find us rolling about on the carpet? No, do not favor that utterance with a reply; for I can tell by your expression that you are about to say something hateful!"

Lord Rupert, thus adjured, contented himself with an ironic smile.

"On a more positive note," conceded her ladyship, "I can see that, should I be fortunate enough to escape the gallows, I need not fear for my reputation; indeed, I shall have no reputation left!"

"In that case, my dear, you and I need have no scruples," said Lord Rupert. "But if you say I must go, then go I shall, and await a more opportune time."

He executed a graceful bow over her hand, turning it in his grasp and twitching back the edge of her black glove so that he might press an ardent kiss onto her bare wrist. It was perhaps unfortunate for Lady Fieldhurst that at this moment the footman reappeared with not only the solicitor, but also Mr. Pickett in tow. Her face flaming, she snatched her hand away from Lord Rupert and dropped a curtsy in the direction of the new arrivals.

"Mr. Crumpton, how good of you to call."

"I trust you will have no objection to Mr. Pickett's presence," the solicitor said, answering her curtsy with a bow. "He called on me to inquire as to the disposition of the viscount's estate. I thought it simplest for all concerned if he joined us for the reading of the will."

"Mr. Pickett has certainly been busy about his investigations," observed her ladyship frostily, acknowledging him with a regal nod.

Pickett noted her sudden coolness, and attributed it to embarrassment at being discovered in what might be considered a compromising situation. He gave her a rather uncertain smile, then bade Lord Rupert a chilly "good afternoon."

"Would you care for a cup of tea, Mr. Crumpton?" she asked, after Lord Rupert had departed. "Mr. Pickett?"

Lady Fieldhurst could only be thankful when they both declined; she felt she had dispensed enough of that noxious liquid today to last a lifetime. Her stiff bombazine skirts crackled as she sank onto the sofa and gestured for the solicitor to do likewise.

"I must apologize, Mr. Crumpton," she said as he seated himself beside her on the sofa. "I confess I had quite forgotten our appointment. I have received so many callers today offering their condolences that at first I thought you were but one more."

Pickett, taking the chair opposite her, wondered bitterly whether society etiquette required that the bearer of condolences salivate all over the bereaved's hand.

"I daresay your husband's heir will be here shortly," Mr. Crumpton said. "Mr. Bertram, not unnaturally, wished to know how matters stood before going to Kent for the funeral."

"Of course," said the viscountess somewhat stiffly.

Mr. Bertram arrived within the quarter hour, along with the dowager Lady Fieldhurst and Mrs. Bertram, who was in a high dudgeon at being summoned to the widow's house. It seemed more fitting, in her opinion (as she later confided to the greater part of her acquaintance) that the solicitor should wait upon the new viscount at his own residence. "I don't say it wasn't most inconvenient, being obliged to go out just when George is trying to prepare for the journey," she complained to Mr. Crumpton, "but of course we must do all we can to ease matters for poor Julia during this trying time, mustn't we, George?"

George Bertram agreed, as was his invariable practice, as Mr. Crumpton spread out his papers on a nearby table.

"As I am sure you are all aware," the solicitor began, "the entailed property, including this house and the principal estate in Kent, as well as smaller holdings in Surrey and Sussex, passes in its entirety to Mr. George Bertram, along with all incomes derived therefrom. Most of the late viscount's unentailed property, both real and personal, also devolves upon —"

A sudden commotion in the hall penetrated the paneled door, and a hearty voice boomed, "No need to stand on ceremony, my lad, no need at all! I'll announce myself!"

Lady Fieldhurst, recognizing the voice, rose from her chair just as the door opened to admit a large, ruddy-faced man with a fine pair of white mutton-chop whiskers, dressed in the expensive yet unashamedly rural costume of the country squire.

"Papa?"

"Ju-ju, my pet!" he exclaimed, enfolding the viscountess in a suffocating embrace. "You didn't think Papa would stay in Somersetshire while his little chick was thrown to the wolves, did you?"

Pickett frowned thoughtfully at this purely rhetorical question and made a notation in his occurrence book.

"I am always glad to see you, Papa, although I could wish for happier circumstances," the viscountess assured her parent. "Does Mama accompany you?"

The squire released his widowed daughter, but retained his grip on her black-gloved hands. "No, no. You know how your Mama is: her health won't permit her to undertake such a journey."

"Particularly at such a pace as you must have made!" she chided. "Really, Papa, you should be more careful."

"I don't spare my livestock where my poppet's well-being is concerned, so you might as well save your breath!"

"Do sit down," she urged, gesturing toward the vacant end of the dowager's sofa. "Would you care for some tea? You remember Frederick's mama, of course, and Mr. and Mrs. Bertram. This is Frederick's solicitor, Mr. Crumpton — and Mr. Pickett, from Bow Street," she added a bit grudgingly. "This is my father, Sir Thaddeus Runyon."

Sir Thaddeus greeted the assembled company in robust accents, declined his daughter's offer of tea, and settled himself on the sofa beside her. Having dealt with the interruption her father's arrival had caused, Lady Fieldhurst begged the solicitor to continue.

"Now, where was I?" Mr. Crumpton muttered, pushing his spectacles higher on his nose and scanning the voluminous document for the place at which he had left off. "Ah, yes! Most of the viscount's property devolves upon Mr. Bertram with some few exceptions, the most significant of these being the dowager's jointure, which will continue to be paid from the estate until the event of her death or remarriage." He smiled benignly upon the late viscount's mother, then turned his attention to Julia. "I am also pleased to assure the present viscountess that she is not to be left destitute."

"No, indeed," agreed the dowager. "Julia is to join me at the Dower House. It is all settled. We will remove there immediately after the funeral."

"Balderdash!" bristled the squire. "She's coming back home to Somersetshire, where she belongs."

"Oh, but I am sure she will be much happier living with us," protested Mrs. Bertram, determined not to be cheated out of her unpaid nanny. "She may have charge of little Edward's care, as if he were her own son. Indeed, the dear boy has his heart quite set on it."

"You are all too kind," protested Lady Fieldhurst in failing accents, feeling that perhaps the gallows was not so very dire a fate after all. "How long may I — that is, must I decide at once?"

Mr. Crumpton blinked in confusion. "No, no, my lady! That is, if you wish to return to your father's house, or to reside with your husband's family, I am sure — but we run ahead of ourselves. You must know that at the time of your betrothal to the late viscount, certain provisions were made in the event of just such an occurrence as has now come to pass."

"Do you mean to tell me, Mr. Crumpton, that my husband *expected* to be murdered?"

"No, no! Of course not!" protested the flustered solicitor, pushing his spectacles higher onto the bridge of his nose. "Surely no one *expects* such a thing! But we live in uncertain times, my lady, and even the peace we enjoyed during those days proved to be a fleeting thing. Your father and your betrothed, as Lord Fieldhurst was then, wished to see that you were adequately provided for."

"I should think so!" interjected the squire. "D'you think I'd give my little girl to a man without making dam — er, dashed — sure he'd take care of her?"

In spite of her father's braggadocio, Lady Fieldhurst could not feel hopeful. As she recalled, her father had been almost as bedazzled by her wealthy and aristocratic suitor as the young Julia herself, especially given her modest dowry and undistinguished pedigree. He had taken rooms in

Bath in the hope that she might form an eligible match — that she might make a brilliant one had never entered his head. But having achieved this unexpected triumph, he was unlikely to have risked offending his future son-in-law by pressing for a lavish jointure for his daughter. As for her husband, time had eventually shown just how cheaply he held her.

"Yes, Mr. Crumpton?" she prompted the solicitor. "How, precisely, do matters stand?"

The solicitor shuffled the papers littering the desk. "According to the terms of your marriage contract, you are to have four hundred pounds per annum for the rest of your life. Such a sum, I believe, will allow you to command life's comforts, if not its luxuries."

The viscountess glanced uneasily toward Pickett and, finding him regarding her steadily, quickly shifted her gaze back to the solicitor. Unaware of the silent exchange, Mr. Crumpton bent his bespectacled gaze to the papers once more.

"It is perhaps fortunate for your sake that your husband apparently never considered the possibility of an early demise, for he did not specify that your jointure cease to be paid, should you marry again."

Lady Fieldhurst's hands clenched in her lap. "Surely no woman having been married to such a man as Frederick could contemplate the prospect of remarriage with equanimity."

The solicitor permitted himself an avuncular smile. "It must seem that way now, my lady, while your loss is still fresh, but you may feel differently someday. In the meantime, however, I wonder if you might be happier in an establishment of your own here in Town?"

Whatever Lady Fieldhurst's feelings on the subject, this suggestion found little favor with the squire. "My little girl, living all alone in London? Poppycock!"

"I am hardly a schoolroom miss, Papa," pointed out the viscountess.

Mr. Crumpton hastened to reassure the affronted parent. "Her ladyship would, of course, wish to hire a respectable woman for companionship."

"And where, pray, am I to find a house in a respectable part of Town, much less household staff, all on four hundred pounds per annum? I fear, Mr. Crumpton, that your notions of life's comforts must differ considerably from my own."

"Given the difference in our respective stations, my lady, it would be very unusual if that were not the case," observed the solicitor wryly. "However, I can set your ladyship's mind at ease on one point. In addition to your widow's jointure, you are to have sole ownership of a modest house in Queens Gardens, Kensington."

"Kensington?" the viscountess echoed in some surprise.

"I had no idea my cousin possessed such a property," remarked Mr. Bertram bitterly, apparently feeling himself cheated out of an inheritance which should have been his.

Mr. Crumpton consulted his notes once more. "It is a small house, purchased in 1805; I drew up the deed myself. At that time he added a codicil to his will, specifying that the house and all its furnishings were to go to you upon his death."

In 1805. Three years after their marriage, when it had begun to be clear that she would never give him the hoped-for heir. She had not expected such a show of generosity, and, while she was suitably grateful, she could not ignore the fact that it placed her present position in quite a different light. Instead of being cast onto the dubious charity of her husband's relations (or the more benevolent but no less smothering generosity of her own), she was now an independent woman of property and substance.

As she pondered the possibilities, the solicitor droned on, reading aloud from an endless list of small bequests.

"— to Mary Smith, nurse, the sum of fifteen pounds sterling . . . to Jim Owen, groom, the sum of fifteen pounds sterling . . . to Harold Gilmore, valet, the sum of twenty pounds sterling . . . to William Rogers, butler, the sum of twenty pounds sterling —"

A sudden movement caught her eye, and she realized that at the mention of the butler's name, Pickett had begun scribbling something in his ubiquitous notebook. Her hackles rose as a new, and most unwelcome, possibility presented itself. If the Bow Street Runner considered a bequest of twenty pounds sufficient motive for murder, what would he make of four hundred pounds per annum plus a house in Kensington?

At last the solicitor exhausted his supply of information, gathered up his papers, and took his leave. The family party broke up immediately thereafter and, after the Bertrams had gone, Lady Fieldhurst walked with her guests as far as the front door.

"But where are your bags, Papa?" she asked, fully expecting to see them awaiting him in the foyer. "I shall have Thomas bring them upstairs at once."

Sir Thaddeus quickly demurred. "No, no! Wouldn't dream of imposing on you at such a time. I'm taking my mutton at Limmer's."

"Are you quite certain? It will not take long at all to have a room prepared for you —"

The squire again declined and, as she had no real desire for houseguests, Lady Fieldhurst accepted his decision with little more than a token protest.

"When do you plan to return to Somersetshire? You will give my love to Mama, will you not?"

For the first time since his dramatic entrance, Sir Joanathan looked slightly ill at ease. "Oh, er, as to that, I haven't quite decided yet. I don't like to go off and leave my little girl in the suds, you know."

"Never mind that, Papa. There is nothing you can do here, and if . . . anything . . . happens, I am sure you will hear of it. Truth to tell, I am surprised the news of Frederick's death reached Somersetshire so quickly."

As Pickett, hovering in the background, had wondered about this very thing, he listened closely for her father's response.

The squire cleared his throat rather loudly.

"Harrumph! Yes, well, I've taken the London papers for years, you know. A man doesn't like to be behindhand with all that's going on in the world."

This remark segued into a brief monologue on his opinions of the war in general and Bonaparte in particular. Having delivered himself of this speech (which most of his acquaintance in Somersetshire had already heard at least once), he bussed his daughter soundly on the cheek, bade her goodbye, and departed for his hotel.

After he had gone, Lady Fieldhurst turned to regard Pickett. "Yes, Mr. Pickett?" she inquired frostily. "Was there something you wanted?"

Thus addressed, Pickett advanced a few paces. "I — forgive me, my lady, but I seem to have offended you. I should like to know what I have done, and — and to beg your pardon."

"As to what you have done, Mr. Pickett, I wonder you should have to ask! Surely you cannot have thought I would be *pleased* to find that you had been asking the better part of my acquaintance for an accounting of my movements? Thanks to you, most of Mayfair awaits with bated breath the news of my arrest for murder."

She had the satisfaction of seeing Pickett

rather taken aback by this revelation.

"If — if that is so, my lady, I am sorry for it," he said at last. "I can't deny that I did question a great many of Lady Herrington's guests, but only so that I might establish that you had not been absent from the ball long enough to have committed the murder."

"And did you do so?"

"Unfortunately, no. There seems to be a quarter-hour during which no one can account for your whereabouts."

"But I told you! The maid —"

"The maid was sacked for, er, flirting with a footman."

"Now that you mention it, I saw them together. But even if she is gone, surely the footman must remember so unwelcome an interruption as I must have been?"

"He was sacked, along with the girl."

"Oh." This unexpected — and unwanted — turn of events left her momentarily weak at the knees. She groped for the side chair positioned against the wall and sank onto it, her black bombazine skirts pooling at her feet. "I see I have misjudged you, Mr. Pickett. I can only wonder that you do not make it easy on yourself and arrest me without further ado, for I cannot but feel it must eventually come to that."

"It is my duty to see that the King's justice is done, my lady," he said. "I fail to see how arresting an innocent woman would accomplish that end."

"Are you so certain, then, of my innocence?"

He dropped to one knee before her chair and looked her squarely in the eye. "As certain as I have ever been of anything, my lady. As God is my witness, I will not let you hang for a crime you did not commit."

The intensity of his brown gaze made her blink back sudden tears. "God bless you, Mr. Pickett," she whispered.

Pickett did not return to Bow Street upon leaving Berkeley Square, but instead sought out the offices of several of the better newspapers, where he made certain inquiries regarding their distribution. Receiving answers that confirmed his own suspicions, he next set out for Limmer's Hotel in Conduit Street. The shabbiest of London's fashionable hotels, Limmer's catered to a clientele more interested in horseflesh than handsome surroundings. In addition to its famous gin punch, it featured plain English food and excellent port, all served in a gloomy coffee room where one might meet any number of like-minded souls. Pickett could see its appeal for Lady Fieldhurst's father, as it was immensely popular among the sporting set, including especially the rich squirearchy.

He inquired at the desk as to Sir Thaddeus Runyon's room number, as well as the date of his arrival, and, armed with answers to these queries, went upstairs and knocked upon the squire's door.

"Yes, what is it?" Sir Thaddeus greeted his caller. "Oh, it's you — Pickens, is it?"

"Pickett, sir."

"Well, what do you want?"

Pickett thought of the boisterous conversations in progress in the coffee room below, and a glint of mischief lit his eyes. "I should like to have a look at your horses."

"My *horses?* What the devil — ?"

"According to the *Times,* the *Morning Post,* and the *Herald,* the issue bearing the news of Lord Fieldhurst's murder would not have reached Somersetshire until this morning. I am curious to see the team that could make a journey of more than one hundred miles in less than six hours. Confess, sir, you were already in London at the time of Lord Fieldhurst's murder — as the hotel register attests."

Sir Thaddeus hesitated for only a moment, then stepped back to allow Pickett entrance.

"Well, let's not stand here jawing for the whole world to hear," he said. "Come in and shut the door."

Pickett obeyed, and the squire closed the door behind him and shot the bolt home.

"All right, I arrived in London two days before Fieldhurst's death. Surely you don't think I came all this way just to kill my daughter's husband?"

Pickett answered his belligerence with a not unsympathetic smile. "Perhaps not, but I do think you wouldn't stop at much where your daughter's happiness is concerned."

"Aye, well, you've the right of it there," conceded the squire. "In fact, it was that very thing that brought me to London. My good lady was convinced our Ju-ju was unhappy, and nothing would serve but that I should go to London and fetch our girl home. Poppycock, I said, but you know what women are once they get a bee in their bonnet."

Pickett, who possessed no such knowledge, merely made a noncommittal noise and encouraged the squire to continue.

"Well, halfway to London, I thought maybe my wife wasn't so far off, after all. Seemed to me this lack of a babe was at the root of the problem, and if we could get past that — well, I decided to ask Fieldhurst if our little Julie could come back to us for a little while. Might make him a bit more attentive — absence making the heart grow fonder, and all that, don't you know. Depend upon it, a few months apart, and in nine months' time she'd be dropping 'em easy as a heifer!" The squire chuckled at his own wit.

Pickett regarded Sir Thaddeus with something akin to horrified fascination. Was it possible for a man to love his own flesh and blood so dearly, yet know her so little? More to the point, would a man so astoundingly obtuse possess the subtlety to free his daughter from an unhappy marriage by making her a widow?

"But they'd been married for six years already," he was moved to protest. "Surely a few months would hardly achieve what six years could not."

"Six years?" echoed Sir Thaddeus incredulously. "Has it really been that long? Stap me if it don't seem like just yesterday I was putting my girl on her first pony — not that she stayed in the saddle for long, for she wasn't much of a horsewoman even then, more's the pity —"

"What did Fieldhurst have to say to this plan, when you put it to him?" asked Pickett, cutting short what showed every sign of being a protracted reminiscence.

The squire wagged his head. "Now, that I don't know, for I never got the chance."

"You never saw Fieldhurst? But you were in London for two days before he died," Pickett reminded him.

"Aye, well, I don't get up to London very often. I had — other business to attend to."

"Sir Thaddeus, I fear I must ask you where you were between the hours of midnight and two o'clock on the night of his lordship's death."

The squire's expression grew so hang-dog that for one moment Pickett thought he was about to hear a confession of guilt. As Sir Thaddeus spoke, however, Pickett realized he was making a confession of quite another sort.

"Here now, young man, my good lady is as dear a soul as ever drew breath," the squire began. "But her health is not what you'd call robust, and — well, a man has his needs. I'll wager you know London pretty thoroughly. Have you ever heard of a woman by the name of Maxine Watkins? She keeps a . . . er, a discreet little house in Sackville Street, just off Piccadilly."

Pickett nodded. "I've heard of it. Can you give me the name of the girl you, er, met with?"

"Something with a *D* — Daphne, was it? No, that was t'other one. Diantha, maybe? Look here, you won't tell Ju-ju, will you?" the squire entreated, clutching at Pickett's sleeve. "My girl thinks the world of me, and if she ever found out, well, it just don't bear thinking of!"

Privately, Pickett thought the state of Lady Fieldhurst's own marriage would have rendered her incapable of being shocked by marital infidelity. Still, he saw no reason to shatter whatever childhood illusions might remain. He promised Sir Thaddeus that he would not reveal the older man's indiscretions, unless the course of his investigations required it, and put forth a tactful recommendation that the squire occupy the remainder of his time in London in seeking out a handsome gift to bring back to his lady wife. Pickett then left Limmer's for Maxine Watkins's house in Sackville Street.

Sir Thaddeus Runyon had not exaggerated when he described Mrs. Watkins's establishment as discreet; no one seeing its stately façade for the first time would suppose it to be anything but a modest but respectable residence. Inside, however, rumor held that neither modesty nor respectability was held in particularly high regard. Pickett, professionally if not personally acquainted with the seamier underpinnings of the Metropolis, was not deceived by the misleading exterior, but raised the polished brass knocker and let it fall.

The door swung open a moment later, and a breathtakingly lovely girl of no more than sixteen peered out and regarded Pickett with wide blue eyes.

"Yes, sir?" she inquired in well-modulated accents. "May I help you?"

Her golden curls were simply dressed, with a single blue ribbon threaded through, and her sprigged muslin gown was modestly cut, with a tiny ruff of fine white linen at the neck. For one bewildering moment, Pickett wondered if he had mistaken the address after all.

"I — I should like to see Mrs. Watkins, if you please," he stammered.

"And whom shall I say is calling?" she asked, stepping back to allow Pickett to enter.

The girl's manner was demureness itself, but a certain calculating gleam in her blue eyes caused Pickett to revise his estimation of her age upward by several years.

"John Pickett," he said. "Bow Street."

The girl gave a sharp gasp, then thrust both her slender arms out at him, clasped together at the wrists, her hands dangling limply. "Take me!" she cried. "Chain me up, lock me away! I am completely at your mercy!"

While Pickett was struggling to assimilate this performance, a second woman, still handsome well into her fifties, entered the room from the back of the house. "Here now, Daphne, what's all this?"

"She's good," Pickett told this woman, jerking his thumb in the fair Daphne's direction. "Your latest virgin in residence?"

"Aye, she came to me from Drury Lane, after the play she'd been appearing in folded. She's an actress," Mrs. Watkins added unnecessarily.

"They should have featured her in a death scene," Pickett observed. "She'd have been packing them in, and not a dry eye in the house."

"Why, thank you kindly, sir," Daphne said, bobbing a coy curtsy.

"She's already packing them in, thank you very much, although I can't vouch for the tears."

"But — do men really believe that?" asked Pickett incredulously.

"Of course they do! Confess, she had you going there for a moment or two. Not only do they believe it, they're willing to pay extra for the privilege of initiating her." The proprietress regarded Pickett speculatively. "I don't suppose you'd be interested — ?"

"N-no, thank you," Pickett hastily demurred.

Mrs. Watkins sighed. "A body would think you'd got ice water in your veins! You're all alike, you men — always wanting to think you're the first."

Pickett thought of a certain widowed lady of his acquaintance. "I should think being the first would be less important than being the last."

"Oh well, to each his own, I suppose. But if you didn't come to see me about Daphne, then which one of my girls is it? No trouble, I hope, for I run a respectable house, and always have."

"No trouble, Mrs. Watkins. Actually, I came to ask you about a man."

"O-ho!" exclaimed Mrs. Watkins, seeing Pickett with new and disapproving eyes. "Well, that explains a lot, but I don't run that kind of house."

Pickett flushed to the roots of his hair. "You don't — I didn't mean — this particular man claims to have been with one of your girls two nights ago. Do you by any chance recall a big, hearty fellow in his midfifties, with white hair, muttonchop whiskers, and a bit of a West Country accent?"

Mrs. Watkins screwed up her face in concentration. "Now that you mention it, I believe I do," she pronounced at last. "He came to us two nights in a row, and he was so free with his blunt the first time that when he came back again the very next night, I offered to let him initiate our Daphne into the arts of love. They like that sort of talk, you know."

"So he would have been with Daphne, then?"

"No, for he took one look at her, and said she was the image of his own little Ju-ju, whoever that might be."

"His daughter."

"Is that it? Well, then, it's just as well he wouldn't have her, for that's the sort of thing I don't put up with and never will!" She paused as a new thought struck her. "Does she? Look like this Ju-ju, I mean."

Pickett shook his head. "Not to me, but then, I'm not a father."

"Anyway, since he didn't want Daphne, I gave him to Dolores."

"May I have a word with Dolores, then?"

Dolores was duly summoned, and soon Pickett and Mrs. Watkins were joined by a raven-haired beauty whose Spanish anteced-ents, unlike Daphne's virtue, might not have been entirely fictitious.

"Oh, yes, I remember him very well," she said in answer to Pickett's query. "He had a mole in the shape of a horse's head, right on his —"

"Never mind, I believe you," Pickett interrupted before he learned a great deal more than he wanted to know. "Do you remember what time it was when you — when he —"

Pickett's question rapidly dissolved into incoherence, but Dolores (who, along with most females of her profession, had dealt with Bow Street before) had no trouble following the thread. "He came to me at about eleven o'clock."

"And how long did he stay?"

"He left at six o'clock the following morning."

"He stayed with you *all night?*"

"He was very — energetic — for a man his age," she purred with a reminiscent smile. "And he paid me well for my time, so I have no complaints."

There followed so detailed a description of the squire's points that Pickett was left in no doubt as to the intimacy of Dolores's acquaintance with the gentleman in question. He thanked her for her cooperation, and resolved to inform the squire that he was free to return to Somersetshire whenever he chose. He would send a note round to Limmer's that afternoon; he did not know how to look Sir Thaddeus in the face, given Dolores's colorful and all too informative recollections.

He supposed he should be disappointed at having yet another promising suspect lead only to a dead end, but such, he found, was not the case; after all, the news that he had arrested her father for murder would be unlikely to win Lady Fieldhurst's gratitude and admiration.

Not, of course, that he was attempting to win any such thing, he reminded himself hastily. He was, as he had informed her ladyship, merely a keeper of the King's peace, doing his best to see that justice was done.

With this end in view, he struck Sir Thaddeus's name from the list of suspects, and turned his attention to those who remained.

CHAPTER 11
IN WHICH JOHN PICKETT SUFFERS FOR A WORTHY CAUSE

"You want me to do *what?*" Lucy demanded some time later, when she was apprised of her most recent role in Pickett's investigation.

It was now late afternoon in Covent Garden's bustling piazza, where the morning's fruit and vegetable sellers had yielded pride of place to the orange girls, flower-sellers, and prostitutes who would offer their various wares to theatergoers later in the evening. Lucy's incredulity was of sufficient volume to cause several of these young women to look her way; a few offering bawdy speculations as to what her companion desired, and generously volunteering to furnish any services which Lucy might be unable or unwilling to render.

"I want you to go to Seven Dials and search the rag shops," Pickett echoed, resolutely ignoring these suggestions, although his ears turned pink. "Ask the barker if he's had a pair of stained white pantaloons from a valet in the Albany."

"Stained with what, pray?"

"Blood, if I'm lucky. Champagne, if I'm not."

Lucy planted one hand on her ample hip. "And what am I to do with these pantaloons, if I find them?"

Pickett pressed half a crown into her free hand. "Buy them and bring them to me."

Lucy, however, was unconvinced. "And why should I be buying clothes for you, John Pickett?" she demanded. "Lud, it's just like I was your wife, only without any of the good parts!"

A second coin joined its brother in Lucy's palm. "And while you're about it, buy something for yourself for your trouble."

Lucy looked down at the riches in her hand and wavered. "Do you have any idea how many bow-wow shops there are in Seven Dials?"

"No, but I'll wager you do."

"I know of six in Monmouth Street alone! And what about you? What are you going to be doing, while I'm out brangling with rag-merchants?"

Pickett could not resist. "What do you think?" he retorted. "Like any good husband, I'll be hoisting a pint at the Coach and Four."

Grinning, he turned and walked away, leaving an indignant Lucy to endure the bawdy hoots of her peers as she stood open-mouthed in the middle of the piazza.

The Coach and Four, as its name implied, had originally catered to the grooms and stable lads employed by the aristocracy, who spent most of their working hours in the various mews tucked away behind the stylish town houses of Mayfair. But, as this establishment's reputation had grown, its custom had expanded to include house servants as well. On any given afternoon, one might find stately butlers enjoying their halfday, or roguish footmen courting flirtatious housemaids, in addition to the more traditional clientele.

John Pickett, entering the tap room at half-past nine o'clock, looked like none of these, and so the proprietor greeted him somewhat curtly with a grudging, "What'll ye have?"

It had been Pickett's experience that publicans were disinclined to view Bow Street operatives with favor; indeed, most of them regarded policing of any kind as a threat to the rights of law-abiding citizens, rather than a form of protection against the lawless. Pickett had, however, been with the Bow Street force long enough to learn that an exchange of silver did much to ensure cooperation, and that a liberal dose of spirits frequently loosened the most tightly-sealed lips.

"A pint of bitter," said Pickett, slapping a coin onto the bar. As the barkeep drew the foaming liquid into a pewter mug, he tossed another coin down and added, "And have one for yourself."

"Thank 'ee, sir, don't mind if I do," said this worthy, much gratified, as he reached for a second mug.

"You've got quite a busy place here," observed Pickett, glancing about the bustling taproom.

As these simple words hinted at an unspoken admiration for his business acumen, mine host unbent sufficiently to admit that, yes, his business was indeed prospering.

"I'll wager you know what goes on in half the great houses in London," continued Pickett.

"I'll not deny it," boasted the barkeep, standing a bit taller and thrusting out his chest. "Why, see that fellow there? He's footman to Earl Grey. And that one in the corner was once stable lad to the Duke of Devonshire."

Pickett leaned in close and lowered his voice to a conspiratorial whisper. "And what of Viscount Fieldhurst, who was murdered? Do any of his staff come here?"

It was a tactical error. The barkeep began to rub down the bar vigorously with a damp cloth, all trace of confidentiality vanished. "Now, listen here, I don't hold no truck with murderers, no siree! This is an honest establishment, God's truth it is, and so any one of these good people will tell you!"

He continued in this vein at some length, and not until Pickett had ordered a second round of drinks were his ruffled feathers soothed to the point of admitting that, yes, the butler Rogers had been one of his regular patrons, but he had not seen the man for some three days. Nor did he wish to see him again, if it were true that he'd snuffed his master. Further questioning brought forth the names of several rival establishments which, he assured Pickett, were not nearly so nice in their clientele as his own.

And so, having learned all he could at the Coach and Four, Pickett made his way first to the Butler's Pantry, then to the Boar's Head, and finally to the Grey Goose. His investigations followed a very similar pattern. Over the first pint, not one of the publicans knew anything about a butler named Rogers; over the second, each somewhat grudgingly recalled having served him on occasion, but could not recollect having seen him since the night of Lord Field-hurst's murder. All were quick to disavow any knowledge of his present whereabouts.

At the Grey Goose, however, something gave Pickett the distinct impression that the proprietor was lying. Precisely what had tipped him off, he could not have said; perhaps it was the simple fact that he spent fully ten minutes drying the same pewter mug. Whatever the reason, Pickett had sufficient confidence in his instincts (although, if truth be told, even these usually reliable faculties were by this time growing a bit blurred around the edges) to order a third pint, and then a fourth, for himself and his host.

"So, what d'ye think?" asked this worthy, wiping the foam from his mouth with his sleeve. "Did this 'ere Rogers really rub out 'is lordship?"

"I don't know that for sure," Pickett demurred. "For all I know, Fieldhurst might have rubbed *him* out instead."

"Well, I can tell you that's what he didn't do," returned the publican, leaning confidingly across the bar. "Poor old Rogers was in here just two days ago, drinking hisself into a stupor and rambling about getting the sack from old Fieldhurst."

Even through the fog which was beginning to cloud his brain, Pickett realized that this was what he had come for. If Rogers had indeed been sacked by the viscount, he had a motive for murder, especially if he knew he was to receive twenty pounds upon Fieldhurst's death. That sum would go a long way toward establishing an unemployed man in a new position. It was true that Lady Fieldhurst had said nothing about the butler losing his position, but it was possible that she had already departed for the Herrington ball when her husband dismissed the butler, and therefore knew nothing about it.

Pickett could not afterwards recall paying his shot and taking his leave, but he must have done so, for he eventually found himself weaving his way down Bond Street in the direction of Berkeley Square. The street was deserted by this time, and he was surprised to discover that the fashionable thoroughfare, which had always remained stationary before, now demonstrated an alarming ability to blur, split in two, and criss-cross before his somewhat owlish gaze. Only with the greatest concentration was he able to remain upright while putting one foot in front of the other, long enough to mount the low steps onto the front stoop of number 12 Berkeley Square. He raised the brass door knocker and let it fall against the strike plate, but the black crape ribbons adorning the knocker muffled the sound. Abandoning this useless device, he pounded hard against the wooden panel with his fist.

Some few minutes passed before the door opened to reveal a sleepy-eyed Thomas, the coat of his blue-and-silver livery hanging open over his nightshirt, breeches, and bare feet.

"Mus' shee — *see* — her la'yship," Pickett pronounced with an effort.

Thomas's sleepy eyes grew round as dinner plates. "B-beg pardon, sir?"

"Lady Fiel'ursht," Pickett reiterated. "Musht ask 'er —"

"Meaning no disrespect, sir, but perhaps you'd best wait till tomorrow," said Thomas, gently but firmly closing the door.

"No, no!" protested Pickett, thrusting his foot into the rapidly closing gap. "Musht ask 'er — Rogers —"

"Thomas?" inquired a feminine voice. "What is the matter? Who is it?"

Thomas, distracted by the query, released his pressure on the door. Pickett, seizing his opportunity, pushed it open and caught a glimpse of Paradise.

Lady Fieldhurst stood at the foot of the stairs, clutching a pink silk wrapper closed over her night rail. Her unbound hair spilled over her shoulders in glorious waves of gold.

"Lucy — too late," he muttered to no one in particular. "Over my head — already."

"Mr. Pickett?" cried the viscountess, recognizing the man reeling on her doorstep. "Have you any idea what time it is?"

Blinking, Mr. Pickett looked around the square, seeing for the first time its dark houses and empty streets.

"Oh dear, I suppose we can hardly cast you into the street at this hour," Lady Fieldhurst conceded. "You'd best come in. Thomas, light a fire in the small guest chamber. Mr. Pickett will be there directly."

Thomas, who knew his duty, took himself from the room, albeit with some reluctance.

Lady Fieldhurst, left alone in the entrance hall with her unexpected guest, regarded Pickett with mingled exasperation and amusement. When she had first realized the identity of her midnight caller, she had recalled his interrogations of Lady Herrington's guests and feared the hour of her arrest was at hand. It was, however, difficult to be frightened of the gawky, rumpled, and absurdly *young* man who stood at the door, swaying on his feet as she approached him.

"Pray, Mr. Pickett, to what do I owe the honor of this visit?" she asked, taking his arm to steady him.

He yielded to the pressure of her hand in the crook of his elbow and allowed himself to be led into the house. "Your name," he said with great deliberation, "ish Julia."

"Yes, it is," she agreed, somewhat surprised that he would have taken notice of what to him must be an irrelevant point, much less that he should call on her in the wee hours of the morning to inform her of it.

"My name," he continued in the same serious vein, "ish John."

Suppressing a smile, the viscountess managed a very creditable curtsey without relinquishing his arm; indeed, she feared that, were she to release her hold on him, he would in all likelihood fall over. "I am pleased to make your acquaintance."

"They both begin with *J*," he said, with the air of one revealing an important discovery.

"Imagine that!"

He blinked as if a new thought had only at that moment occurred to him. "Am I jug-bitten, d'you think?"

"I should not be at all surprised," she said soothingly, steering him in the direction of the staircase. "But Thomas has gone to prepare a room for you, where you may have a good night's sleep. In the morning, you shall no doubt feel much more the thing." As she recalled the effects of her own over-indulgence on the night her husband was slain, however, honesty compelled her to add, "Eventually."

Chapter 12
In Which Is Seen the Power of the Written Word

Pickett awoke the next morning with the distinct impression that someone was pounding his head with a sledgehammer. Opening his eyes, he discovered that he was alone in an unfamiliar bedchamber. The hangings were open, and from his supine vantage point he could see a small writing desk and chair positioned beneath a window through which poured an indecent amount of brilliant sunshine. Turning his head away from the offending light, he saw a small table outfitted with a large porcelain bowl and pitcher, with a rectangular looking-glass mounted on the wall above. Gradually he realized that the sound reverberating off the robin's egg blue walls was in fact no hammer at all, but someone tapping on the door.

"Come in," he croaked.

"Begging your pardon, sir," said Thomas, entering the room with a can of hot water, which he emptied into the pitcher, "but her ladyship is at breakfast and invites you to join her."

Pickett recognized Lady Fieldhurst's footman, and certain of the previous night's events came rushing back to his consciousness. He lurched forward to a sitting position and instantly regretted his haste, wincing at the pain that shot through his abused head. "I'll be there in five minutes — no, best make that ten."

"Yes, sir."

As the door closed behind the footman, Pickett flung back the counterpane. Glancing down at his rumpled person, he was relieved to find that he had at least managed to remove his coat and boots before collapsing — or had Thomas removed them for him? He could ask, but he was not at all certain he wanted to know. His neckcloth was untied and draped across the back of a chair, along with his coat and waistcoat, but his wrinkled shirt and breeches bore the unmistakable signs of having been slept in.

He staggered out of bed and lurched across the room to the looking-glass to survey the damage. The image that met his bleary-eyed gaze resembled nothing so much as a death's head on a mop stick. His brown eyes were bloodshot and his complexion pasty. His queue had come undone at some point in the night, and his hair now stood up from his scalp in all directions. His chin was shadowed with faint stubble; too late he wished he had requested of Thomas the loan of a razor.

But there was no good to be found in repining over what could not be helped. Pouring some of the water from the pitcher into the bowl, he made his ablutions as best he could, and felt rather better for the feel of warm water on his face. A prolonged search through the bedclothes at last unearthed the black ribbon that had held back his hair. If it was sadly crumpled from the night's misadventures, it was at least in better shape than his neckcloth. At last, having arrayed himself in his creased clothing, thrust his feet into his scuffed boots, and retied his queue, he was forced to acknowledge the fact that there was nothing else he could do to make his appearance less repugnant. Thus, with mingled dread and anticipation, he left the room and staggered forth to meet her ladyship.

He found her awaiting him in the breakfast room, reading a letter and sipping chocolate from a delicate Sèvres cup. The lusterless black of her mourning gown comprised the only dark spot in the sunny yellow chamber — and, consequently, the only spot upon which he could fix his gaze without hurting his eyes.

At his entrance, she set her cup down and laid her letter aside. "Good morning, Mr. Pickett. Would you care for bacon and buttered eggs?" she asked, precisely as if she entertained inebriated Runners at her breakfast table every day of the week.

She raised the lid of a silver chafing dish, and the smell of the proffered bacon assailed Pickett's nostrils. His stomach lurched.

Lady Fieldhurst, seeing his pallid countenance change to a queer shade of green, lowered the lid hastily. "Or perhaps a bit of dry toast and some coffee —"

"Just — just coffee, if you please."

"I have just received a most curious communication from Limmer's hotel," she continued, filling another one of the ornate china cups with steaming dark liquid. "It seems that Papa intends to leave London this very afternoon, and wishes me to suggest something that he might purchase for Mama as a gift."

Pickett, receiving the cup with hands that shook slightly, found her quizzical gaze fixed upon him and felt it behooved him to offer some sort of explanation. "Perhaps, having seen your situation for himself, he wished to reassure your mama on that head."

"I daresay that must be it. He pays you the compliment of saying that I appear to be in good hands. Although," she added, noting the way his cup rattled against its saucer, "it appears those hands are not as steady as they were when he saw them yesterday."

"My lady, about my conduct last night, I can't say how sorry I am —"

She shook her head, dismissing his half-formed apology out of hand. "Not at all. I daresay most men over-imbibe from time to time. Certainly my late husband did so with sufficient frequency to prevent my being shocked by seeing another in that condition."

Pickett was moved to protest a comparison he considered highly unflattering. "I don't know anything about your late husband's habits, my lady, but I can assure you that they are not mine."

She said nothing, but raised one skeptical eyebrow in a manner that made him all the more painfully aware of his unkempt appearance, the lingering proof of last night's excesses.

"As to that, it wasn't by my choice, believe me," Pickett put in hastily. "I was trying to find some trace of the missing butler. I visited several pubs he'd been known to frequent, and when one of the proprietors proved tight-lipped, I had to, er, lubricate his tongue a bit."

"If he was half as well-lubricated as you were, I wonder he was coherent at all," observed the viscountess, but the severity of her tone was belied by a lurking twinkle in her eyes.

"Yes, and I was a regular addle-pate not to realize he was trying to drink me under the table. It was unforgivable of me to foist myself on you in such a condition, my lady, and if I said or did anything to offend you —"

" 'If,' Mr. Pickett?" she echoed in tones of exaggerated surprise. "Do you truly not remember?"

The Runner's bleary eyes opened wide, his expression so replete with mortification that she could only wonder what the poor man might imagine he had done.

"I was only roasting you," she assured him hastily. "You were none too steady on your feet, I grant you, but no fault could be found with your manners." Seeing that he was still far from convinced, she quickly turned the subject. "But you were searching for Rogers, you say? Tell me, did you find him?"

"No, but I found something else. Lady Fieldhurst, were you aware that your husband intended to sack the butler that evening?"

"Sack — you are asking if he meant to discharge Rogers? Impossible! He has served the Fieldhursts all his life, like his father before him."

"And yet he told the publican at the Grey Goose that he'd been given the boot." A possible explanation presenting itself, Pickett suggested, "Perhaps your husband caught him trying to nab the family silver."

"Nonsense! Rogers would no more steal from Frederick than he would murder him." She frowned over this last declaration. "But if it is true that Frederick dismissed him, it would seem Rogers has a motive for that, too."

"Let's just say it casts his disappearance in a very odd light."

"But if he did kill Frederick — *not*, mind you, that I believe for one moment that Rogers could commit such a heinous act! — then why should he bolt? He would be better served to pretend nothing had happened, thus retaining his position, collecting his bequest, and deflecting suspicion away from himself."

"Perhaps he panicked when he realized

what he'd done," suggested Pickett.

"Perhaps," Lady Fieldhurst conceded doubtfully, "although blind panic does not sound like Rogers any more than theft or murder does. Clearly, he must be found."

"My thoughts exactly — which, I hope, will explain why I spent most of last night swilling ale at the Grey Goose."

"Yes, but you must not do so again, for should Rogers return to that establishment, the proprietor will certainly inform him of your visit."

"Believe me, I have no desire to repeat the experience, but in the absence of a better idea —"

"Oh, but I have a better idea," declared her ladyship, her blue eyes sparkling in anticipation. "We shall set a trap for him!"

" 'We,' my lady?" echoed Pickett with some misgivings.

"Most certainly 'we,' Mr. Pickett. Rogers was *my* butler, Fieldhurst was *my* husband, his body was found in *my* bedchamber, and it is *my* neck that is likely to be placed in the noose. Surely you cannot mean to insult my intelligence by trying to convince me that the matter need not concern me?"

"No, but the Grey Goose is no place for a lady —"

"Which is just as well, since I do not

intend to go there. But there is another possibility. You will remember that my husband left me a small house in Kensington. Provided that I contrive to escape the gallows, I intend to remove there after the investigation is complete. Naturally, I will require some staff. Camille will accompany me, and perhaps Thomas, in his role of footman. Why should I not advertise for a butler? Rogers must be in need of a new position, and so would be quick to answer such an advertisement."

"Surely he'd get the wind up when he recognized the house number and street," Pickett objected.

"No, for I should interview applicants at the house in Queens Gardens. Then, after I have reassured Rogers that he is not in imminent danger of arrest, but wanted only for questioning, I shall send for you." Seeing that Bow Street was not entirely convinced, she added, "I make the suggestion not only to assist you in your investigation, Mr. Pickett, but to repay a kindness. When I was first wed, Rogers was very kind and patient with a green girl who knew nothing of the management of a great house. If he is in some sort of trouble, I should desire to offer him my assistance."

Pickett wavered. He had no doubt that,

provided Rogers took the bait, Lady Fieldhurst's proposal was likely to be far more
successful than anything he might accomplish at the Grey Goose. Still, he could
not overlook the fact that the butler now
had a motive for murder. No matter how
much she might feel she owed him, the
viscountess must not be left alone to confront a man who might well be a killer.

"Very well," he said at last, "you can place
your advertisement under one condition: I
will accompany you to Queens Gardens and
remain with you throughout the interview."

Lady Fieldhurst frowned. "But Rogers
may prove reluctant to speak with you
present, and — oh, I see! You want the ele-
ment of surprise, is that it?"

Better, he decided, if she should think that
was his only concern. "Yes, that's it."

Lady Fieldhurst rose from the breakfast
table, signaling the end of the interview.
"Very well, Mr. Pickett, we have an agreement. Now, if you will excuse me, I must
pen an advertisement for the *Times*."

Pickett took his leave in as punctilious a
manner as his condition would allow, and
Lady Fieldhurst turned her efforts to com-
position. She had scarcely finished this task
and laid aside her pen when Thomas entered
the room, bearing the morning's post on a

silver tray. She leafed half-heartedly through the thick stack of condolence cards — all of which would have to be answered later — but stopped abruptly when she reached a card noticeably different from its fellows. While the others were written in elegant script on fine vellum, this one was scrawled in pencil on cheap, coarse paper. Turning it over, she broke the seal (a single blob of yellowish tallow dropped from a burning candle) and spread the single sheet open.

I know what you need and I can help. Bring 25 shillings to the Sailor's Rest in Upper Well Alley off Wapping Street. Ask for Jane.

A Friend.

Lady Fieldhurst's initial reaction was one of fear, for she had never before received a blackmailing letter. A second, closer reading, however, gave her reason to hope that herein lay her salvation. There was, after all, no implied threat, merely an offer of help in exchange for a relatively modest sum of money. Furthermore, although her experience was admittedly limited, she suspected that extortionists rarely identified themselves as friends of their victims.

Eager to share this most recent development with young Mr. Pickett, she instructed Thomas to send for the carriage, then rang for Camille to fetch for her a shawl and a deep-brimmed bonnet with a long black veil which covered her face and trailed down her back. Thus arrayed, she allowed Thomas to hand her into the waiting carriage and gave the driver directions to set her down at Number 4 Bow Street.

Alas, she had quite failed to anticipate the effect of a crested carriage, occupied by a heavily veiled lady, upon the inhabitants of that venerable address. She entered the building to find every man-jack in the place on his feet and staring at her with ill-concealed curiosity. Of Mr. Pickett there was no sign.

"I should like to see Mr. John Pickett, if you please," she informed the Runner nearest at hand, a man of about thirty-five with straw-colored hair and an indefinable air of command.

"Aye, so should we all, but he's not in yet." He looked her up and down appreciatively. "The name's Foote. Perhaps I might be of assistance, Mrs. — ?"

"My Lady Fieldhurst, I presume." A white-haired man arose from the magistrate's bench and stepped down to meet her. "Mr. Pickett is not here at the moment, but

I expect he will arrive at any time. If you would care to wait —"

At that very moment, the door opened behind her and John Pickett entered the room, looking rather better for the recent use of a razor and a change of clothes. One glimpse of his unexpected caller, however, was sufficient to reduce him to stammering idiocy.

"My — my lady!" he exclaimed. "What are you — what brings you — ?"

She pushed back her veil, and the sight of the flower-like face lifted to Pickett's brought knowing grins to the faces of his peers, and a look of pained understanding to the magistrate.

"I received a letter by this morning's post," she said, withdrawing it from her reticule. "I thought you should see it."

Mr. Colquhoun, seeing that the crowd of appreciative Runners showed no inclination to disperse, thought it politic to intervene. "Perhaps you should take her ladyship into my office, where you may be private."

"Yes, sir — thank you, sir."

The group reluctantly broke up with much shuffling of feet and more than one whispered remark, followed by ribald laughter. Pickett, his ears turning slightly pink, led the viscountess into a tiny, cluttered room behind the magistrate's bench. In the privacy of this chamber, she handed him the letter. He carried it to the single window, through which pale sunlight streamed, and studied it for a long moment before looking up at her.

"I don't like it, my lady."

"Nor do I, Mr. Pickett, but I like the idea of perishing on the gallows even less."

"The courts hold a very low opinion of purchased testimony."

"Even so small a sum? Surely twenty-five shillings is little enough to offer in exchange for one's life."

Useless, he supposed, to tell her that the denizens of the East End docks, where the Sailor's Rest was located, might well live their entire lives without ever possessing such a sum.

" 'Ask for Jane,' " he read aloud, consulting the letter once more. "I think we've found Lady Herrington's maid, in any case."

"But of course!" exclaimed Lady Fieldhurst, much struck by this deduction. "It all fits: the poor girl is no doubt sorely in need of funds, having lost her position, and sees a way in which we both might benefit."

"Nevertheless, paying her to establish your alibi would do you a great deal more harm than good. Notice that she never says that she actually saw you, only that she is willing to 'help' you for a price. It would be assumed that you paid her to present a false testimony."

"I see your point," she conceded, crestfallen. "I fear I fail to understand the workings of the criminal mind."

"And a very good thing, too, or you should likely be in Newgate by now."

He succeeded in surprising a smile out of her. "*Touché,* Mr. Pickett. So what are we to do now?"

He slapped at the letter in his hand. "We go to this Sailor's Rest in Upper Well Alley, and we ask for Jane."

Upon hearing these words, Lady Fieldhurst was at first gratified that Pickett made no attempt to dissuade her from accompanying him. Later, however, when a hired hackney set them down at the foot of Upper Well Alley (she had sent her own carriage back to its Mayfair mews, correctly assuming that what was too conspicuous for Bow Street must be doubly so for the East End waterfront), she began to wish he had insisted she return to Berkeley Square. Branching at a right angle off Wapping Street, which ran parallel to the river, Upper Well Alley was a dank, narrow passage smelling strongly of fish, along with other odors perhaps better left unidentified. It appeared to cater to stevedores and others in the seafaring trade, lined as it was with rundown pubs, residences of the meaner sort, and cheap boardinghouses where a sailor might find a room in which to tumble a willing wench while he was in port. Directly opposite Wapping Street, along the riverfront, a ship bearing the name of *Dolphin* strained at its moorings, as if impatient to put back out to sea. Lady Fieldhurst could readily understand its eagerness; she felt no inclination to linger in the area herself. Edging a bit closer to Pickett, she tucked her hand into the crook of his arm.

Pickett, feeling a slight pressure on his sleeve, glanced down to discover her ladyship's black-gloved hand resting in the curve of his elbow, and for a moment heard all heaven's bells bursting forth in glorious melody. He was slightly embarrassed to realize that it was only the bells of the *Dolphin* and her sister ships, in combination with the church bells of St. John at Wapping, marking the hour.

The Sailor's Rest, when they found it, proved to be one of the better boardinghouses, "better" being, in this case, a relative term. Although the paint on its façade had long since peeled away, cheap lace curtains hung in its windows, and a pot of brave, red geraniums adorned the front stoop. Pickett ushered the viscountess inside, and together they approached the matron.

"I should like to see Jane, if you please," Lady Fieldhurst addressed this worthy. "She said I might find her here."

The woman regarded her with suspicion not unmixed with awe. Clearly, it was not every day her house entertained veiled ladies of obviously genteel birth. Apparently satisfied with what she saw, she barked an order to a small, barefooted girl in a worn and patched apron, and the child scampered up the stairs in search of the establishment's newest tenant.

Jane herself descended the stairs a moment later, twisting her apron in restless hands. She eyed Pickett warily, but addressed herself to Lady Fieldhurst. "Did your ladyship bring what I asked for?"

It was Pickett who answered her. "Miss Mudge — it is Miss Mudge, is it not? — you must know that her ladyship cannot pay you to testify on her behalf. To do so would only make her look guilty."

Jane's wary gaze grew belligerent. "And who might you be? The boy-friend? Didn't let any grass grow beneath your feet, now, did you?"

"This is Mr. Pickett, the Bow Street Runner who is investigating my husband's murder," Lady Fieldhurst said in a frigid tone calculated to put the insolent maid in her place.

It worked only too well. At the mention of Bow Street, Jane sucked in her breath and took a quick step backward, as if poised for flight.

"You have nothing to fear from me," Pickett hastened to reassure her.

"Not me — my Davey," Jane stammered. "When he got the boot from my lady, he pinched my lord's snuffbox to hock — something to live on, he says, until we can get back on our feet."

"I assure you, I am not interested in petty thievery," Pickett said. "An innocent woman's life is at stake. Surely it is the duty of every citizen to do whatever he can to prevent such a miscarriage of justice."

Jane's gaze shifted to the viscountess behind her black veil and back to Pickett. "What do you want me to do?"

"I believe you did some sewing for Lady Fieldhurst on the night of the Herrington ball. Is that correct?"

The maid's eyes narrowed in mistrust. "And what if it is?"

"I would like you to come back to Bow Street with me and sign a statement specifying when, precisely, Lady Fieldhurst was with you on the night of the Herrington ball."

"I'll not have to appear in court?"

"If her presence in Portman Square at the crucial time could be established, I doubt her ladyship could be brought to trial at all."

"And you'll not arrest my Davey?"

"Not unless Lord Herrington reports the theft of his snuffbox and prefers charges."

Jane appeared to weigh her options for a long moment, then said, "Let me go upstairs and put on my bonnet."

She climbed the stairs back up to the floor above, while Pickett and Lady Fieldhurst waited below.

"Well!" said her ladyship, with a sigh of relief. "That was not so very difficult, after all."

"No," Pickett concurred with a thoughtful frown. "In fact, it was almost too easy."

The minutes ticked by but, although various boarders came and went, there was no sign of Jane. At last Pickett, with growing unease, turned to the viscountess. "I wouldn't know, having never worn one, but does it really take that long to put on a bonnet?"

He could not see her face, concealed as it was by yards of black netting, but her shoulders stiffened as his own suspicions communicated themselves to her. "Mr. Pickett, you don't suppose — ?"

"Oh yes, I do!"

With one mind, they hurried up the stairs, footsteps pounding on the uncarpeted boards. A door halfway down the corridor stood ajar, and Pickett ran down the narrow passage and burst into the room, Lady Fieldhurst following hard on his heels. As he had expected, the room was unoccupied. Signs of hasty flight were evident in the gaping drawers of a scarred bureau and, most telling of all, the raised sash of a single, grimy window overlooking the back of the building. He muttered something under his breath (which Lady Fieldhurst wisely refrained from asking him to repeat), then crossed the tiny room in two strides and thrust his head and shoulders out the window.

"Here, now!" panted the matron, red-faced and breathless, from the doorway. "I run an honest house here, and I'll not have any havey-cavey doings under my roof!"

Pickett ignored her and addressed himself to Lady Fieldhurst instead. "She's flown. There's a drainpipe outside the window; no doubt she climbed down it."

"Gone!" cried the matron, outraged. "Why, she owes me twenty-five shillings for room and board!"

"Hadn't we better search for her?" Lady Fieldhurst asked, joining him at the window.

Pickett shook his head. "We'd never find her. The waterfront offers a thousand places for a fugitive to hide."

"So what do we do now?"

Pickett sighed. "We'd better hope Rogers turns up soon, for we'll not be getting any help from Jane."

CHAPTER 13
THE MATTER OF THE
MISSING BUTLER

The following day, Lady Fieldhurst confronted her late husband's solicitor in the room that had once been his study.

"Well, Mr. Crumpton? Did you bring the keys, as I requested?"

The solicitor withdrew two identical brass keys from the pocket of his waistcoat, but appeared reluctant to relinquish possession. "As his lordship's widow, Lady Fieldhurst, your wish must be my command. Still, I cannot think it wise —"

"Never mind, I'll announce myself!"

A reedy voice in the foyer interrupted Mr. Crumpton's protestations, and a moment later the study door burst open. Mr. George Bertram stood on the threshold in a state of deep perturbation, his brow damp with perspiration and his color high. Lady Fieldhurst's heart sank. She had not wanted an audience for this interview, and she had no doubt as to what circumstance she owed this unwelcome visit from her cousin by marriage. Indeed, the folded newspaper under his arm confirmed her worst suspicions.

"*There* you are!" Without waiting for an invitation, he strode into the room and flung the newspaper onto the viscount's desk. "What, pray, is the meaning of this, Cousin Julia?"

She did not have to look at the newspaper to understand his inquiry, for she knew the words from memory. Indeed, she had composed the lines herself:

Help wanted, mature man of good character and sober habits to serve as butler to widowed lady. Experience necessary, references requested. Apply in person between the hours of 2 and 4 of the clock, 11 Queens Gardens, Kensington.

"I should think it would be obvious," she replied with some asperity. "I cannot be expected to occupy a house without adequate staff. You need not fear I shall be a burden to you, George. I am quite capable of paying his wages myself, as Mr. Crumpton can attest."

The solicitor coughed discreetly, and Mr. Bertram, suddenly conscious of the presence of a third party, had the grace to look embarrassed.

"You never could be considered a burden, my dear cousin. But surely the dowager Lady Fieldhurst's staff is sufficient to the needs of two widowed ladies, while as for her ladyship's butler, she would be highly offended should you attempt to replace Phelps."

"I am sure she would be," conceded the viscountess. "Fortunately for her peace of mind, I have no such intention. I mean to hire a butler of my own."

Mr. Bertram scowled. "Two butlers for the same household? Now, Cousin Julia —"

"Pray disabuse yourself of the notion that I am to make my home with Frederick's mama. I am quite certain we should make one another miserable."

"*Not* reside with — but it is all settled!"

"Then it is a great pity no one thought to consult me in the matter."

"But the dowager — what will she do for companionship? One cannot but fear for her, living all alone —"

"She is not alone at all, for she has Phelps."

"An elderly retainer can hardly take the place of a beloved daughter-in-law," protested Mr. Bertram.

Privately, the viscountess doubted the "beloved" part, but had no doubt the dowager would welcome the presence of an unpaid drudge whom she could browbeat.

"If she requires a woman for companionship, why should she not hire one? Or," she added in the tone of one inspired, "since you are worried about her, perhaps you would feel better if you hired one for her."

This shaft struck home, for Mr. Bertram's face grew mottled, and he muttered something about the difficulty and expense of hiring good servants.

"Very true, which is why I am advertising in the *Times*." Some demon of mischief prompted Lady Fieldhurst to add, "Would you like for me to draft a notice? I am sure money must be no object with you, for anyone who can afford to erect a Gothic ruin in the rose garden will not wish to be niggardly where the dowager's well-being is concerned."

"But where will you live? Caroline spoke of your coming to us, but I fear it would be painful for you to live in the same house you once shared with my cousin."

"Most painful," agreed Julia. "I shall take Mr. Crumpton's advice and remove to the house Frederick left me in Kensington. Indeed, that is the purpose of his visit today.

He has brought me the keys, and I intend to take possession of the house today. You did say you had brought the keys, did you not, Mr. Crumpton?"

Mr. Crumpton, still clutching the brass keys, cleared his throat, muttered something unintelligible, and cleared his throat again. "I must beg you not to be too hasty, my lady. Surely now, while your grief is still fresh, is not the time to make such a momentous decision. There is much to be said for your cousin's suggestion. Then, perhaps later, after your year of mourning is completed —"

Lady Fieldhurst regarded the solicitor with confusion, and no small sense of betrayal. "But Mr. Crumpton, it was your suggestion that I set up my own establishment in the first place! What, pray, has caused this reversal of opinion?"

Mr. Crumpton tugged at his cravat. "Since we last spoke on this subject, I have been to inspect the house, and found it, er, unfit for occupation by a lady."

"Unfit? In what way? Is it structurally unsound? Do the chimneys smoke? Or perhaps the roof leaks?"

"No, no! Indeed, there is no reason why you might not sell the house for a handsome sum."

"You behold me agog with curiosity, Mr. Crumpton," said her ladyship, although her voice was pitched at a tone more indicative of annoyance than inquisitiveness. "If the house is fit for others to dwell in, why should not I?"

The solicitor cleared his throat, then threw a pleading glance in the direction of the heir. Finding no help from that quarter, he plunged into apologetic speech. "It is a matter of the furnishings, my lady. These, I am persuaded, would not be at all to your tastes."

"I did not realize you were so well-informed as to my tastes." As the solicitor opened his mouth, she raised a black-gloved hand to forestall further protests. "Understand this, Mr. Crumpton, and you too, George. Although you may have your own opinions as to what I should do, I am not bound by your suggestions. You, Mr. Crumpton, may offer me advice — indeed, sometimes I may even ask you for it — but I am under no obligation to follow your recommendations. As for you, George, although you may be the head of the family, you have no real legal authority over me, nor do you control my purse-strings."

The end of the interview was never really in doubt. All her life she had been under the domination of a man — first her over-bearing father, then her cold and distant husband. Now that she was finally free to do as she pleased, she would not yield her independence to anyone.

By the time her visitors (one still bluster-ing, the other still fretful) took their reluctant leave some quarter-hour later, the keys to the house in Queens Gardens rested snugly in the bottom of her reticule.

Queens Gardens was a quiet *cul-de-sac* tucked away off the Brompton Road. Its distance from London precluded it from attracting the attention of the fashionable world, but its neat, narrow houses exuded an air of upwardly mobile respectability. Aside from the possibility that she might find herself rubbing shoulders with an ambitious City man, Lady Fieldhurst could find nothing in her surroundings to support Mr. Crumpton's sudden qualms.

The now-familiar figure of Mr. Pickett awaited her on the front stoop of Number 11 and, as the carriage rolled to a stop, he came forward to meet her.

"Well, Mr. Pickett, you are certainly prompt," she observed, taking the coach-man's proffered arm as she disembarked from the vehicle. "I hope I have not kept you waiting long."

"Not long at all," he assured her, wishing he had thought to offer his arm before the coachman could provide this service.

Lady Fieldhurst dismissed the driver with instructions to return for her at four, then turned her attention back to Pickett. "I beg you will forgive my tardiness, Mr. Pickett. It took rather longer to obtain the keys than I expected." Without quite knowing why, she found herself recounting the interview with her solicitor. As she had noted before, Mr. Pickett had a way of leading one to say far more than one had intended.

"And so he did his best to discourage you?" said Pickett at the end of this recitation. "Why? Did he know, or suspect, your real purpose in coming today?"

"I am convinced he could not, for I never said a word to anyone but you. He would have it that the house was not suitable for a lady, or some such nonsense. As for George, I daresay he is simply envious. He had hoped to inherit everything, lock, stock, and barrel. Between the pair of them, I was half afraid you had given me up."

"Not at all, my lady," he assured her. "It still lacks ten minutes to the hour. You did have one prospect arrive early, though."

Lady Fieldhurst paused with one foot on

the stoop and turned to regard him hopefully. "Rogers?"

Pickett grimaced. "I hope not, for I sent the fellow away. He was seventy if he was a day, and I had the impression our man was younger."

"Yes, certainly," said Lady Fieldhurst. "I daresay I should have furnished you with a description. But it is a very odd thing about servants. Even though one sees them every day, one rarely *sees* them. I can say with certainty that Rogers is less than seventy years old, and that he is not stout or bald or cross-eyed, but, as far as telling you what color his eyes are, or whether he is above average height, I should find myself at a loss."

Fitting the brass key into the lock, she turned the knob. The door swung open with a groan, revealing a shadowy entryway which stretched into darkness at the rear of the house. "It — it's rather a creepy place, isn't it?" Her voice echoed down the empty passage, and she instinctively moved closer to Pickett.

Determined not to let this opportunity slip, he cupped his hand around her elbow. "The hinges need oiling, that's all."

Against the wall on the right, stairs climbed into blackness; on the left, a wide, arched doorway beckoned. Lady Fieldhurst turned toward this, then froze on the threshold. "Oh! Oh dear!"

The furniture was swathed in Holland covers, but the ghostly appearance was somewhat negated by the fact that, over the fireplace, a large portrait of a nude female stared haughtily down at the intruders. Overhead, plump, winged cherubs chased scantily-clad damsels across elaborately plastered ceilings.

Pickett coughed discreetly. "Er, friend of your husband's?"

"It would certainly appear so," acknowledged Lady Fieldhurst, averting her gaze from flashing dark eyes and tumbled ebony locks.

Mr. Pickett, by contrast, studied the portrait with an interest which to the viscountess seemed unwarranted. "Something about her looks familiar."

"Why, Mr. Pickett!" cried her ladyship, much shocked. "I am surprised at you!"

Pickett flushed deeply. "Her *face,* I mean," he amended hastily. "Something about her *face* looks familiar!"

With an effort, Lady Fieldhurst fixed her gaze on the female's dark, heavy-lidded eyes, determinedly ignoring the lady's more obvious attributes. "Yes, I see what you mean. I daresay we have both seen her on the Covent Garden stage. I understand gentlemen often choose their mistresses from among the thespians. At any rate, Mr. Crumpton's objections would appear to be explained." She gave a rather shaky laugh. "I suppose I should be thankful that Papa did not remain in London long enough to help me inspect my inheritance."

Pickett drew one finger along the surface of a small table near the door, then studied the faint coating of dust on the tip of his finger. "If it's any consolation, my lady, the house appears to have been unoccupied for some time —"

She held up a hand to forestall him. "You are very thoughtful, Mr. Pickett, but pray do not think my husband's infidelity comes as a shock to me. I have known of it for years. Indeed, he has never made any effort to keep it secret. If this house has stood empty in recent months, it only means he was keeping his trysts at some other location."

Pickett was not sure which he found the most shocking: the late viscount's amorous habits, or his wife's resigned acceptance of them. "His death must have come as a welcome release!"

"One would think so," confessed her ladyship. "And yet, as long as Frederick lived, there was a chance, however slight, for reconciliation. Now, however, I can only wonder what went wrong, and what I might have done differently — oh, bother!"

Tears were springing to her eyes faster than she could blink them away. As she fumbled through her reticule, searching in vain for a handkerchief, Pickett thrust his own into her hand. She took it and dabbed at her eyes, annoyed with herself for this display of emotion before a relative stranger — a stranger, moreover, who under the circumstances held the power of life and death.

"Will you think me impertinent, my lady, if I suggest that perhaps the blame best lies with your husband?"

She smiled somewhat cynically. "Impertinent, no; accommodating, yes. Certainly no one would guess by your manner that you suspect this display of sensibility is nothing more than a belated attempt to divert suspicion by playing the grieving widow."

"I wasn't thinking any such thing —" protested Pickett, painfully aware that Mr. Colquhoun would have been quick to draw that very conclusion.

It was perhaps best that he was interrupted at this point, as a knock on the door heralded the first of the applicants for the position of butler. While Pickett went to admit the caller, Lady Fieldhurst snatched the dust cover off the nearest piece of furniture. The sofa underneath proved to be a virulent shade of green, but there was little she could do to amend matters at this point. Grimacing at the unknown light-skirt's execrable taste, she bundled up the white linen covering and draped it over the portrait, then seated herself on the sofa and spread her narrow, black bombazine skirts to cover as much of the upholstery as the current fashion would allow. When Pickett entered the room with a tall, hook-nosed man of somber mien, Lady Fieldhurst was the picture of demure widowhood.

"Good afternoon," he said, inclining his slightly stooped shoulders. "I have come to present myself as a candidate for the position of — of — of —"

As the man's voice trailed off, his eyes grew increasingly wider, and his gaze appeared to be fixed at some point over her right shoulder. Even as she turned to identify the cause of his consternation, Julia knew with a sinking feeling what she would see. Alas, the dust cover was slipping, displaying inch by inch the abundant charms of the painted female adorning the mantle.

"Well!" the offended butler bristled, drawing himself up to his full height with an air of outraged dignity, "I was given to understand that this was a respectable household! I can assure you, madam, that you could not offer me sufficient wages to persuade me to toil within a — a den of iniquity!"

Pickett, correctly surmising that this personage was not the missing Rogers, seized the impertinent butler by the collar.

"Here now, no one's going to offer you anything but a bit of the home-brewed, unless you start showing some respect for her ladyship!"

Lady Fieldhurst leaped to her feet, the color of the sofa cushions long forgotten. "No, Mr. Pickett, pray do not! His is an honest enough reaction, for were we not ourselves saying something very similar only moments ago?"

She might have saved her breath. The butler continued to denounce his present company, prophesying a series of gruesome fates, not only for her ladyship, but for all those who rejoiced in iniquity. Pickett, being a young man of action rather than words, twisted his fist more tightly into the man's collar and bore him inexorably toward the door. Lady Fieldhurst's protests were lost in the sounds of a scuffle and, finally, the slamming of the door.

"Well, that's taken care of *that*," pronounced Pickett with no little satisfaction as he re-entered the room.

"Are you injured, Mr. Pickett?" asked Lady Fieldhurst, watching with growing concern as he wiped a red substance from his knuckles. Surely that was blood he now wiped from his knuckles with the same handkerchief that had so recently dried her tears?

"Not at all. The fellow's nose — it, er, sprang a leak."

Lady Fieldhurst cocked a skeptical eyebrow. "And I suppose your hand became bloodied when you helped to stanch the flow. Really, Mr. Pickett, it was badly done of you! What else was the poor man to think, with that — that *creature* there?" She glanced toward the portrait, immediately regretted it, and looked hastily away.

"I know how to deal with her," declared Pickett. He crossed the room in three strides, then lifted the portrait from its nail above the mantel and set it on the floor with its face turned toward the wall.

When the next applicant appeared, they were better prepared. The Holland covers had been removed from the rest of the furniture, and the viscountess, seated in stately dignity before the fireplace, received each applicant as Pickett presented him. As he called out the name of each hopeful, Pickett gave Lady Fieldhurst a questioning look, which she answered with the slightest shake of her head. In this manner, he would know when — or if — the fugitive Rogers finally presented himself.

They spent two full days in this manner, and Pickett, who had always fancied that he knew London well, was forced to concede that he had never dreamed the Metropolis contained so many unemployed butlers. They had seen dozens of butlers: old ones and young ones, tall ones and short ones, thin ones and fat ones, bald, periwigged, and bespectacled ones. They had seen so many butlers that at last Lady Fieldhurst threw up her hands in mock dismay and declared that they had mingled into such a blur in her brain that if Rogers should appear on the instant, she was not at all certain she would recognize him.

In this, at least, she was mistaken. For when, at half-past three on the third day, Mr. Pickett ushered in a man answering to the name of Brown, Lady Fieldhurst's arrested gaze told Pickett all he needed to know. One glance at the man Brown confirmed Pickett's hopes. The erstwhile butler stared at the viscountess in abject horror, then, before she could say a word, darted for the door. Pickett moved quickly to block his exit and, while the two men struggled in the doorway, Lady Fieldhurst abandoned her place by the fire and hastened to reassure her former servant.

"Pray calm yourself, Rogers! There is no need for this outburst. You are in no danger here. Indeed, I have been very worried about you."

To the dismay of his captors, these comforting words had the unhappy effect of causing the butler to burst into tears. As great, wrenching sobs racked his frail body, the viscountess placed an arm about his stooped shoulders and guided him to one of the hideous green chairs.

"There, there! Sit down and tell us all about it, and you will feel much better directly," she said soothingly, as if she were speaking to a child.

"I didn't kill him!" he protested, instinctively directing his denial at Pickett. "I swear I didn't!"

"Of course you did not," said her ladyship. "You have always been unfailingly loyal to the Fieldhursts, just like your father before you. Indeed, Frederick left you a bequest of twenty pounds in his will."

"I don't deserve that he should leave me anything," sobbed Rogers, abandoning, in the throes of strong emotion, the refined accents he affected in his role of butler. "Nor would he, if only he'd lived long enough to change his will."

"Surely it could not have been as bad as all that! To be sure, Frederick had a cutting tongue at times, but he would not have been so cruel — to you," she added after the slightest of hesitations.

"Aye, that he would have, my lady," insisted Rogers, his sobs subsiding at last to a sniffle. "Turned me off without a character, he did, just a few hours before he — well, when I saw him lying there, I said to myself, 'they'll think I done him in, they will, and no mistake.' So I cleared out. I know it was wrong, and I'm sorry, but it was all I could think of."

"But why should he do such a thing? Why, your family has served the Fieldhursts for generations!"

Rogers fumbled in his inside coat pocket and withdrew a folded and creased sheet of paper. It bore the signs of repeated readings, and the ink was smudged in several places. "I'll never forget that day as long as

I live, my lady, and that's a fact. This letter came for me in the evening post."

Lady Fieldhurst took the paper and scanned it. "It is from the War Office," she told Pickett quite unnecessarily, as he was reading over her shoulder. " 'We regret to inform — your son, William Rogers — killed in action — siege of Scilla — oh, poor Rogers! If you were perhaps derelict in your duties that evening, surely no one could blame you after having received such dreadful news!"

"His lordship never knew, my lady. A new shipment of brandy had arrived that afternoon from Berry Brothers, and so I — well, I reckon you could say as how I was drowning my sorrows. When his lordship rang for me to show his visitor out, and saw the state I was in, he dismissed me on the spot. I went to my room and packed my bags, then went to find his lordship and beg him to give me another chance. When I saw he was dead, I was that scared, I just ran."

Lady Fieldhurst glanced at Pickett and found him scribbling furiously in his notebook. She wondered what he thought of the butler's story. Surely he must believe it, for who could feign such raw heartbreak?

"You have had a very difficult time, Rogers, but now you must come back home," she said, patting the butler's trembling hand. "We have all missed you very much, and we want to help you."

Rogers blinked back fresh tears. "But — but I've been dismissed," he reminded her.

"*Fieldhurst* dismissed you," she pointed out. "But Fieldhurst is dead, and I find myself in need of a butler. So, what is it to be, Rogers? Will you come back?"

"Aye, my lady," he said, bowing his head as if in benediction. "Aye, that I will."

"One moment," said Pickett, speaking up for the first time since Rogers's arrival. "This visitor you were to show out — who was he?"

Rogers cast a questioning glance at the viscountess, as if awaiting instructions. She gave him an encouraging nod. "You need not be afraid to answer."

"Very well, my lady, since you wish it. His lordship's guest was his colleague at the Foreign Office, Sir Archibald Stanton."

Chapter 14
In Which
John Pickett
Storms the Citadel

"Sir Archibald Stanton?" echoed Pickett, looking sharply from the butler to the viscountess. "Was Sir Archibald a frequent visitor?"

"I should not call his visits frequent, but they were not unusual," said her ladyship. "I know little of my husband's duties for the Foreign Office — his was not a confiding nature, even in the early days of our marriage — but I cannot think it strange that he and Sir Archibald should confer from time to time."

Nor could Pickett. Indeed, he could find nothing remarkable at all about Sir Archibald's presence that night — except for that brief glimpse of Sir Archibald's hand in his pocket, and a letter that was no longer where it should have been.

"What time would you say it was when you were summoned to show Sir Archibald out?" Even as Pickett asked the question, he had to wonder how reliable an answer he could expect from a man who had been, by his own admission, drunk at the time of the summons.

Here, however, he did Rogers less than justice. "It was twenty minutes past twelve," the butler stated decisively.

Pickett, jotting down notes in his notebook, looked up. "You seem quite sure of that, given your, er, condition at the time."

Rogers gave a discreet cough. "Begging your pardon, sir, but it was because of my condition that I noticed. When the bell rang I imagined, in my confusion, that it was the clock. I was momentarily puzzled that it should be chiming at such a peculiar time."

Pickett duly noted the butler's testimony, but his mind was already racing ahead on quite another track. Twenty minutes to twelve . . . and his lordship dead by two . . . The times fit. Sir Archibald could have called in the hopes of retrieving the letter and, failing in his object, returned later to take the letter by force. But if so, why would he kill the viscount in Lady Fieldhurst's bedchamber and leave the letter to lie on his lordship's desk until morning?

One thing, at least, was clear. It behooved him to call again upon Sir Archibald Stanton, and this time he would not be so easily brushed aside.

Lady Fieldhurst's coachman returned for her promptly at four; by which time she had given her once and future butler a few shillings and sent him on his way with instructions to set his affairs in order before returning to Berkeley Square.

"I congratulate you, my lady," said Mr. Pickett as the viscountess locked up the house behind them, leaving it once more in the sole possession of the naked brunette. "You said you would root him out, and you did."

"And, unlike some people I could name, I shall not suffer a sore head in the morning," she returned with a mischievous smile. She bent to drop the key into her reticule, and when she looked up again, her expression had grown serious. "I must thank you, Mr. Pickett, for not being too hard on Rogers. It was most considerate of you."

Pickett, though gratified, was somewhat embarrassed to be the object of such praise. "The man just lost his son, my lady. Only a brute would terrorize the poor fellow, under the circumstances."

"Perhaps. But after all your fruitless efforts to locate him, the temptation to bully him must have been great."

"Not at all. Why should I stoop to bullying, when you were doing a far better job at getting information out of him than I ever could?"

Lady Fieldhurst turned quite pink with pleasure. "Was I, indeed?"

"You were — and I thank you."

They had by this time reached the viscountess's carriage, where Drayton stood, waiting to hand her in. Lady Fieldhurst placed her hand on Drayton's outstretched arm and mounted the single step before turning back. "May I offer you a ride back to Bow Street, Mr. Pickett?"

He shook his head. "You are most kind, my lady, but no, thank you."

"Surely there is no need for you to walk so far," she persisted, still perched precariously on the step.

"I can always hire a hackney," he pointed out.

"Come, Mr. Pickett, this is false pride! Why should you spend your hard-earned wages on hackneys when you have been offered a ride *gratis?*"

Mr. Pickett, too painfully aware of the fact that he earned his bread by turning over his fellow man to the unloving arms of the Law, might have bristled at this unflattering observation had it not been swiftly followed by her ladyship's most enchanting smile.

"Unless," she added, "you decline my offer because you have already endured more than enough of my company for one day."

Who could resist such an entreaty? Mr. Pickett, at least, was not proof against it. "No, no!" he stammered hastily. "If that is truly what you think, then I have no choice but to accept your offer."

Lady Fieldhurst, having won her point, seated herself inside the carriage and swept her skirts aside so that Mr. Pickett, entering the equipage in her wake, might occupy the facing seat.

"Drayton," she called to the coachman, "you may set Mr. Pickett down in Bow Street."

Although elegantly upholstered and emblazoned with the Fieldhurst crest, her ladyship's personal carriage was not large. Pickett discovered this fact very quickly after settling himself on the rear facing seat, where he was soon lost in bemused contemplation of the fact that he sat in such close proximity to the viscountess that their knees were all but touching. Upon hearing her ladyship's instructions to her coachman, however, his mind was jolted back to more pressing matters — specifically, his unfinished business with Sir Archibald Stanton.

"Not Bow Street, my lady," he protested. "Curzon Street, if you would be so kind."

Lady Fieldhurst gave Drayton a nod of confirmation as he closed the carriage door. Alone with Pickett, she regarded the Runner with a quizzical expression. "Curzon Street? That can only mean you intend to pay a call on Sir Archibald."

"Can you wonder at it, after what Rogers told us?"

"No. But I cannot help feeling a bit sorry for Sir Archibald."

"Sorry for him? Why?"

"If you could but see your own face, Mr. Pickett, you would not have to ask! Yes, I definitely feel sorry for poor Sir Archibald, blissfully unsuspecting that you are about to descend upon him with the light of battle shining in your eyes."

Pickett gave a somewhat sheepish laugh. "Let's just say I don't enjoy being played for a fool."

"Hmmm," said Lady Fieldhurst, regarding him appraisingly. "I wonder if anyone could."

"They not only could; they are," he said bitterly. "Every last one of them — Sir Archibald Stanton, Lord Rupert Latham, even —"

He broke off abruptly.

"Even?" she prompted.

Even you, he had almost said. But that would never do. "Even the tapster at the Grey Goose," he finished lamely.

"I think you underestimate yourself, Mr. Pickett. I suspect the problem lies, not in your ability, but in your years — or, more specifically, your lack thereof."

"I'm no green youth," protested Pickett. "I am four-and-twenty."

"Practically in your dotage," retorted Lady Fieldhurst. "Depend upon it, Mr. Pickett, people underestimate you because of your youth. I confess, when Thomas sent for Bow Street on the night Frederick was murdered, I fully expected him to bring back a considerably older man. But I assure you, whatever doubts I may have entertained as to your competence have long since been laid to rest."

"I'm pleased to hear that, at any rate," said Pickett, somewhat mollified. "When did that happen?"

She pondered the question for a moment before answering. "I think it must have been the last time I saw Lord Rupert. He was furious with me for revealing the incident of the spilled champagne. Not until then did I realize that you had tricked me very neatly into exploding not only my own alibi, but his as well."

However flattering, Pickett could not agree with this assessment of his talents. "I never resorted to trickery, my lady!"

"Oh, I don't hold it against you. In fact, I think it was quite clever of you."

"If you think I was trying to trick you into incriminating yourself —"

"Now, *that* I do not, for I am well aware that I was — and still am, for that matter — quite incriminated already. No, I think you must believe in my innocence, for I suspect you would have me in irons quickly enough, if you truly believed that I murdered Frederick. Or —" Her gaze grew speculative as a new thought occurred to her. "Perhaps you do intend to arrest me, and it is you who are playing me for a fool. Giving me more rope to hang myself with, as it were."

Pickett, lapsing into incoherent denials, could only be grateful when the carriage turned into Curzon Street. Sir Archibald, with his undisguised hostility, was easier to cope with than the enchanting Lady Fieldhurst, who muddled his mind and bewitched his senses until he no longer knew whether he was coming or going. As the coach rolled to a stop before Sir Archibald's domicile, Pickett thanked the viscountess for her hospitality and took his leave of her, then exited the vehicle. As the carriage bowled up the street and out of sight, Pickett strode up the broad, shallow stairs of Sir Archibald's residence, and rapped sharply on the door. It was opened by the same dour-faced butler who had admitted him before, and who now gestured toward the cold little sitting room with its uncomfortable chairs. "If you will wait here, sir, I will inform Sir Archibald —"

"Not this time," interrupted Pickett, pushing past him into the house.

"Stop! You must not —"

Sir Archibald, hearing the commotion at his front door, emerged from a room on the left. "Here, now! What's all this — not you again!"

"I want answers, Sir Archibald, and I mean to have them," Pickett informed him without preamble. "Were you at Lord Fieldhurst's house on the night he was murdered?"

Sir Archibald's face grew dark with fury. "Who says so?"

"The butler who admitted you."

"Oh, so he's turned up at last, has he? And you would take the word of a drunken sot over that of a British diplomat?"

"How would you know the butler was drunk, unless you had seen him that night?"

"Very well, I was there. It proves nothing!"

"No, but it does cast a certain letter in a different light. We are at war with France, and you are in a position of trust. A letter written in French left lying about could prove a bit awkward, could it not?"

Sir Archibald crossed the room to the bell pull and tugged at it violently. The butler's swift appearance led Pickett to believe he must have been listening at the keyhole. "Mr. Pickett is leaving," Sir Archibald informed his servant. "Have the goodness to show him out."

Having been ejected from Sir Archibald's domicile in none too gentle a manner, Pickett was more than ever convinced of the significance of the disappearing letter. Having encountered a brick wall at the diplomat's residence, it remained only for him to go over Sir Archibald's head — to the Foreign Office, in fact, where there might be those (Foreign Secretary Canning, for one) who would take no little interest in the knowledge that Sir Archibald Stanton had taken from the late Viscount Fieldhurst a letter written in the language of Britain's mortal enemy.

Upon being set down in Downing Street,

where the Foreign Office had been head-quartered for the last fifteen years, Pickett was surprised to discover that the corridors of power were not so very different from the environs of Bow Street. The street itself was narrow and cramped, with government offices both major and minor competing for space with pubs, livery stables, and cheap boardinghouses. Emboldened by this realization, he took the front stairs two at a time and entered the edifice that had once been the town residence of Lord Sheffield.

At Pickett's entrance, a clerk looked up from a desk littered with papers. This individual, although underpaid and overworked, was nonetheless a junior member of an ancient (albeit impoverished) family, and knew his place in the hierarchy of British society. He took one look at Pickett, assessing at a glance his shabby clothing and unfashionable queue, and dismissed him as a creature of no importance.

"May I help you?" he inquired in bored accents.

"I'd like to see Mr. Canning," said Pickett.

The clerk's bored expression vanished. "My good fellow, there is a war on," he protested, torn between exasperation and amusement. "One can't just stroll in off the street and demand to see the Foreign Secretary."

"Then who can I see?" asked Pickett, undaunted.

"I should say that depends upon the nature of your business."

"My 'business' is the murder of Viscount Fieldhurst," stated Pickett, presenting his card. "John Pickett, of the Bow Street police office. I have some questions to ask regarding the viscount and Sir Archibald Stanton."

At this revelation, the clerk's face grew pale. "One moment, please. If you will — excuse me —" He crossed the hall with a carefully measured tread, but his inner turmoil was betrayed by the furtive glances he cast over his shoulder at Pickett.

As the clerk disappeared behind a closed door at the opposite end of the hall, Pickett could not but wonder whether it was the viscount's name or Sir Archibald Stanton's that provoked such a pronounced reaction. He was sorely tempted to press his ear to the door, but even as he pondered this course of action, the door opened and the clerk reappeared. His manner was calmer now, but beads of perspiration shone on his forehead.

"If you will come with me, Mr. Pickett,"

he said, sweeping his arm in the direction of that half-closed door.

Pickett followed and was shown into a room embellished with fine linen-fold paneling and tall windows which reached from floor to ceiling. Positioned before the windows was a massive oak desk, behind which sat a distinguished-looking man with silver-streaked hair and rather cold blue eyes.

"Ah, Mr. Pickett. Come in and sit down."

As Pickett advanced into the room, hat in hand, he heard the click of the door as the clerk shut it behind him and realized he was being granted a private interview — although it seemed more like an inquisition. All at once he felt nine years old again, a charity school pupil called on the carpet for some long-forgotten misdemeanor. Repressing the old feeling of inferiority, he lifted his chin, looked the older man squarely in the eye, and demanded with well-feigned bravado, "And your name is — ?"

The man shook his head. "Not important. Mr. Pickett, you are no doubt aware that the viscount was highly placed within the Foreign Office. We regret his passing, and are naturally shocked at the violent manner in which he died, but we have nothing more to say to the matter."

"But an innocent woman's life may be at

stake!" insisted Pickett.

"You refer, I presume, to Lady Fieldhurst. Her ladyship's involvement is unfortunate, but there is nothing we can do."

Pickett placed both hands on the desk and leaned across it, towering over his cold-blooded adversary. "You would let her hang for a murder she never committed?"

"Regrettable, of course, if such a thing were to come to pass, but in matters of national security, it is sometimes necessary to place the good of the many over the good of a few."

Pickett felt a sudden chill in spite of the sunlight streaming through the windows. "Do you mean to say — ?"

"To be blunt, Mr. Pickett, better men than Lady Fieldhurst have died for the sake of their country."

Pickett could only stare in mounting horror.

"I realize this must sound harsh," continued the man in placating tones, "but someday you will understand. You are very young —"

"I'm old enough to know when I'm being patronized," retorted Pickett, finding his tongue at last. "Who is it you are so determined to protect? Is it Sir Archibald Stanton? Or perhaps Fieldhurst himself?"

"I have said all I intend to say on the subject," the man said brusquely, ringing for the clerk. "Now, if you will excuse me, there is a war on, and I am very busy. Good day, sir."

"You haven't seen the last of me," Pickett vowed, his voice rising in helpless fury. "I'm going to find out who killed Lord Fieldhurst, and I don't care who I have to bring down in the process!"

"Good day, sir," said the man again, as the clerk opened the door and very pointedly held it open.

Finding himself expelled from the premises for the second time in less than two hours, Pickett was forced to concede defeat and turn his steps eastward. It was now obvious that he could expect no help from the Foreign Office. He must return to Upper Well Alley, where he hoped to find Jane Mudge returned to roost. Several of her modest possessions had been strewn about the untidy room; surely she must come back for them. And when she did, he would have a sworn statement from her, if he had to drag her all the way to Bow Street by her heels.

"Not you again!" exclaimed the matron as he entered the boardinghouse.

"I was wondering if I might see Jane," he

said. "Has she come back?"

"Aye, for all the good it'll do you. She come back an hour ago and paid me what she owed, then packed up her gewgaws and cleared out."

"Did she say where she was going?"

"No — leastways, nothing that made no sense. Some rubbish about her and her Davey going to ride a dolphin. Faugh! As if anyone could!"

"A *dolphin,* did you say?"

Without waiting for a reply, Pickett ran out of the house and back down the street toward the river. The tide was going out, and the *Dolphin,* her sails billowing, glided on the ebbing waters toward the Thames estuary and the open sea beyond.

"You, there," Pickett called to one of a group of brawny men coiling up the heavy cables that had tethered the ship to the dock. "Where's she bound?" A jerk of his thumb indicated the departing *Dolphin.*

"New South Wales," came the reply. "It'll be three months or more ere she makes port there."

Pickett's heart fell to his boots. Even if the treacherous maid survived the voyage around the Cape of Good Hope — by no means a certainty even in times of peace, let alone now, when the French navy prowled the coasts — Lady Fieldhurst might well be brought to trial long before Jane's feet once more touched solid ground.

It was past seven o'clock by the time he reached Bow Street and the sun was beginning to set. Clearly there was no point in stopping by the police office to report this unwelcome turn of events to Mr. Colquhoun, as even that most diligent of magistrates would by this time have sought the comforts of hearth and home. Deciding to do likewise, Pickett made his way to Drury Lane and his hired lodgings.

As he fitted an iron key into the lock, he wondered what it might be like to come home to a woman every night, a woman who would welcome one with a warm smile and a hot meal. He shook his head as if to clear it. His solitary state had never bothered him before; perhaps it was the thought of Mr. Colquhoun surrounded by family that made him feel uncharacteristically lonely by comparison. Or, whispered a little voice somewhere inside his head, perhaps it had more to do with an afternoon spent with Lady Fieldhurst in her modest Queens Gardens house; apart from the army of servants and the other trappings of aristocracy which emphasized the difference in their stations.

As he turned the key and opened the door, an odor wafting within drove these unprofitable thoughts from his head. He glanced around the empty room, noting that the candles had been lit, and spied a steaming meat pie in the center of the plain deal table.

"Mrs. Catchpole?" he called.

"Aye, Johnny, here I am," she returned, waddling out of the bedchamber. "I brung up your clean linen, along with a bite for your supper."

"More than a bite, I'd say," said Pickett, eyeing the pie with anticipation as he seated himself at the table. "And a good thing, too! I'm hungry enough to eat a horse."

She chuckled richly at this not very original witticism. "No horse here, ducky, just a good English kidney pie and a mug of ale to wash it down."

"You're an angel!" declared Pickett around a mouthful of pie.

"Lawks, no!" protested Mrs. Catchpole, blushing rosily all the same. "I didn't do nothing a good wife wouldn't do. Now, my niece Alice is in service to Lady Dalrymple, and she can make a black pudding that will melt in your mouth!"

"Who, Lady Dalrymple?" asked Pickett,

seeing what was in the wind.

"Lawks, no! Who'd expect a lady to do her own —" Mrs. Catchpole broke off abruptly, returning Pickett's limpid gaze with eyes narrowed in suspicion. "Oh, I see what you're about, Johnny! You're trying to pull my leg!"

Pickett, who could think of few pastimes which held less appeal, suppressed a shudder at the mental image which rose to his brain. Alas, Mrs. Catchpole, having determined that her niece would make the perfect wife for her handsome young boarder, would not be so easily distracted. Fortunately for Pickett, her catalog of Alice's numerous charms was interrupted by a knock on the door. Mrs. Catchpole, abandoning the subject with considerable regret, said with a sigh, "You go ahead and eat, Johnny. I'll get it."

She bustled over to the door and opened it. After exchanging a few curt words with the person on the other side, she turned back toward Pickett, disapproval writ large upon her usually cheerful countenance.

"Female says she has to see you, Johnny."

Pickett choked on his ale, and leaped to his feet so quickly he knocked the chair to the floor. At that moment, Lucy breezed into the room with some light-colored garment draped over her arm and a purple bonnet of surpassing ugliness adorning her head.

"About time you were coming home, John Pickett," she scolded. "How's a girl to make an honest living going around carrying a man's breeches? Makes it look like she's spoken for, it does, and that's bad for business!"

"Lucy! You found them!" he exclaimed, firmly tamping down the pang of disappointment he'd felt when he realized that his caller was not, in fact, Lady Fieldhurst. For why would her ladyship come looking for him, even if she had known where to find him?

"Aye, I found 'em, and bought 'em, and had enough left over for this bonnet," she declared proudly. "Can't imagine why anyone would want to get rid of it, but then, there's no understanding the nobs, is there?"

"None at all," agreed Pickett, although he was no longer paying attention. Instead, he spread Lord Rupert's pantaloons out on the table and held the candle aloft, the better to examine them. Apparently his lordship's tale of spilled champagne had been the truth, or near enough as made no odds. There were no telltale bloodstains marring the finely tailored garment. "Good job, Lucy."

Lucy, elbows on the table, leaned forward until her bosom threatened to tumble out of her bodice and into his kidney pie. "Is that all you have to say, John Pickett?" she pouted. "Just 'good job'?"

Pickett bundled up the breeches and stuffed them into her gaping neckline. "How about, 'You can keep these for your troubles'?"

"And what, pray, am I going to do with a man's breeches? Didn't I just say —"

"Sell them to another rag shop," suggested Pickett. "Or give them to your Frog."

The reminder of her Frenchman had the happy effect of making Lucy forget her grievances. "Aye, I'll do that this very night! I wonder what he'll think of my new chapo?" she said, patting the crown of her hideous bonnet. "Good evening to you, John Pickett — or should I say, 'Bone sewer'!"

After Lucy had gone, Pickett turned back to the kidney pie and found Mrs. Catchpole quivering with righteous indignation. "Well! That you would allow a creature like that under my roof —"

"Mine is not a pretty business, Mrs. Catchpole, and sometimes I have to take help wherever I can find it," he said, hiding a smile as he addressed himself to the kidney pie. "But you were about to tell me about your niece — Alice, I think it was?"

"Never mind!" cried Mrs. Catchpole, her large, square hands fluttering, as if to brush away such an abhorrent suggestion. "Now that I think on it, it wouldn't be such a good idea, after all. I wouldn't have my Alice exposed to such as that creature; no, not for love nor money I wouldn't!"

"I was afraid of that," said Pickett mournfully. "Now you see why I have no wife."

"Indeed, I do, Johnny, and I'm sorry for it, but I can't have Alice rubbing shoulders with women of that stamp, even for — well, I just can't, and that's all there is to it! Good night, Johnny. Just leave the dirty dishes there on the table and I'll get them in the morning."

"Good night, Mrs. Catchpole," Pickett said with deceptive meekness as the door closed behind her.

I can't have Alice rubbing shoulders with women of that stamp . . . Nor could he imagine Lady Fieldhurst doing so, even if everything else were equal, which it most emphatically was not. And yet, when presented with that painting in her house, the viscountess had shown herself to be surprisingly resilient. She had been embarrassed, naturally, but she had not fallen into hysterics nor had a fit of the vapors. As he turned his attention back to the cooling kidney pie, Pickett had to smile. He had gotten his wish, after a fashion. He'd been welcomed home by both a hot meal and a warm smile, although neither had come from the source he might have chosen.

CHAPTER 15
IN WHICH JOHN PICKETT PROPOUNDS A THEORY

"Well, well, if it isn't young Lochinvar," observed Mr. Colquhoun when Pickett reported to him the following morning.

"I beg your pardon, sir?"

"Lochinvar," repeated the wily Scotsman with a twinkle in his eye. "Hero of Walter Scott's new poem. Romantic young fellow who gate-crashes a wedding and makes off with the bride."

"I fail to see the connection, sir," Pickett said stiffly.

"Do you? And here I thought you one of the more intelligent men of my acquaintance. No, no, don't go all muffin-faced on me! I'm only roasting you. Now, what did you discover yesterday?"

"A dead end where the maid is concerned, although we were at last able to locate the butler, Rogers —"

Pickett's use of the plural pronoun was not lost on Mr. Colquhoun, even though that worthy appeared to be deeply engrossed in the notes he scribbled onto a blotter. "We?" he echoed without looking up.

"Lady Fieldhurst and I," explained Pickett.

The scratching of Mr. Colquhoun's quill ceased, and he regarded the erring Runner from beneath ominously lowered brows. "I was not aware that the viscountess was acting as your partner in the investigation."

"Her ladyship is not acting as my partner in anything, sir, but she had an idea for smoking out the butler; and since I'd had little enough luck in that quarter myself, I thought it couldn't hurt to let her have a go at it."

"On the contrary, Pickett, it could hurt you a great deal. Your reluctance to arrest the lady — who is still generally held to be the most promising suspect, regardless of your unwillingness to see her as such — has not gone unnoticed in certain quarters. You have a promising future in Bow Street, my boy, but not if you persist in compromising your integrity for the sake of a pretty face."

"Begging your pardon, sir, but I am not compromising anything. If she was in fact guilty, why should she offer to help me locate the butler? For Rogers turned up on her very doorstep, just as she predicted, and through him we — or rather, *I* — discovered that the late-night visitor was none other than Sir Archibald Stanton, the same one who'd pinched the letter from Lord Fieldhurst's desk."

Mr. Colquhoun gave a grunt. "And so the butler appears, complete with a motive for murder and evidence incriminating Sir Archibald. Convenient for her ladyship, at any rate."

Pickett wisely chose to let this comment pass. "I paid a call on Sir Archibald, hoping to question him further, but meeting with no success there, I stepped 'round to the Foreign Office."

"The Foreign Office?" echoed Mr. Colquhoun, startled. "And what, pray tell, did you do there?"

Pickett's gaze slid away from the magistrate's. "I, er, seem to have accused Sir Archibald of spying."

"You *what?*"

"Or maybe it was Lord Fieldhurst who was spying, and Sir Archibald was onto him. They're protecting someone, sir. I'm sure of it."

"And what, pray, was the Foreign Office's response to this extraordinary accusation?" asked Mr. Colquhoun, his eyebrows lowering ominously.

"They, er, they threw me out on my ear," confessed Pickett, belatedly adding, "sir."

"As well they might! Have you run mad, man?"

Pickett looked up, his earlier embarrassment forgotten. "That letter means *something*," he insisted. "I would swear to it. What was Fieldhurst doing with it in the first place, and why would Sir Archibald take it from his desk and then try to fob me off with a cock-and-bull story about her ladyship —"

"What cock-and-bull story was this?"

Too late Pickett recognized his error. He had not told Mr. Colquhoun about his first interview with Sir Archibald, painfully aware that he had not shown to advantage in the encounter. Now, however, an explanation was clearly called for. "He tried to convince me that the letter was from a French mistress of Fieldhurst's, and he'd taken it to spare Lady Fieldhurst's sensibilities."

"It seems reasonable enough. God knows there are plenty of French emigrées trying to earn their bread any way they can."

"Yes, sir, but his tender concern for the viscountess struck me as false. For one thing, her ladyship has no illusions about her husband's character, and so does not need Sir Archibald's protection. For another, I find his fit of gallantry a bit self-serving, seeing as it attempts to clear him of suspicion, while at the same time crediting her ladyship with an additional motive for murder."

"You, on the other hand, would insist upon her innocence even if you had discovered her standing over the body with the bloodied weapon in her hand," the magistrate remarked dryly.

"You wrong me, sir, but that is beside the point. I have a theory which I should like to put to you, if I may."

Mr. Colquhoun threw up his hands in resignation. "I daresay I shall be forced to hear it whether I would or no, so by all means, Pickett, let us hear your theory."

"Espionage," declared Pickett. "Either Fieldhurst or Sir Archibald is spying for the French, and the other found out and pinched the letter as proof. Sir Archibald has my vote. Fieldhurst could have set up the meeting to confront Sir Archibald with his crimes, and Stanton, seeing the game was up, murdered him to keep him quiet."

"An interesting theory," conceded the magistrate, "but for the fact that Fieldhurst was very much alive when the butler showed Sir Archibald out."

"He could have come back later, after Fieldhurst had retired upstairs for the night."

"Then why pursue the viscount upstairs? Why should not Sir Archibald just go into the study, take the letter, and go?"

"He probably didn't know it was there until the next morning, when he called on Lady Fieldhurst and saw it lying on the desk. Perhaps he assumed Fieldhurst had the letter on his person, and followed him upstairs in the hope of persuading the viscount to give it to him. Or perhaps Fieldhurst was blackmailing him, and Sir Archibald saw his chance to do away with the blackmailer *and* retrieve the letter. So he stabs Fieldhurst, then rifles the pockets of his coat, but the letter isn't there."

The magistrate's silence was deafening.

"All right, forget the blackmail theory," Pickett said with a sigh. "Let's say Fieldhurst was the spy. Sir Archibald confronts him with his crimes, finds the viscount unrepentant, and returns later to eliminate the breach to national security."

"Thus cheating the hangman? Why, if Fieldhurst's death is to be the end result either way?"

"To spare the Foreign Office a black eye when it becomes known that one of their own is spying for Boney. Can you imagine the scandal? The Foreign Office might well have deputized him to rid them of the embarrassment before it came to light."

"That is quite an accusation, young man!"

"Not an accusation, sir, just a theory based on my own lack of welcome at the Foreign Office."

Mr. Colquhoun scowled into space, pondering the extraordinary scenarios presented for his consideration. "Even if Sir Archibald did return to murder the viscount, for whatever reason," he said at last, "how did he leave the house without being seen? No one on the opposite side of the square reports seeing anyone exit the house through the front door, and had he attempted to leave through the servants' entrance, he must have passed through the downstairs dining hall at the very hour when the staff was gathered for the evening meal."

"He may have simply been lucky," Pickett pointed out. "No one across the square recalled seeing Sir Archibald leave at twenty past twelve, although it seems fairly obvious that he must have done so. Or he might have gone up the servants' stair to the attics, and thence to the roof. The houses are so close together that an agile man might leap from one to the next without much fear of falling."

"Unfortunately, the most promising theory is worthless without solid evidence to back it up," observed the magistrate, albeit not without sympathy. "Having made yourself *persona non grata* at the Foreign Office, where will your investigations take you next?"

"St. George's, Hanover Square."

"What the devil for?" thundered Colquhoun. At the mention of one of Mayfair's most fashionable churches and the site of more than one Society wedding, his expression assumed so forbidding an aspect that Pickett could not but wonder if the magistrate suspected him of absconding with the viscountess to the nearest altar *à la* young Lochinvar.

" 'The tomb of Deacon Toomer,' " quoted Pickett, reading from his notes. "I have no idea who the fellow was or where he is buried, but since St. George's is the viscount's parish church, the crypt there seems to be the best place to start searching."

"I don't know," muttered the magistrate, as the purple faded from his countenance. "It seems little enough to go on."

"I agree, sir, but since the footman Thomas heard the words spoken in anger from her ladyship's bedchamber shortly before the time of death, it apparently means something to someone — a meeting place, perhaps; or perhaps Toomer's death is somehow tied to Fieldhurst's."

"Another spy, in other words," grunted Colquhoun. "Have a care, Pickett, or you are likely to see one lurking behind every tombstone!"

"I shall naturally do all I can to help poor Lady Fieldhurst," declared Mr. Robert Hodgson, rector of St. George's, Hanover Square. His voice bounced eerily off the walls as he and Pickett descended the stone stairs into the crypt.

The Runner, carefully picking his way down steps only dimly seen in the drunkenly bobbing light of the rector's lantern, was obliged to wait until his feet touched level ground before asking, "Were you well acquainted with the viscountess?"

"I should not say I was well acquainted with her ladyship, although naturally we exchanged greetings every Sunday after services. She seemed to me to be a gentle lady, incapable of such a violent act."

"She attended services regularly?"

"Until her husband's death, yes."

"Some would take her absence since then

as evidence of a guilty conscience," observed Pickett.

"The mean-spirited might, I daresay. For my part, I attribute her absence to her recent bereavement — along with, perhaps, a perfectly natural reluctance to offer herself as fodder for the gossips."

Pickett looked up sharply. "Gossips, you say?"

Mr. Hodgson gave an unecclesiastical snort. "Oh, they say nothing to her face — they haven't the courage for that! — but the scandal sheets print the most revolting insinuations, while as for the sketches in the printing shop windows — really, one finds it an embarrassment to walk down Oxford Street! But as I recall, you yourself have not escaped their censure. Allow me to assure you that I, for one, respect you for your restraint in the matter."

"I, er, thank you," said Pickett, somewhat baffled by the rector's reassurances.

His eyes had by this time grown accustomed to the darkness of the crypt and could now distinguish individual tombs. Some were no more than large stone slabs, while others bore elaborately carved memorials to the deceased.

"As I told you when you first questioned me, I cannot recall a Deacon Toomer interred here, although I believe there is a William Toogood along the right-hand wall about halfway back. Whether he was a deacon or not, I cannot say. Feel free to look as long as you wish. I shall be upstairs in the vestry, if you should have need of me."

He left the lantern with Pickett, assuring the Runner that he had climbed the staircase often enough to have no need of its assistance. Left to his own devices, Pickett lost no time in locating William Toogood's modest stone slab. The hope, never very strong, that the rector had misread the name proved a futile one, as the crudely carved letters were clearly legible. To this disappointment was added the discovery that the subject had shuffled off this mortal coil in the year of our Lord 1746, forcing Pickett to absolve both Lord Fieldhurst and Sir Archibald of having any hand in good Billy's demise.

Deprived of this promising lead, he set about examining each of the remaining tombs in turn. It was a monotonous task, relieved only by one harrowing moment when a draft from an unseen crack in the crypt wall snuffed out the feeble lantern and plunged him into stygian darkness. Only by cupping his hands around the wick and blowing gently was he able to coax the flame back to life. By the time this operation was completed, however, he found he had lost all taste for his present company. He made short work of the remaining tombs and, finding no sign of an occupant named Toomer or any evidence that any part of the crypt had been used for meetings of a clandestine nature, abandoned the dark of the vault for the sunshine above.

He should have gone next to investigate the crypt of Sir Archibald's parish church, St. Martin in the Fields; he'd had every intention of doing so, had not certain of Mr. Hodgson's words taken root in his brain and refused to be dislodged. *The sketches in the print shop windows . . . you yourself have not escaped their censure.* Finding himself only a short walk from Oxford Street, he decided to see for himself those sketches which had so embarrassed the rector.

He soon wished he had not. To be sure, most of the window space was taken up by the usual unflattering representations of the Prince of Wales and his amorous activities, along with a number of caricatures criticizing Wellington's progress (or lack thereof) against Bonaparte. But it was a drawing of quite another sort which held all of Pickett's attention, one which featured a fair-haired woman whose ample bosom spilled over the abbreviated bodice of her low-necked, high-waisted gown. With her left arm, she embraced a rakish gentleman dressed in the wasp-waisted coat and high shirtpoints of the fashionable set — Lord Rupert Latham, presumably — while with her right, she plunged a scissors into another man's neck. This gentleman, however, appeared oblivious to the threat to his life, so engrossed was he in fondling the doxy sitting upon his knee. The caption at the bottom of Mr. Gillray's masterpiece read: "The Modern Marriage."

"A lot he knows," muttered Pickett to no one in particular. "She's not that top-heavy."

A print by Thomas Rowlandson was displayed nearby, this one even more offensive than Gillray's offering. For here was Lady Fieldhurst dressed in the black mourning gown of the recent widow — although Pickett sincerely doubted any widow had ever displayed so much bared bosom. A noose hung loosely about her neck, but far from dreading her fate, she smiled coyly at the leering fellow who held the other end of the rope — a man in a shallow-crowned hat and the red waistcoat of the Bow Street foot patrol. The lady held a bloody scissors imperfectly concealed behind her back, but the Runner, ogling her cleavage with bulging eyes, took no notice of them. The caption read: "Bow Street Investigates."

Two gentlemen passed the shop from the other direction, one pausing before the window just long enough to make a ribald remark to his companion, who laughed heartily as they continued up the street. Pickett, feeling more than a little ill, hardly noticed them. This, then, was what Mr. Colquhoun had feared. The insult was not aimed at him personally; the artist (if one could call him that) had apparently made no attempt to portray the particular officer investigating the viscount's murder, but instead had resorted to a generic but readily recognizable type. In the process, he called into question not only Pickett's integrity, but that of the entire Bow Street force.

With a heavy heart, Pickett realized what he must do. He would follow this last lead as far as it would take him, but if the deceased Deacon Toomer failed to lead him to the murderer, he would have no choice but to arrest the viscountess.

John Pickett was not the only person to take exception to the sketches adorning the local shop windows. Another found them equally objectionable and this worthy, unlike Pickett, was in a position to take corrective action. He strode into the shop, demanded of the proprietor a copy of each of the offensive drawings and, armed with these, paid a call of ceremony in Berkeley Square.

Lady Fieldhurst, entertaining the Countess of Dunnington over morning chocolate, received him in the breakfast room. It was unlike Lord Rupert to be out and about so early (he had more than once complained in Lady Fieldhurst's presence of being obliged to rise before noon), so when the newly restored Rogers entered the breakfast room to announce a visitor, the viscountess had expected to see someone of more matutinal habits — someone, for instance, like John Pickett.

"Good morning, Rupert," said Lady Fieldhurst, feeling vaguely disappointed. "This is an unexpected pleasure, to be sure."

Lord Rupert did not deign to admire how the sunlight pouring through the east-facing windows turned her hair to burnished gold, nor did he comment on the contrast between her ladyship's angelically fair skin and the unrelieved black of her mourning gown. He likewise ignored the hand she offered for his kiss, except to thrust two sheets of foolscap into it, along with the command that she "look at that!"

Thus adjured, Lady Fieldhurst set aside her china cup and studied the two drawings in silence for a long moment before pronouncing, "This looks nothing at all like Mr. Pickett."

"The devil take Mr. Pickett! It is the other one that most concerns me."

"Yes, Rupert, I can see how it would," agreed Lady Dunnington, examining the drawings over her hostess's shoulder. "Mr. Gillray has quite failed to capture your good side."

Lord Rupert refused to dignify this sally with a response. "Damn it, Julia, all of White's is abuzz, while as for the betting book, its pages are filled with private wagers on your guilt or innocence."

"Do the odds run in my favor?" asked the viscountess with detached curiosity. "Perhaps you would be willing to place a small wager on my behalf."

"No, my dear, I would not! I am far more concerned with scotching the scandal. I came today for the express purpose of asking you to marry me without delay. I have already taken steps toward acquiring a special license, so we may be wed at once."

"Why, Rupert, such passion!" exclaimed Lady Dunnington. "I vow, I am quite overcome!"

Lord Rupert glared at Emily. "Can you not grant us a moment of privacy?"

"Oh, never mind me," Lady Dunnington said soothingly. "Julia assures me I am quite like one of the family."

Lady Fieldhurst had been sipping her now tepid chocolate, but at Lord Rupert's inelegant proposal, she set her cup on the table with sufficient force to send the light brown liquid spilling over the side. "You presume too much, Rupert! How, pray, will I avert a scandal by marrying you before Frederick is cold in the ground? Surely such haste would only add credence to this," she said, gesturing toward the drawing.

"At least the world would know that my intentions were honorable."

She had to smile at the elasticity of his morals. "I am sorry to inform you, Rupert, that there is no 'honor' in paying court to a married woman; any more than there was 'honor' in my encouraging your attentions. I am flattered by your offer, but if I am made uncomfortable by gossip linking my name with yours, it is perhaps no more than I deserve."

Lord Rupert's gaze shifted from the risqué sketches littering the table to the complacent woman sipping cold chocolate as if she were taking tea with the Queen.

"Are you truly so hardened, Julia?"

She nodded. "Oh, quite! Six years of marriage with Frederick has that effect on one, to say nothing of being suspected of murder."

"Perhaps I should tell you, then, that odds are running four to one against you."

The fragile china cup rattled against its saucer, but her voice remained steady. "In that case, you must certainly place a wager for me. I could earn a rather tidy profit — provided, of course, that I live long enough to enjoy it."

"Will you at least tell me whether your rejection of my offer is more in the nature of a 'not yet' than a 'no'?" demanded Lord Rupert.

"Since you will have it, Rupert, no, no, a thousand times no!" declared Lady Fieldhurst in a voice that brooked no argument. "I have not been released from one marriage, only to rush headlong into another. Believe me, the last thing I need in my life right now is a man!"

"Very well, Julia," said Lord Rupert, throwing up his hands in mock surrender. "Say no more! I trust, however, that you will forgive me for observing that this show of independence would be more convincing did your life not at this very moment rest in the hands of a man — if one may so describe a cub not yet old enough to shave."

Lady Fieldhurst, recalling the faint but unmistakable beard adorning Pickett's chin on the morning following his overindulgence, could not let this animadversion pass unchallenged.

"Oh, he shaves," she assured him, then blinked at the two scandalized faces regarding her across the breakfast table. "Now, what have I said to make the pair of you look at me like that?"

CHAPTER 16
IN WHICH
JOHN PICKETT
UNDERTAKES A
JOURNEY

After leaving Oxford Street, Pickett, in a frenzy of righteous indignation, not only examined the crypt at St. Martin in the Fields, but the tombs at Westminster Abbey as well, the close proximity of that historic edifice to the Foreign Office rendering it a promising meeting place for political intrigue. Alas, though he made the acquaintance of numerous Toobys, Tuckers, and Trueloves, not one Toomer could he find.

With the air of one clinging to a vain hope, he hired a hackney to convey him to the City. St. Paul's Cathedral, he knew, was so popular with tourists that two or more men might meet in its crypt without occasioning a second glance. Upon being set down in front of this historic edifice, he dropped a sixpence into the poor box (the requested remuneration for touring the premises) and fell into step behind a group of fashionably dressed young people descending into the crypt. One of these, a young lady fetchingly attired in a pale blue pelisse and a straw bonnet with matching ribbons, exclaimed with ghoulish delight that it was exactly like something in one of Mrs. Radcliffe's novels. As her companions flitted eagerly from tomb to tomb with morbid relish, Pickett addressed the curate whose unenviable task it was to point out the genius of Christopher Wren and the tombs of John Donne and Dr. Johnson to sightseers more interested in gothic horrors.

"Do you have many repeat visitors?"

"Oh, yes," said the curate. "Many make an annual pilgrimage. There are those who do not consider their stay in Town to be complete without a visit to the Whispering Gallery."

"What about the crypt? Does one visit per season usually suffice?"

Pickett was obliged to repeat his question, for farther into the vault, one of the young men leaped out from between two large monuments, sending the ladies of the party into shrieks of mock terror that reverberated in the cavernous depths.

The curate, observing with disfavor the hilarity which ensued, gave a weary sigh. "Lord Nelson's tomb is always popular, but yes, one visit to the crypt usually satisfies all but the most voracious appetite for the macabre."

"If there were regular visitors, then, you would probably have noticed them," Pickett observed, "especially if they were interested in one particular tomb, such as that of Deacon Toomer."

"Deacon Toomer?" echoed the curate, his brow puckered in concentration. "I cannot recall that we house such a tomb at all, although I would hesitate to claim intimate knowledge of every single one. If you would care to search for it, you are welcome to do so."

Pickett thanked him with a sinking heart. The crypt was cavernous, and he had already wasted far too much time poking about the tombs at Westminster Abbey. Fortunately, he received assistance from an unexpected quarter, as the young lady in blue enthusiastically squealed out the name on every memorial she examined. But even with this unscheduled aid, he failed to locate a single Toomer, deacon or otherwise, among the inhabitants of St. Paul's crypt.

The sun was riding low in the western sky when he left St. Paul's, and Pickett knew that at the Bow Street office, the night patrol would have come on duty. He was free to go home, but the prospect of Mrs.

Catchpole's good-natured meddling filled him with dread. Delaying the inevitable, he traversed the mile or so from the City to Covent Garden on foot. As he drew abreast of a pub, scents wafting through its open doors made his stomach growl, and he realized with some surprise that he had not eaten in six hours or more. He stepped inside, ordered a ploughman's dinner and a pint of ale, and took a seat at a corner table where he might be alone with his thoughts — none of which, it must be said, made for very congenial company.

"Is this seat taken?"

Lost in melancholy reflection, Pickett started at the sound of the familiar voice. Mr. Colquhoun stood there with his hand on the back of the opposite chair, clearly awaiting an invitation to sit down.

"It's yours, sir, if you want it."

Apparently the magistrate did, for he drew it out from the table and made himself comfortable. "I saw you come in," he told his most junior Runner. "From your gloomy demeanor, I gather your investigations were fruitless?"

"Utterly. If the tomb of Deacon Toomer ever existed — or the deacon himself, for that matter — you could never prove it by me." He paused and took a long pull of ale.

"I did accomplish one thing, though: I stopped in Oxford Street and took a look in the shop windows."

He wished Mr. Colquhoun would say something. Even an "I told you so" would be better than that look of wordless sympathy.

"I'm sorry, sir," Pickett continued. "I had no idea. I hope you know I would never do anything to damage the reputation of the Bow Street force, at least not intentionally. I owe you too great a debt to repay you so shabbily."

"Faugh!" snorted the Scotsman. "Any debt you owed me was paid in full long ago, so let's hear no more of it."

Pickett could not help smiling a little, well aware that Mr. Colquhoun was uncomfortable with any suggestion of sentimentality. "As you wish, sir." His smile faded. "Still, I don't want to discredit the force. I am prepared to do my duty, but I wonder if you would give me three days' grace."

"Why three days?"

"I'd like to travel to Kent, sir."

"Kent? What is in Kent, pray?"

"Fieldhurst's estate. I'd like to have a look at the church yard, the family crypt, that sort of thing."

Colquhoun's bushy white brows rose.

"You still expect to find Deacon Toomer?"

"To be honest, sir, no. But it is the only clue I have to go on, and until I have exhausted every avenue —"

He broke off, and the two men sat in silence for a long moment. "Very well," said the magistrate at last. "You have your three days."

Pickett looked sharply at him, almost afraid to hope. "You'll not send someone else while I'm gone?" Seeing the look of affronted dignity on his magistrate's face, he quickly demurred. "No, I know you would not. I beg your pardon. Thank you, sir! I'll take the first stage to Maidstone tomorrow. Now — if you'll excuse me — I'd best go home and pack!"

Filled with a new sense of purpose, Pickett leaped up from his chair, pausing only long enough to stuff a crust of bread into his mouth, then headed for the door in such haste that he tripped over the table leg and only narrowly avoided sprawling spread-eagled on the tavern floor.

Colquhoun, observing his ungainly departure with ill-concealed amusement, plunged a hand into his coat pocket and withdrew a bulging coin purse. "Oh, John?"

The use of his Christian name, while not unheard of, was sufficiently unusual to cause Pickett to pause in mid-flight. "Yes, sir?"

"A little something in advance," said the magistrate, pressing a few silver shillings into his hand. "To offset the expenses of the journey."

"Thank you, sir." Recalled to propriety, Pickett bobbed a rather awkward bow and took his leave in a slightly more restrained fashion.

Left alone with Pickett's abandoned dinner, the magistrate reached across the table and broke a bit of cheese off the forgotten chunk on his plate. "The lad is besotted," he muttered, shaking his head sadly. "God help him."

Pickett, disembarking from the stagecoach at Maidstone, took a moment to stretch his cramped muscles before going into the nearest public house and inquiring as to the location of Lord Fieldhurst's principal seat.

"That would be over to Fieldhurst village, it would," said the publican. "If you be needing a ride, Old Ben will be heading in that direction shortly. Won't you, Old Ben?" he added, pitching his voice so that it might be heard by someone apparently half a mile away.

The heavy tread of hobnailed boots heralded the entrance of Old Ben into the taproom. Pickett, who had been expecting a fellow in his dotage, was somewhat amused to discover that Old Ben was in fact no older than Mr. Colquhoun. "Aye, I can offer you a lift, if a Londoner like yourself won't mind the smell of a farm wagon."

"Not a bit," Pickett assured him. "But how did you know I was from London?"

Everyone in the pub seemed to find this question wonderfully funny. "Lord love you, you've got 'City' written all over you!" said Old Ben, still chuckling. "We can spot 'em at fifty paces."

Far from being offended, Pickett took an instant liking to Old Ben and, on the leisurely drive to Fieldhurst village, seized the opportunity to inquire as to the origins of his misleading name.

"Oh, that would be to tell me from my firstborn, Young Ben," explained the farmer, as if this were the most logical thing in the world. "He's the wrestling champion hereabouts, and a great favorite with the females, too. But though he could have his pick of the local girls, he's in no hurry to settle down. He'd be about your age, I'd say. And what about yourself? Be there a London lass pining for your return?"

Pickett could only wish it were so. "No,"

he said. Then, painfully aware of the abruptness of his denial, he pointed out over the fields stretching out to both left and right, where tender green plants climbed poles higher than a man's head. "What's growing there?"

As a ploy, it worked brilliantly, for Old Ben forgot all about lasses, rural and otherwise. "There's a Londoner for you," he said, chuckling. "Them's good Kentish hops, the finest in England."

This quite naturally led to the subject of farming. Old Ben enthusiastically cataloged the local crops, along with his predictions for the year's harvest in each one, and Pickett in return described for him the open-air fruit and vegetable markets of Covent Garden. Having established a rapport, Pickett judged it time to broach the subject most occupying his thoughts.

"Is this Lord Fieldhurst's land?"

"Aye, all this and more."

"Is he a good landlord?"

"Can't rightly say. I work my own place," the farmer said with simple pride. "He seems to do right by his tenants, though, and her ladyship gives a fine harvest festival round about Michaelmas. I guess there won't be no festival this year, what with his lordship dead and all."

"Perhaps the new viscountess will carry on the custom next year," suggested Pickett, although what he knew of Caroline Bertram made him think it unlikely that she would be eager to spend money on persons unable to advance her social ambitions.

"Aye, mayhap she will. But even so, it won't be the same."

Pickett could not dispute this home truth. "You must know just about everybody who lives in these parts," he observed, steering the conversation in a more fruitful direction.

"Aye, that I do. Country folk are like that. We don't have secrets from each other here in Fieldhurst — or if we do, we don't keep 'em long," added Old Ben, laughing heartily at his own witticism.

"Is there any family around here by the name of Toomer? Someone connected with the church, perhaps?"

Old Ben scratched his chin while he pondered this question. "Not that I can think of," he said at last. "The sexton is Tom Tilney, and the curate is Paul Trotter, but I never did hear of a Toomer in these parts. You're sure of the name?"

Pickett shook his head. "I thought I was, but I daresay I was mistaken. It's of no importance, at any rate."

Old Ben accepted this explanation without comment, and soon drew the wagon to a halt before an establishment called the Hart and Hare, where, he said, Pickett might be assured of a room for the night as well as a hot meal in the evening.

"For there aren't many visitors hereabouts, leastways not this time of year," he observed. "Harvest time, now, there's another story. But no one's staying at the Hart and Hare now, saving a Mrs. Bertram. Now that I think on it, she's from London, too, so I'll wager the two of you'll soon be thick as inkle-weavers."

Pickett had no confidence in the accuracy of this prediction, but owned himself more than a little taken aback by the presence of Mrs. Bertram in the vicinity. He had no idea the lady meant to accompany her husband to the funeral; still less did he understand why she should be putting up at a public inn, rather than staying at the ancestral home that now belonged to her husband. It would appear that, far from resolving the Bertrams' quarrel, Mr. Bertram's inheritance of the title had only served to exacerbate it.

As if reading his passenger's mind, Old Ben chose that moment to volunteer the further information that if Pickett wanted to have a look-see at the Big House, he should take the right fork at the foot of the High Street and follow it north until just past the bridge. He steadfastly refused to accept payment for the use of his wagon, but as Pickett prepared to climb down, he asked, "So, was it her ladyship what done it?"

Pickett, taken by surprise by this question, missed the step and landed rather heavily on the ground. "Beg pardon?"

Old Ben laughed aloud at his confusion. "Lord love you, I knowed you was Bow Street the minute I clapped eyes on you! We had a couple of Runners come to Maidstone a few years back, looking to break up a gang of highwaymen. All the same, the lot of you — not but what you're a mite younger than I would've expected. So, what do you think? Was it her ladyship?"

Pickett knew he should deny any knowledge of the case, but something about the man's candor demanded the same sort of honesty. "Some think so, but I don't believe them."

Old Ben nodded. "That's all right, then," he said, and with this benediction, drove away.

Pickett spent the better part of the afternoon

combing the churchyard for deceased Toomers. When this yielded no new information, he returned to the Hart and Hare for the evening meal, where he questioned everyone he could find, from the old men lingering over foaming tankards of ale to the comely village lasses who dispensed it. Alas, here too his efforts were fruitless: no one had heard of anyone by the name of Toomer, dead or alive, deacon or no. The only bright spot in a wasted day lay in the fact that he managed to avoid an encounter with Mrs. Bertram; it seemed to Pickett that she could do him considerable harm if she took exception to his presence and set the locals' backs up.

On the second day, he followed Old Ben's instructions and walked to the Big House, as the Fieldhurst mansion was known locally, and requested the housekeeper to show him about the place. He had no very clear idea of what he hoped to learn from this exercise, but by this time was quite frankly grasping at straws. He did discover two facts, neither of which had any bearing on the case: first, that the destruction of Lady Fieldhurst's beloved rose garden in favor of a Gothic ruin would indeed be a travesty; and second, that any lady who had once been mistress of such a majestic pile as Fieldhurst Manor would be unlikely to spare a thought for a man who lived in two hired rooms above a chandler's shop.

He kept these observations to himself, however, responding to the housekeeper's litany of the house's history, furnishings, and past and present inhabitants with suitably admiring or regretful noises, as the commentary dictated. They mounted the stairs to the second story and, as they entered the long portrait gallery running along the back of the house, he was much startled to find Lady Fieldhurst herself awaiting him at the other end. Abandoning the housekeeper in the middle of a long anecdote about crusading Bertrams in the Middle Ages, he hurried forward to meet the viscountess, unmindful of the disapproving eyes of earlier generations of Fieldhursts looking down on him from their framed canvases on the wall. He was halfway down the length of the gallery before he realized, to his chagrin, that it was not her ladyship at all, but a very skillfully executed likeness.

"That's the most recent viscountess when she was still Miss Runyon," explained the housekeeper, unaware of the pang of disappointment piercing the Runner's breast like a pair of nail scissors. "It was painted by Thomas Lawrence just before her marriage.

It's held to be very like her, as most anyone who has ever seen her ladyship will tell you."

Pickett, at least, could not argue the point. The artist had portrayed his subject seated in a flower-filled bower, her white skirts (slightly fuller than the current fashion) billowing about her. He thought she had not changed much over the intervening six years, at least not physically, yet there was something different. He could not have said exactly what it was, but he could see it in her eyes. The wide-eyed girl on the canvas smiled at him with all the eager innocence of youth; the lady in Berkeley Square concealed her innermost self beneath a sophisticated veneer. The girl possessed great charm and beauty, but Pickett found the woman infinitely more alluring.

"Very — very nice," he told the housekeeper, then quickly inquired as to the identity of the dour-faced Cavalier on an adjacent canvas.

Thus applied to, the housekeeper immediately launched into the checkered history of Sir Roderick Bertram, Baronet; leaving Pickett free to steal furtive glances at the youthful viscountess to his heart's content. He could not help wondering whether the critical gazes of her husband's distinguished relations preyed upon her spirits; he knew that, were he to be subjected to them for any length of time, they would prey upon his.

"There's also a picture of Sir Roderick's lady, if you'd care to see it," said the housekeeper, coming at last to the end of her narrative. "She defended this house against invading Roundheads, all by herself. Her portrait is near the other end, if you'll just step this way —"

"Perhaps," suggested Pickett as they traversed the length of the gallery, "Sir Roderick would look less bilious if his lady were not so far away."

The housekeeper blinked at this suggestion, then chuckled richly. "And so he might, at that! Lord bless you, Mr. Pickett, I think you must be a romantic!"

"Who, me?" said Pickett, taken aback by this candid (and, had he but known it, uncannily accurate) reading of his character. "Not at all, I assure you!"

They came at last to the long windows overlooking the rear of the house, and Pickett stopped for a moment to study the extensive grounds. In the distance, an ornamental lake gleamed blue and gold in the sunlight, while nearer, Lady Fieldhurst's rose garden added splashes of pink and scarlet to the vivid green of the hedges. A movement among the blossoms caught Pickett's eye, and a moment later a man and woman stepped arm in arm out of the shrubbery and onto the gravel path.

The housekeeper, following the direction of his gaze, spied the couple in the rose garden. "That's the new viscount," she explained, "come down from London yesterday for the funeral."

"And the woman?" Pickett asked.

The housekeeper shook her head. "I haven't been properly introduced, but I should think it was her new ladyship — although why she wants to put up at the Hart and Hare, instead of staying in the big house with his lordship, I don't understand and never shall."

Pickett made no reply beyond a noncommittal grunt. From his second-story vantage point, he easily recognized Mr. Bertram, but as for the woman, he could be certain of only one thing. She was not the lady he knew as Mrs. George Bertram.

Chapter 17
In Which Pickett
Makes a Surprising
Discovery

While the housekeeper conducted him through those rooms open on certain occasions to the public, Pickett wrestled with the meaning of his latest discovery, and wondered how and when to confront Mr. Bertram. The latter decision, at least, was taken out of his hands. For when he left the housekeeper and returned to the hall at the end of his tour, the front door opened and George Bertram entered the house, along with his fair companion. At the sight of the Bow Street Runner whom he had supposed to be more than forty miles away in London, Mr. Bertram froze on the threshold and stared at Pickett with mingled horror and guilt.

"*You* here?" he demanded, when at last he found his tongue. "Good God, is there no escaping you? What are you doing here?"

"I might ask you the same question," said Pickett, glancing at the woman. Seen at close range, she was perhaps forty years old, with the sort of bland prettiness which rarely survives beyond the first blushes of youth. Still, the expression on her plump face was sweet, and she possessed a surprisingly genteel manner.

"As you are no doubt well aware," said Mr. Bertram, fairly bristling, "my cousin will be buried upon the morrow. I am here to represent the family."

"And carrying on the fine old family tradition, apparently," observed Pickett. "Tell me, how did you persuade Mrs. Bertram to stay home?"

"It wasn't difficult; I just gave her a hundred guineas for refurbishing her wardrobe," said the new viscount, casting an apologetic glance at his companion. "Look here, Henrietta, I must talk to this fellow alone. If you will excuse me, I shan't be above a moment."

"Of course, George," she said serenely.

George Bertram led Pickett into one of the formal drawing rooms he had toured earlier with the housekeeper, and closed the door behind them.

"I know what you're thinking," Mr. Bertram said as soon as they were alone, "and let me tell you, you're wrong."

"Am I?" asked Pickett, carefully noncommittal. "I know only that your, er, companion is lodging at the Hart and Hare under an assumed name."

"You are impertinent, sirrah, as well as mistaken! The name she gave at the Hart and Hare is her legal name. She is my wife."

Pickett was momentarily bereft of speech. Fortunately, Mr. Bertram apparently recognized that some explanation would be required of him, and thus continued his narrative.

"I met Henrietta when we were both quite young," he said, his gaze unfocused, as if seeing again that long-ago meeting. "I was an ensign in the Army, stationed near Bath. Henrietta was making her come-out there, as her parents lacked the funds to provide her with a London Season. We loved at first sight."

"But your families disapproved?"

George Bertram gave a snort of derision. "*My* family disapproved! Not only was Henrietta penniless, but also the daughter of a curate — not a suitable match for the second in line to a viscountcy. My cousin had not yet come into his title in those days, but still there was much speculation about when he would marry and beget an heir. It was hammered home to me that until he did, I must conduct myself in a way appropriate to a future viscount. But we fooled them all, my Henrietta and I! We married in secret. I won't bore you with the details, but suffice it to say that we were so successful in keeping our secret that no one suspects to this day."

"And then?" Pickett prompted, when Mr. Bertram lapsed into reminiscent silence.

"Then Lord Fieldhurst died — my uncle, you know — and my cousin inherited the title. Since he still showed no inclination to marry, it became imperative to the family that I should do so, and thus ensure the continuance of the line. A match was arranged with Caroline Deering, eldest daughter of a Lancashire baron. It was by no means a brilliant match, but it was a respectable one by Fieldhurst standards, and her portion was said to be sizeable."

"And so you made a bigamous marriage."

"I've done nothing that the Prince of Wales himself hasn't done," insisted Mr. Bertram. "He abandoned his Mrs. Fitzherbert readily enough for Princess Caroline, after Parliament made it a condition for increasing his funds."

Pickett wondered how many times over the past two decades George Bertram had justified his actions by making the royal comparison. "Perhaps," he said, conceding the point. "But — begging your pardon — you, sir, are no prince."

George Bertram's face grew dark with impotent fury. "I might have known you would not understand! You cannot possibly imagine the sort of pressure placed on the heir presumptive to an ancient title. At last I saw they would not be persuaded by any argument I could put forth, and so I put aside my dear Henrietta, and married Caroline."

"If the lady I loved agreed to marry me," Pickett said slowly, "I don't think I would give her up, no matter what sort of pressure was brought to bear."

"Fine words, Mr. Pickett, but they put no bread on the table! Have you any idea what an ensign is expected to support himself on?"

Pickett did not, but as he suspected it compared rather favorably to a neophyte Runner, he found it difficult to drum up much sympathy for Mr. Bertram's plight.

George Bertram, seeing that his audience was not convinced, hastened to put himself in the best possible light. "In any case, I did not abandon Henrietta utterly. I continued to see her whenever I could, and when her parents cast her off after it was discovered that she was with child, I hired a small cottage where she might live with a respectable woman."

"All at your second wife's expense," observed Pickett dryly.

"Yes — not that Caroline's dowry was nearly as large as my family had been led to believe. At any rate, once the boys were old enough to be sent to school — we have two sons, Henrietta and I, so I have done my duty to the family by begetting legitimate heirs of the body — I moved her to London to be near me. Now that my cousin is dead, I am head of the family, and I intend to restore my lawfully wedded wife to the position that should have been hers all along."

"And the other Mrs. Bertram? Does she know?"

"She does not. I will allow, however, that the situation is no fault of hers, and I intend to do right by her, as well as I am able. When I learned that my cousin had left a house in Kensington, I had hoped to install her in it, but unfortunately, that property was left to his widow."

"On the night of the murder," said Pickett as a new idea occurred to him, "you were with your first wife."

George Bertram bowed his head. "I was. I stayed at White's long enough to establish my presence there, in case Caroline should become suspicious, then left by the back door — a long-standing arrangement worked out with the doorman, for reasons which should be obvious."

"You realize that I must question —" What to call her? Pickett wondered. "— Mrs. Henrietta Bertram."

"Of course," Mr. Bertram said with a sigh "In a way, it will be a relief, giving up the double life I have led for twenty years."

Pickett privately suspected Caroline Bertram would soon enough disabuse her bigamous husband of this notion, but he wisely held his tongue. Within a few minutes, Henrietta Bertram was seated in the chair vacated by her husband.

"Yes, George was with me that evening, from about eleven o'clock on," she said. "It was not his usual night — he usually came to me on Tuesday and Thursday — but he had quarreled with Caroline and was very much perturbed."

"And you were not?" asked Pickett, amazed by her calm acceptance of her husband's betrayal. "Did you never resent his treatment of you?"

She laughed then, a musical sound that recalled the carefree young girl she had once been. "I assure you, Mr. Pickett, I am no saint! I sometimes resented it very much.

You will say George was weak and cowardly, and so he was — and so he still is, for that matter — but I could not expect him to be other than what he is. Oh, I admit, in the early days of our marriage, I sometimes longed for George to make a grand gesture; renouncing his family and his claim to the title, and acknowledging me before the world as his wife. But even if he had done so, it would not have answered. We should have been penniless, for his family would not have hesitated to cut him off without a shilling. He would have ended by hating me."

Privately, Pickett thought George Bertram did not deserve such loyalty. "Now that you are free to claim your rightful place, why did you put up at the Hart and Hare, instead of staying here with your husband?"

Her brow puckered in a thoughtful frown. "George tried to persuade me to do so, but it did not seem right to me to push myself forward at such a time. There will be ample opportunity for all that later, and most of it will be extremely unpleasant. I do feel rather sorry for Caroline; it seems to me that she is the one who will suffer the most from George's lack of courage. But for now, I will not think of that. For now, I will enjoy strolling about the grounds with George and planning our future here together. Have you seen the rose garden? You must allow me to show it to you before you go. The present viscountess laid it out herself, I believe."

Pickett recalled a snatch of conversation he had overheard one morning in the breakfast room in Berkeley Square. "Then — you don't intend to dig it up?" he asked, liking Mrs. Henrietta Bertram better by the moment.

"Good heavens, no! Who could do such a wicked thing? It must grieve Lady Fieldhurst very much to lose it. I wonder if she would like to have cuttings of some of the more unusual species."

Pickett smiled. "I think she would like that very much, your ladyship."

Mrs. Bertram's answering smile was pathetically bewildered. "How very odd that sounds! I have lived so long as a fallen woman, I wonder if I shall ever grow accustomed to anything else."

On the following day, having exhausted all other options, Pickett packed his meager belongings and retraced his route to Maidstone, conveyed this time by Young Ben, whose father was on this occasion occupied in the fields. Like his father, Young Ben was by nature loquacious, but this time Pickett found it difficult to enter fully into the farmer's amiable chatter. His three days were over, and he had found nothing of use to Lady Fieldhurst. In fact, he had done nothing at all beyond proving the bigamous George Bertram blameless in the murder of his cousin.

Some three miles from Maidstone, Young Ben spied a red-haired damsel in calico, walking toward the village with a basket on her arm. He drew the cart to a halt as it came abreast of her, calling as he did so, "Becky! Come ride with me, sweeting!"

Pickett, recalling Old Ben's boasts of his son's popularity with the local female population, was not surprised to hear Becky accept this offer with every indication of eagerness. Upon being admonished to "make room, do!" he squeezed up sufficiently to make room for the new passenger, and offered a hand to help her up. Once Becky was settled between the two men with her basket on her lap, Young Ben set the cart in motion, and the three continued on their way.

Finding herself surrounded by handsome young men, Becky lost no time in making Pickett's acquaintance, and spent the remainder of the journey making herself agreeable to each of her companions in turn. Alas, she was soon obliged to concentrate her efforts on Young Ben, for her coy blushes and inviting smiles were quite wasted on Pickett. Although he responded mechanically to her coquetries, he could think only of how abysmally he had failed. *As God is my witness, I will not let you hang.* . . . What right had he to make such a promise, when he could not keep it?

It was a relief to at least two of the three travelers when Pickett was finally set down in Maidstone. Young Ben was convinced that his father must have been having him on, for the lively tales of London life which he had been assured would spill forth from Mr. Pickett's lips had never materialized. Becky, for her part, was unaccustomed to being all but ignored by the local blades, and saw no reason why she should tolerate such cavalier treatment from a Londoner, be he never so handsome.

As for Pickett himself, he was beyond feeling much of anything at all. He thanked Young Ben for his hospitality, bade the petulant Becky farewell, retrieved his battered valise from the back of the wagon, and soon boarded the stagecoach that would take him back to London. He obtained a seat beside the window and spent the journey staring out at the passing scenery, unmindful of the occasional efforts of his fellow passengers to engage him in conversation.

He reached his Drury Lane lodgings in the afternoon. Mrs. Catchpole, hearing an unusually slow and heavy tread on the steps, waddled out of her workroom at the back of the shop, and called up the stairs, "Johnny? Is that you?"

No response issued from overhead except for the thud of Pickett's valise striking the uncarpeted floor. A moment later, the door at the top of the stairs opened, and Pickett once again descended to the shop below.

"*There* you are, Johnny! I thought it was you." Mrs. Catchpole lifted a steaming teakettle from the hearth by means of her apron wrapped around its handle. "And just in time, too! Sit down and have a cup of tea, and tell me all about your journey."

Pickett did not answer. Mrs. Catchpole, glancing around at him to repeat the invitation, saw in her boarder's face a look of such bleak despair that, as she confided later to her niece Alice, it gave her such a queer turn as she'd never had in all her life. In fact, Pickett did not even seem to notice she was there, but left the shop without a word and turned his steps in the direction of Bow Street.

At any other time, the girls with their baskets of apples and the men pushing their carts of cabbages might have made him smile to think of Old Ben and his farm wagon. Today, however, he neither saw the street vendors nor heard their cries. He spoke to no one and looked neither right nor left until he entered the Bow Street office and approached the magistrate's desk.

Mr. Colquhoun looked up and smiled as Pickett stopped before the wooden railing. "Well, John, how was your sojourn in the country?"

Pickett, unsmiling, gripped the railing so tightly his knuckles turned white. "Sir, I would like to request a warrant for the arrest of Lady Fieldhurst for the murder of her husband."

CHAPTER 18
LADY FIELDHURST
MAKES A DISCOVERY

An unnatural hush seemed to fall over the usually bustling office. Two members of the foot patrol, discussing the latest issue of the *Hue and Cry,* seemed very far away; their voices no more than a distant hum. For Pickett, there was no sound except the scratching of the magistrate's quill on the parchment that would send Lady Fieldhurst to Newgate, and thence, in all likelihood, to the gallows. At last Colquhoun laid the quill aside, shook sand over paper to absorb the wet ink, and handed the document over the railing to Pickett, who scarcely glanced at it before rolling it up and storing it inside the hollow wooden tipstaff he carried expressly for this purpose.

"Do you want me to send someone else, John?" the magistrate asked quietly.

For a moment, Pickett was tempted. He dreaded the task that lay before him, and if there were any way he could honorably avoid it, he would not hesitate to do so. Yet the thought of placing the viscountess's fate in the hands of a stranger was intolerable. She deserved, at the very least, the comfort of a familiar face. *As God is my witness . . .* He shook his head. "No, sir. If it must be done, I — I'd rather do it myself."

"There is still a chance," Colquhoun pointed out. "She might be fortunate in her jury. Men have been known before now to be moved by the plight of a beautiful woman. Or new evidence might turn up before the trial. Stranger things have happened."

Pickett nodded, well aware that neither of them truly believed it. Like one in a trance, he turned and left the Bow Street office.

The brilliant May sunlight outside seemed to make a mockery of his despair. The distance to Berkeley Square was long and the day uncomfortably warm, but he elected to walk nevertheless. He wanted only to delay the inevitable for as long as possible.

"One of these days, John Pickett, you're going to step right in front of a carriage and be put to bed with a shovel," scolded Lucy, looping her arm through his. "Where have you been keeping yourself?"

He managed to summon up a bleak smile. "In Kent."

"*Kent?* What have you been doing in Kent?"

The smile vanished. "Nothing," he said bitterly. "Not a bloody thing."

"Don't swear in front of a lady," Lucy said primly, even though she herself possessed a vocabulary that would embarrass most sailors.

"I beg your pardon. I'm afraid I'm not very good company today."

Lucy squeezed his arm. "Maybe I could put you in a better mood."

"I doubt it."

"All right, be that way!" she retorted, withdrawing her arm abruptly. "*Some* men know how to appreciate a woman!"

"Your Frog, for instance?"

"Wee-wee," Lucy agreed cheerfully, lapsing into atrocious French. "Why, just last night —"

"I don't want to know," interrupted Pickett, holding up a restraining hand.

"— He said, 'Lucy, mon cur, shut the door!' "

"If he called you a cur, I hope you told him to shut it himself."

"You don't know nothing about the French, do you?" retorted Lucy with a snort of derision. " 'Mon cur' means 'my heart,' and 'shut the door' means 'I love you.' "

Pickett regarded her skeptically. "Are you sure about that? Seems to me 'shut the door' wouldn't be a very —" He broke off abruptly as a light, dim at first, but growing steadily brighter, began to dawn. "What did you say?"

"I said, 'shut the door' means 'I love you' in French," Lucy repeated impatiently. "Honestly, John Pickett! Just because *some* men don't know how to treat a lady —"

She got no further, for Pickett seized her by the shoulders and planted a quick, hard kiss on her half-open mouth. "Thank you, Lucy! You're a brick!"

"And don't you forget it!" she called after him as he ran down the street.

Lady Fieldhurst, ignorant of the grim fate that awaited her, was occupied with troubles of a different sort. Pacing the floor of the best guest chamber, she reread the note hand-delivered by a liveried footman only moments earlier, then flung the offending square of vellum onto the counterpane. It missed the bed completely and fluttered to the floor, but her ladyship paid no heed.

"Can you believe the cheek of the woman?" she demanded of her lady's maid, who was restoring her mistress's freshly laundered gowns to the clothes press.

"Quelle femme, madame?" inquired the Frenchwoman without pausing in her labors.

"Mrs. Bertram — the viscountess, as I suppose I must accustom myself to calling her. She cannot wear sparkling stones until her mourning is complete, so why must she have the Fieldhurst jewels today? And to demand them in such a way!" She pitched her voice in a very fair imitation of her cousin-by-marriage's shrill tones. " 'George — my dear Fieldhurst, you must know! — will call for them upon the morrow, after he has returned from Fieldhurst Hall.' As if she feared I might flee with them during the night! I wonder she does not come to collect them herself, so that she might count the silver while she is about it."

"C'est très difficile, madame, but she is within her rights, *n'est-ce pas?"*

"Indeed she is, although far outside the bounds of good taste," Lady Fieldhurst admitted grudgingly. "And that is why, when George Bertram calls tomorrow, I shall surrender the family jewels with a smile on my face, even if it kills me." A fresh concern occurred to her, and she added, "My jewel case is still in my own bedchamber, is it not?"

"Oui, madame. As *madame* cannot wear

the jewels at present, I saw no need to fetch them. Shall I do so now?"

For a moment, she was tempted. She had been careful to avoid the room since the night of her husband's murder, and she did not look forward to entering it now. But tomorrow the Fieldhurst heirlooms would pass to new hands, and one part of her life would be irrevocably over. She would collect the jewels herself, in memory of the young bride who had once been so dazzled by the man who had bestowed them upon her.

"No, thank you, Camille, your forbearance has been tried far enough by my ill humor," she said with a sigh. "You may go now."

"*Merci, madame.*" The lady's maid bobbed a stiff curtsy and exited the room through the servants' door.

Alone with her thoughts, none of which were pleasant, Lady Fieldhurst retrieved the note from the floor and read the offending message once more. What a pity that one of the Bertrams could not be arrested for the murder! To be sure, it was difficult to picture poor, dull George as a killer; she could not conceive of him having the imagination to concoct such a scheme, much less the courage to carry it out. Caroline, however, was another matter entirely. George had been subject to petticoat rule for as long as she had known him, and Caroline certainly possessed ambition enough for two. Yes, she could readily imagine Cousin Caroline hounding her poor husband to murder, just like Lady Macbeth.

I must ask Mr. Pickett if he can somehow pin it on Caroline, she thought, and smiled to picture his reaction to this request. But Mr. Pickett had been making himself very scarce of late; indeed, she had not seen him at all since that day in Queens Gardens. She supposed his absence meant there was no new evidence in the case. Or perhaps there *was* new evidence, and he was busy pursuing a lead. How gratifying it would be if that were so, and the case was soon solved. It would be a relief to put all this behind her, to go somewhere far away where no one had ever heard of the murdered Lord Fieldhurst or his notorious widow. Still, it was strange to think that, with justice served, the surprisingly youthful Bow Street Runner, with his unfashionable queue and slightly crooked nose, would pass as completely out of her life as if he had never existed.

With a sigh, the viscountess wadded the vellum note into a ball and tossed it into the grate. The afternoon was advancing, and her bedchamber, facing northeastward across the square, would soon be growing dark. She had no desire to be in the room after night had fallen.

Although her vacated bedchamber was only a short distance down the corridor from the guest room she now occupied, she might as well have been stepping into another world. The servants refused to enter this room, so it remained exactly as it had been on the night of Frederick's death. The cold ashes had not yet been swept from the grate, and the curtains remained slightly askew from Mr. Pickett's examination of the window for signs of forced entry or hasty exit. The indirect afternoon sun turned the room's cream-and-rose splendor to burnished gold, recalling all-too-vivid memories of the firelight that had danced across the viscount's lifeless body.

"Stop it at once!" she chided herself as she closed the door. "You are behaving as foolishly as the silliest chambermaid!"

Nevertheless, she carefully averted her gaze from the dark stain on the Aubusson carpet. She sat down at the dressing table, noting that here too almost everything was just as it had been on that night, the one exception being the nail scissors which had been taken as evidence. She removed the small key from its hiding place underneath the edge of the table, fitted it into the lock of the polished mahogany jewel case, and raised the lid.

Cut stones gleamed dully in the dim light. Sapphires, rubies, and emeralds all rested regally in their velvet-lined compartments, each ready to adorn the ears and throat of the new viscountess, uncaring of the fate of the old one. The opals had once belonged to her mother, and Caroline Bertram would have them over her own dead body. This thought not unnaturally gave rise to another: that of Mrs. Bertram claiming the pale stones after her predecessor had perished on the gallows. She scolded herself for allowing her imagination to run away with her. For all she knew, Mr. Pickett might even now be preparing to arrest someone — Sir Archibald Stanton, perhaps — for her husband's murder. Resolving to keep a tighter rein on her thoughts, she forced her attention back to the task at hand.

As a diversionary tactic, it left much to be desired, for the next jewels to catch her eye were the same diamonds she had worn on the night of her husband's death. She could not recall taking them off — many of the events following the discovery of her husband's body remained a blur — but assumed the faithful Camille must have returned them to their rightful place.

Removing them from their case for perhaps the last time, she held them up to her throat and regarded her reflection in the mirror. The white stones glinted against the black bodice of her mourning gown. It seemed a lifetime ago that Frederick had stood here beside her as she prepared for the ball, his cold fingers stroking her neck. She shuddered at the memory, just as she had shuddered at his touch. He had found her revulsion amusing and had offered to summon the chambermaid to light the fire. And she had said no . . .

The diamonds slipped through her fingers and fell to her lap as the significance of this memory began to dawn. He had offered to have the fire lit, and she had said no. Why, then, had there been a fire burning when she returned from the ball to find Frederick dead? Who had entered her room and started a fire against her wishes, and for what purpose?

She rose from the dressing table, dropping the diamonds into quite the wrong compartment, and moved slowly to the fireplace, where she knelt before the grate.

The powdery gray cinders gave away no secrets, but several small, round lumps caught her attention. She reached in and plucked one from the ashes. It was hard and round, and when she wiped it clean on the skirt of her gown, she discovered two tiny holes on one side. It was a button; a button which, made of metal, had survived unscathed the fire that had consumed the garment it had once adorned. How very odd, and yet somehow familiar. Where had she seen such buttons before? She reached into the ashes again and found another, and still another. There were ten of them in all — ten small, round buttons, enough to fasten a woman's gown from neck to waist.

Mr. Pickett must be told. But what could she do? She would not embarrass him by bursting into the Bow Street office again and demanding to see him, especially not as she appeared now, with her skirt and hands and — yes, a glance at her mirror confirmed it — even her face liberally dusted with powdery gray ash. No, she must write him a note instead, and instruct Thomas to deliver it at once. Seating herself once more at the dressing table, she pushed the jewel case away — she had no time to waste on such trivial matters now — withdrew crested stationery, pen, and ink from the top drawer, and began to write.

"Dear Mr. Pickett," she began, then frowned. The greeting seemed rather too intimate. She wadded up the paper, withdrew a clean sheet from the drawer, and began again.

Mr. Pickett, something has come to my attention that may have a bearing on the case. Please call in Berkeley Square at your earliest convenience.

She underscored these last two words three times for emphasis. She then signed it, shook sand over it, sealed it with wax, and was just reaching for the bell pull when a faint sound behind her caused her to whirl around in surprise.

"Camille," she said with a shaky laugh, discovering her lady's maid standing just inside the service door. "How you startled me!"

Camille made no reply, but advanced silently into the room.

"As I said before, I am quite capable of sorting through the jewelry myself," said Lady Fieldhurst in what she hoped was a tone of firm dismissal. "You may go."

"What are you doing, *madame?*" Camille asked, sounding more like the mistress than the servant.

The viscountess gauged the distance to the door, and thought it politic to answer the question, however impertinent. "I am writing a letter for Thomas to deliver. I was just about to ring for him when you came in."

"Give it to me, *madame,*" Camille said, holding out her hand. "I will see that he gets it."

"That will not be necessary." Seeing Camille's gaze shift to the little pile of buttons on the dressing table, Lady Fieldhurst realized she had not the luxury of awaiting Mr. Pickett's arrival. Her best — indeed, her *only* — course of action was to engage the abigail in sympathetic conversation while she inched toward the door. "I found your buttons in the ashes, Camille. Why did you burn your dress?"

"It was necessary because of the bloodstains, *madame,*" replied the lady's maid with a Gallic shrug. "But I think you already know this, *n'est-ce pas?*"

"Oh, my poor Camille," breathed Lady Fieldhurst. "You should never have made such a sacrifice."

"Sacrifice?" Camille's tone was one of contempt. "You think I killed him for your sake, because you quarreled with him? No, this thing I did for myself, because I loved him!"

To Lady Fieldhurst, confronted with her servant's defiant tilt of the chin and her flashing, dark eyes, it seemed as if she was looking into the face of a stranger. But no, this woman was no stranger. She had seen her once before, gazing passionately out from a painted canvas, her long, dark hair, as yet untouched by silver, spilling over her bared bosom. "You were his mistress."

"Long before you were his wife!" Camille spat. "You, who could not even give him the son he wanted so desperately! If not for the Revolution, I might have looked far higher than an English viscount for a husband, but no! My family's lands were confiscated and I — I, Camille de la Rochefort, who might have married whomever I pleased — was forced to earn my bread on my back, while *le vicomte* married a country nobody too green to realize he had another woman."

"Perhaps," Lady Fieldhurst said, taking a small step toward the door, "perhaps he loved both of us, in his way."

Camille, reliving past grievances, seemed not to hear her. "He was a man unlike other men, and so when he asked me to betray my homeland, I said, 'Why not?' Why should

I not betray those who made it impossible for me to marry the man I loved?"

"You spied for England?"

"For England? Bah! What care I for England? I spied for my lover. It was one thing that you, his wife, could never do for him, just as you could never give him a son. And all the while, I said *'oui, madame'* and *'non, madame,'* and laughed because I possessed a part of him that you never could."

"Then why —" The viscountess forced the question past lips that had suddenly gone dry. "Why did you kill him?"

"Because his love was false!" cried Camille, as if the words were torn from her throat. "Because it was all a lie! On that night I heard him talking to Monsieur Stanton below stairs, and I realized that he had been using me all these years. It was England he loved, not Camille de la Rochefort. I would have done anything for him, given him anything he asked, because I loved him. He did not have to lie to me."

"Poor Camille," murmured the viscountess, almost within reach of the door. "He betrayed us both."

"His betrayal of me was worse," Camille said, advancing purposefully upon her mistress. "For now he is dead, and you have his name, and his position, and the house where we once loved with such passion. And me, I have lost my lover and now I have nothing. And you will win again, for it is you who will join him in death."

Realizing that her moment had come, Julia sprang for the door, but in that fraction of a second when she fumbled for the knob, the woman was upon her. The viscountess was ten years younger than her maid, but Camille was several inches taller and outweighed her mistress by more than two stone. Although Julia fought with every ounce of strength she possessed, kicking and clawing for all she was worth, the outcome was never in doubt. Camille seized her by the throat and flung her backwards onto the bed, then grabbed one of the thick goose down pillows and pressed it over her face.

CHAPTER 19
IN WHICH
ALL IS REVEALED

There was, as Pickett had observed to Lucy on an earlier occasion, never a hackney around when one needed it. But as he was suddenly possessed of a burning impatience to reach Berkeley Square; and thus disinclined to stand on the corner waiting for such a vehicle to miraculously appear, he set out on foot. It was perhaps just as well, for he needed time to consider the possibilities raised by Lucy's abominable French, to fit them together like pieces of a puzzle until a coherent pattern appeared. By the time he had reached the fashionable environs of Mayfair, such a pattern had indeed emerged, with only a few pieces missing. As he neared Berkeley Square, his steps quickened. He could not shake the growing conviction that, if his theory was correct, the viscountess might face a far more immediate danger than the warrant he carried in his tipstaff. By the time he reached the

Fieldhurst town house, he was more than ever convinced of the need for haste. He bounded up the shallow steps onto the front stoop and pounded on the door knocker as if the Furies were at his heels.

There was no answer. Pickett could only assume that Rogers was polishing silver in his pantry, or else the butler was pickled again. As he reached once more for the knocker, a loud thump sounded from somewhere above and to his immediate left — if his sense of direction did not mislead him, the very room in which Lord Fieldhurst had died. Flinging propriety to the winds, Pickett released the knocker and seized the knob instead. In the space of a moment, he had flung open the door (not troubling, in his haste, to close it behind him) and crossed the hall, then took the curving stairs two at a time. Upon reaching the top, he burst through the nearest door and stood transfixed at the sight that met his horrified gaze.

Camille de la Rochefort, her lips twisted in grim determination, crouched on hands and knees on the bed as she pressed a plump white pillow over the face of a writhing female figure, a creature who struggled so mightily against her aggressor that her black bombazine skirts were by now rucked up about her knees.

Pickett, who had seen those shapely, silk-clad calves all too frequently in his dreams, could not fail to recognize them now. Casting his tipstaff aside, he seized Camille by the shoulders and dragged her off the viscountess. The abigail immediately focused her efforts on this new adversary, kicking and clawing like a woman possessed. Indeed, it was only by pinning the woman's skirts to the mattress with his knee that Pickett was able to avoid quite a painful kick in a most vulnerable location. Deprived of what was arguably the most powerful weapon in her arsenal, she tossed frantically to and fro in an effort to escape his grasp, and once succeeded in raking her fingernails down his cheek. She paid dearly for this temporary victory, however; for he seized both her wrists in a vise-like grip, then wrenched both arms behind her back and hauled the woman to her feet.

The immediate crisis averted, he became aware of the sound of running footsteps, and turned to discover Rogers, wearing an apron over his black suit and twisting a polishing cloth in his hands. Behind him, Thomas the footman stared goggle-eyed at the scene, while a hysterical housemaid sobbed gustily onto his shoulder. Beyond Thomas, two new arrivals pushed their way past the motley crew into the room. Pickett blinked at the sight of the two men clad in the distinctive red waistcoats of the Bow Street foot patrol.

"Mr. Colquhoun told us to follow you," one offered by way of explanation. "He thought you might need help."

"And so I do, but not for the reason he expected," acknowledged Pickett, panting slightly.

Camille took advantage of the distraction to administer a swift kick to his shin.

Pickett flinched, but did not falter. "Take her to Mr. Colquhoun, and tell him I want her held on charges of murder and attempted murder." True, the arrest warrant was in Lady Fieldhurst's name, but Pickett had every confidence in the magistrate's ability to make it right. "And be careful with her — she's a regular Tartar."

But even as he voiced this caveat, Camille's bearing changed. She ceased struggling in his grasp and stood as straight and proud as if she were making her curtsy at Versailles. "You may unhand me, *s'il vous plaît.* I will come quietly, *oui,* even willingly. *Alors* —" Her gaze shifted to the bed, where the viscountess still lay, limp and gasping for breath. The smile she bestowed on her former mistress was almost pitying. "— I will soon be reunited with my lover."

She swept from the room with her handsome head erect and, although Pickett did not think she would so demean herself as to attempt an escape, he was glad to note that the foot patrol still held her by the elbows. Rogers, displaying a degree of tact which did much to explain Lady Fieldhurst's loyalty to him, shooed the other servants back to their duties while Pickett turned his attention to the viscountess. He sat down on the edge of the bed and took one of her cold hands in his, then wrapped a supporting arm about her shoulders and gently raised her to a sitting position.

"Are you all right, my lady?" he asked.

"Oh, yes — or I very soon will be." Her voice was raspy, and her throat already showed the beginnings of bruises, but she appeared otherwise unhurt. She looked up at him, and touched gentle fingers to his face. "But you are bleeding!"

A discreet cough from the doorway reminded Pickett of the butler's presence. "Perhaps my lady would be the better for a glass of sherry?" suggested Rogers.

Lady Fieldhurst, suddenly conscious of her exposed limbs, busied herself with shaking down her skirts. "Sherry would be lovely, Rogers. I daresay Mr. Pickett would not object to a glass, either, along with a cold compress for his injured cheek."

Mr. Pickett, suddenly realizing that he was sitting on her bed with his arm still encircling her waist, leaped to his feet as if scalded by her touch. "Ob-object?" he stammered. "N-no, not at all. It — it would be much appreciated."

Rogers bowed and withdrew, leaving the Runner and the viscountess the task of filling an awkward silence.

"A most timely arrival, Mr. Pickett," said her ladyship, somehow contriving to look elegant in spite of her ash-streaked gown and ravaged coiffure. "I congratulate you."

Pickett, noting her ladyship's heightened color and the determination with which she avoided his gaze, wondered if she too was aware of Mr. Rowlandson's handiwork in the windows of Oxford Street.

"Timely?" he echoed, the word finding no favor. "If I'd not been gadding about all over Kent, you should never have been placed in such a position." His choice of words was unfortunate, as it recalled to his mind the precise position her ladyship had occupied, sprawled on the bed with her lower limbs gloriously displayed.

"What were you doing in Kent?" she asked. Finding him oddly distracted, she was obliged to repeat the question before receiving an answer.

"Chasing after mare's nests," he said bitterly. "On the night of the murder, the footman Thomas was passing by your bedchamber when he heard the words, 'The tomb of Deacon Toomer may shut the door on the poor sod' shouted by an unknown speaker. I've scoured half the crypts in London, not to mention the Kentish countryside, trying to locate the tomb. It wasn't until I returned to London that, er, someone made me realize that 'shut the door' and the French words for 'I love you' sound very much alike."

Lady Fieldhurst observed the rich color that stained his cheeks as he spoke these words and drew her own conclusions. She wondered who had been whispering French endearments into Mr. Pickett's ear and, perhaps more importantly, why it should annoy her that she might owe her life to a pretentious City lass not above putting on airs to impress her beau. Whoever she was, she was not the only woman in London with a little French at her command, as Mr. Pickett would soon discover.

"*Je t'adore,*" she said in an accent Lucy would scarcely have recognized. "Yes, I can see how it might be mistaken for 'shut the door' by someone who did not speak the language, especially when heard through a closed door."

"What about Deacon Toomer, then?"

"I daresay we shall never know for certain, unless Camille chooses to tell us her exact words. But based on what she told me before you arrived, I should hazard a guess on something along the lines of, *Tu m'as dit que tu m'aimais'* — in English, 'You told me that you loved me.' "

The words hung in the air between them like a tangible thing, and for a moment it was almost as if they were no longer discussing the lady's maid and her doomed passion. It was perhaps fortunate that Rogers appeared at this juncture to inform her ladyship that the requested sherry awaited them in the drawing room.

"I should have guessed, by the way Fieldhurst's coat was pushed off his shoulders," Pickett remarked, once they had exchanged the charged atmosphere of the bedchamber for the more decorous setting of the drawing room. "He was apparently taking it off prior to — er —"

Seeing that this line of reasoning was rapidly leading into deep waters, he decided a change of subject was in order. "You never realized she was his mistress?"

"No, although I was aware that Frederick was unfaithful. I did not even recognize her portrait when I saw it in Queens Gardens," she added ruefully, taking a sip of sherry.

"It was painted years ago, and she'd had a hard life since then."

"She was spying for him too, did you know?"

He nodded. "That explains the letter Sir Archibald Stanton took from your husband's desk. Apparently the Foreign Office hoped to retain Camille's services after the viscount's death. What I took for evidence of guilt on Stanton's part was no doubt his attempt to preserve her cover."

"His efforts would have been fruitless, in any case," said the viscountess. "Oh, he might have preserved her anonymity, but she would never have continued spying. She was more jealous of Frederick's country than ever she was of me, his wife. What I fail to understand is, why now? She had been his mistress, as well as his partner in espionage, for years. Why did she turn on him so abruptly?"

"I think I may have the answer to that," said Pickett. "I was in your — upstairs — on the morning after the murder, when Sir Archibald called to pay his condolences. I could hear the two of you speaking quite plainly through the chimney flue. If Camille was indeed working in your bedchamber when Stanton called upon your husband, as she said when I interviewed her, she could have heard enough of their conversation to realize she had been deceived in Lord Fieldhurst's affections."

He was obliged to abandon this promising theory, however, as a new prospect occurred to him. "No, that can't be right. There was a fire in the grate that night, so the sound would not have carried."

"Oh, but there was not!" cried Lady Fieldhurst. "That is, there was certainly a fire by the time you arrived on the scene, but it was not lit until after Frederick was dead."

She gave the bell pull a tug, and when Thomas answered the summons (Rogers having returned to his pantry and the unpolished silver), she instructed him to go to her bedchamber and fetch the small, round buttons on her dressing table.

"I found them in the grate, among the cinders," she explained to Mr. Pickett, when these had been given over into his custody. "When I realized they were Camille's, I wrote a note asking you to call as soon as possible, but Camille surprised me before I could instruct Thomas to deliver it. She realized at once what I was about and made no attempt to conceal her guilt. She even told me how she had burned the blood-stained dress and put on a castoff gown I had given her earlier in the evening."

"She told you all this?"

"I tried to keep her talking while I edged toward the door. It wasn't difficult; all I had to do was make sympathetic noises whenever she paused for breath. Unfortunately, when she realized I meant to escape —" She shuddered at the memory and took restorative sip of sherry. "When I heard someone at the front door, I — I rather hoped it was you."

A tremulous smile accompanied this confession, and Pickett was not quite certain whether the warmth that suddenly flooded through his veins was due to the unaccustomed beverage (superior, certainly, to anything served in the Covent Garden pubs) or to the lady sitting beside him on the sofa. Alas, in either case, he had obligations awaiting him in Bow Street, as well as a magistrate who would no doubt be expecting a full accounting of the unexpected turn of events. Reluctantly, he set down his wine glass and took his leave of the viscountess.

"I cannot allow you to leave without thanking you for all you have done," she said, accompanying him as far as the door.

"It is not often one meets cleverness combined with kindness."

He snorted derisively, unimpressed by this flattering view of himself. "Clever! I'm a clunch for not figuring it out a week ago!"

"You are too hard on yourself, Mr. Pickett. Had you been less clever, or less kind, I should have found myself clapped in irons any time this past se'ennight. You have saved my life twice over — once from the scaffold, and once from Camille — and for that I must always be grateful," she said, holding out her hand to him.

He knew a moment's panic when his fingers closed over hers. Would it be presumptuous of him to kiss her hand? Did saving a lady's life give one the right to take certain liberties? If not, then it should; Parliament should pass a law. But even as he wrestled with this dilemma, she withdrew her hand from his, and the moment was lost.

He stammered something — he could never afterwards recall precisely what — bowed once more to her ladyship, and betook himself back to Bow Street.

The trial was something of a nine days' wonder. Hastily printed and bound versions of Camille de la Rochefort's purported life story now held pride of place in the shop windows of Oxford Street. As for John Pickett, he had undergone a miraculous metamorphosis in the public eye; transformed by Mr. Rowlandson's pen from a lecherous buffoon to an avenging angel pictured rescuing a terrified Lady Fieldhurst (this time attired in virginal white) by cutting the hangman's rope just as the trapdoor dropped.

Indeed, such was the uproar surrounding the trial that it seemed as if the whole of London was crammed into the Old Bailey for the grand finale. One person, however, was conspicuously absent: in vain did Pickett search the crowd for a glimpse of Lady Fieldhurst. The only representative of the Fieldhurst clan was the new viscount — taking notes, no doubt, in preparation for his own trial for bigamy. Pickett could have set his mind at ease; such cases were rarely prosecuted, and it was unlikely that a jury of peers, many of whom had likewise made loveless marriages to appease their families, would bring in a conviction against a man they no doubt envied for finding a way to eat his cake and have it, too. Caroline Bertram, in the meantime, had left London altogether; rumor had it that she had buried herself in the wilds of Cornwall.

Camille de la Rochefort was less fortunate.

She was found guilty of the murder of her lover, the Viscount Fieldhurst, and sentenced to hang by the neck until dead. As she had so confidently predicted, she would soon be reunited with her lover. Pickett hoped she would nag him mercilessly for all eternity.

Ironically, now that the quest that had consumed his every waking moment had come to so successful a conclusion, Pickett was strangely blue-devilled. He lingered in the courtroom until the last of the crowd had dispersed, and he could no longer convince himself that he might yet spy her ladyship among the fashionables making their exits. At last, with the sigh of one reluctantly abandoning a forlorn hope, he made his way through the narrow door of the bail dock and into the street. As he stepped out of the shadow of the massive building and into the sunshine, a hand fell heavily on his shoulder. He turned and saw Mr. Colquhoun, puffing slightly from the effort of catching up with the much younger man.

"Well, Pickett, what did I tell you?" asked the magistrate, falling into step beside him. "Lovers' triangle, crime of passion — I said so all along."

The twinkle in the magistrate's eyes

robbed the words of any arrogance, and Pickett's lips twitched in spite of his melancholy.

"Indeed, you did, sir."

"Now, about that reward money —"

Pickett shook his head. "I'm not interested in the money."

"Just as well, for you'll not be getting any," said the magistrate with his usual candor. "I'm afraid the Foreign Office does not love you, John."

"I don't doubt it, after I burst in like a raving lunatic, accusing everyone and his Aunt Charlotte of espionage — or worse."

"Actually, you were far too close to the truth for their liking. Mr. Canning and his cronies probably guessed the truth as soon as they learned of the circumstances surrounding Lord Fieldhurst's death. But they were hoping to retain Mademoiselle de la Rochefort's services — her political services, that is; I can't speak for her personal ones — and you posed a threat. In fact, you robbed the Foreign Office of one of its most valued agents — for which they do not thank you."

"Could a woman in her position really know so much?" asked Pickett, somewhat taken aback by this revelation.

"Not military secrets, no. But she maintained ties in France, friends and family members who lay low during the Terror and later aligned themselves with Bonaparte. The most trivial scrap of court gossip can yield volumes to those who know what to look for. And now," he added, jerking a thumb in the direction of the Magpie and Stump across the road, "I could do with a spot of tea — or maybe something a bit stronger. Will you join me?"

"Thank you, sir, I will."

As they neared the pub, Pickett reached into the pocket of his good black coat for his stocking purse, but the scrap of fabric he withdrew held no coins within its folds. It was a lacy square of finest lawn, embroidered with the ancient crest of a noble house picked out in blue and silver threads.

He recognized it at once, but it took him a moment to think how it came to be in the pocket of his best coat. It was on the night of the murder, the night he had first seen Lady Fieldhurst. He had removed the handkerchief from the face of her dead husband and, distracted by the lady's beauty, stuffed it into his pocket, where he had promptly forgotten all about it. He should return it to her at once.

On second thought, no, he would not. Her ladyship was now carrying the black-bordered handkerchiefs of the recent widow, and would not need this one for some time yet. He would keep it for now, and someday, when the temptation to see her became too great to resist, he would call in Kensington and place it in her hands himself. Until then, he would be patient.

He tucked the handkerchief back into his pocket with a much lighter heart. He would see her again, and that was enough — for now.

ABOUT THE AUTHOR

Sheri Cobb South is the author of five young adult romances, all published by Bantam as part of its long-running Sweet Dreams series. More recently, she has turned her attention to the regency genre, her first choice for reading ever since she discovered Georgette Heyer at the age of sixteen. Her regency novels include the critically acclaimed *The Weaver Takes a Wife* and the award-winning *Miss Darby's Duenna.* She is a graduate *summa cum laude* of the University of South Alabama, where she earned a B.A. in English and won the William R. Harvey Award for excellence in the study of English literature. She lives in Mobile, Alabama with her husband and two children. Sheri loves to hear from readers. She may be contacted at Cobbsouth@aol.com.

The employees of Thorndike Press hope you have enjoyed this Large Print book. All our Thorndike and Wheeler Large Print titles are designed for easy reading, and all our books are made to last. Other Thorndike Press Large Print books are available at your library, through selected bookstores, or directly from us.

For information about titles, please call:
    (800) 223 1244

or visit our Web site at:
    www.gale.com/thorndike
    www.gale.com/wheeler

To share your comments, please write:
    Publisher
    Thorndike Press
    295 Kennedy Memorial Drive
    Waterville, ME 04901

2. ~ 26.4.00